Learning to Love *Again*

A *Huron Cove* Series Romance by

ROB SHUMAKER

This is a work of fiction. Names, characters, places, and incidents either are the products of the author's imagination or are used fictitiously. Any resemblance to actual persons, living or dead, events, or locales is entirely coincidental.

Cover design by Blue Water Books

Also by Rob Shumaker

The Angel Between Them

Turning the Page

Christmas in Huron Cove

"Trust in the Lord with all your heart
and lean not on your own understanding;
in all your ways acknowledge him,
and he will make your paths straight."

Proverbs 3:5-6

CHAPTER 1

Huron Cove, Michigan

"Dad, when are you going to get married again?"

After a quick look in his rearview mirror, Luke Spencer took his foot off the gas pedal and flicked on his turn signal before coming to a stop at the intersection. *Really? This is what she asks me?* He could feel a rumble of dread echoing through his stomach. *This is not going to be good.* He looked both ways and then let off the brake.

"Are you excited about going back to school?"

Kayla Spencer sighed like only a pre-teen girl could. Then she leaned forward in the front passenger seat, her eyes narrowing as she glared at her dad. "You're deflecting."

Luke cast a sideways glance at his daughter. She was eleven going on eighteen. And between her and her best friend Emma with their endless barrage of questions, he couldn't seem to change the subject like he did in the past. Spoiling her with offers of pizza or ice cream or the latest must-have toy didn't cut it any longer because the inquisitive Kayla wouldn't let him get away with it. Now she wanted answers, and he was stuck in the driver's seat with no way out.

Still, dear old dad thought he had a few tricks up his sleeve when he wanted to run out the clock and hope she'd drop whatever it was that was making him so uncomfortable. "I'm what?"

"You're deflecting. Changing the subject." Her seatbelt was

the only thing restraining her from wagging her finger in front of his face.

How did she get so smart? Isn't she supposed to be talking about the latest Barbie doll or newest boy band or something? Anything other than asking when I'm going to get married again. Why would she think of such a thing?

He shook his head. "That doesn't sound like something I'd do, sweetie." He reached over, patted her on the arm like she was a good little girl, and then returned his eyes to the road.

Kayla sighed again. "Now you're just stalling."

Behind the wheel of his police SUV, Luke silently wished for a call to come across the radio. He'd take anything at the moment. A speeder, a jaywalker, a cat up a tree. Anything that would require his immediate attention and give him more time to get out of the latest jam with his daughter. *Just wait until she's a teenager!*

He had been a widower for almost half a decade now. Although his mind told him it had been five years, his broken heart made it feel like it was yesterday. Not a day went by without him thinking of Maria, his beloved wife who was taken at the age of thirty after losing her battle with cancer. Kayla was six at the time. Old enough to know what was going on and old enough to feel the pain of losing her mother. But for the last month, she had been asking him pointed questions that were guaranteed to make him uncomfortable—questions about love and dating and relationships.

And now the worst of all—when he was going to get married again. Not *if*, mind you. *When*.

"I'm waiting."

Luke tightened his grip on the steering wheel. The hum of the Ford's engine masked the churning in his stomach. He couldn't keep deflecting or stalling any longer. "We've had this conversation before, Kayla. My sole focus in life is you. You're all that matters to me and all I have time for. I have to work hard to make sure you're taken care of. You're my only daughter, and I love you with all my heart."

He sat back in his seat, the beginnings of a smile creeping out of the left side of his mouth which Kayla could not see. He felt proud at coming up with an answer, although, in all honesty, he meant every word. But surely now she'd drop it when he told her how much he loved her and she was all that mattered. *Let's see you come back on that one, kiddo!*

"Did you ever think I would like to have a new mom?"

A wince flashed across his face. There was no hiding it from her. He felt like his deflated body was melting into the faux leather seat. He wished she had reached over and punched him in the stomach. That would have been better than the blow she had just delivered to his heart.

"Sweetie, I know it's tough to understand. But finding a woman who wants to be a wife and mother is not an easy thing to do, especially here in Huron Cove. There aren't a lot of single women out there."

"It couldn't hurt to try, Dad."

As a trickle of sweat rolled down the left side of his face, he pulled to a stop outside of the Stones' house on the shores of Lake Huron. He wanted to answer her truthfully, but he knew better.

Luke Spencer had spent the last five years doting on his only daughter and doing everything in his power to make sure she was healthy, safe, and loved. That was his mission in life. Nothing else mattered. Sure, the issue of dating had been tossed around by his friends. But he couldn't imagine ever loving another woman after Maria. He didn't want to. He wanted to remain true to her forever, even if it meant growing old without anyone to share his life with. So he decided to lock his heart for good and focus all his energies on Kayla. *That was good enough. Wasn't it?*

He turned to look at her. "And don't forget, there are a lot of people around town who love nothing more than being able to treat you like a daughter. Olivia's one of them."

Kayla's eyes looked down at her hands folded in her lap. Her shoulders slumped and she whispered. "I guess." With little energy, she unbuckled her seatbelt and opened the door.

Luke could feel his heart shattering into a million pieces. He tried desperately to cheer up his daughter, but he could only think of using the tired old bribe angle. "Olivia's going to take you and Emma shopping for school clothes. Get whatever you want, and I'll take care of it."

With sad hound dog eyes, she nodded. "Okay."

"I love you, sweetie."

Kayla shut the door without offering a response. She turned and walked away, dragging her backpack on the ground behind her like a sad hobo kicked off the train with only his bindle.

Man, can I be any worse of a father? He wiped the sweat off his face as he watched Kayla walk inside the Stone residence. She didn't even give him a parting glance or a wave goodbye.

The radio crackled to life and the dispatcher asked his whereabouts. Apparently, the chief wanted Luke to watch for speeders when his shift started. He checked his watch and then grabbed the microphone on his lapel. "I'll be there in five minutes, Judy. I'll head straight out there."

"Everything okay, Luke?"

Luke took a deep breath before responding. *No, everything is not okay. Apparently my daughter will never be happy again in life unless I find myself a wife and her a mother. All I need now is a miracle.* He pressed the button to reply. "Yeah, it's fine, Judy. I was just dropping off Kayla."

* * *

"I wish you wouldn't have moved all the way out to the middle of nowhere."

Lily O'Leary sped down the interstate toward Huron Cove and switched her cell phone from her left hand to her right. When she saw the exit approaching, she turned on her signal, cranked the wheel to the right, and then returned her focus to her sister Rose in Chicago.

"I know, sis. You've only told me that very thing a thousand times in the last week." She jammed on the brakes at the first intersection. "I wish I didn't have to move six hours away from home either, but this is the closest teaching job I could get on such short notice."

"You could have taken that job in Minneapolis. At least they have an airport up there." Rose added an additional reason. "And they have the Mall of America up there, too. Think of the shopping you're going to be missing out on."

Lily kept one hand on the wheel as she picked up speed toward Huron Cove. "It was about the same distance. But can you imagine how cold it would get in the winter. I'd probably freeze to death taking my bags to the car."

Rose sighed through the phone. "Michigan isn't a tropical paradise either, Lil."

"I know, I know." Lily saw the sign that announced there were only ten more miles to Huron Cove. Ten more miles until she reached her "new home." She shook her head in disgust but quickly recovered. "Just remember. It's only temporary. A year at the most." She looked at the trees going by in a blur and corrected herself. "Not even a year. August to May and then I'll find something closer to home. I didn't even bring all my clothes, only what I could stuff in the backseat of the car. And I've already started looking for job openings. There are always a lot of teachers announcing their retirements in January and February, so I'll be ready to pounce when any vacancies are posted for the next school year."

"I still don't like it."

"You can come up here and visit sometime." Lily passed the sign that said Huron Cove was five miles straight ahead. "Although from the internet search, I can already tell you there's not going to be much to do."

Her car whizzed by the billboard announcing the upcoming Apple Festival. With the distraction of her sister, she didn't see it.

She didn't see the police SUV idling beneath the billboard either.

Her older sister continued with her lecture. "And make sure you don't meet any guys up there. You don't want to get involved with someone and be forced to put down roots in the boonies."

"I won't, Rose. I have no desire to meet a man in Huron Cove. Like I said, one year and then I'm out of here."

With the mile marker indicating she only had a mile to go, she thought about telling Rose she had to hang up. But she now had a new distraction—the red-and-blue police lights filling her rearview mirror. "Oh, great," she muttered under her breath. She eased her foot off the gas pedal. "You have got to be kidding me. I knew I was going to hate this town."

"What's wrong?"

Lily gulped and told her sister the truth. "There's a cop pulling me over."

In an instant, Rose yelled through the phone. "Be careful! It could be a trick. I saw it on an episode of *Law & Order* once."

Lily pulled her car to a stop on the side of the road and had the wherewithal to roll her eyes. "That's only on TV, Rose. It's probably some Barney Fife character looking to meet his quota for the month."

"Or maybe he likes to prey on hot twenty-eight-year-old women!"

"I'll be fine." Out of her side mirror, she saw the officer exit his vehicle. Even with the quick glance, she could tell the guy didn't look like Don Knotts. "I'm going to have to go here in a minute, Rose. The officer's coming."

"Keep me on the line just in case there's trouble!"

Lily flinched at the knock on the window. She held up a finger like she'd be with the officer in a minute. Or two. Whenever she got around to it.

He knocked again, harder this time. She turned her head and frowned, miffed at the man's impatience. He made a motion for her to roll down the window.

"I gotta go, Rose."

Lily clicked off the phone and pushed the button to lower her window. It gave her time to size up the man and her situation. The officer filled out his uniform well, and that was even considering the bulletproof vest he was probably wearing. She'd bet he was at least six-two and not afraid to hit the gym at the end of his shift. What she couldn't tell was how he dealt with drivers who had a lead foot.

"Morning," Luke said.

Lily looked up from her seat and squinted at the officer. She couldn't see the man's eyes behind his dark sunglasses. He had a nametag that said Spencer. She didn't know whether it was his first or last name. She noticed his strong jaw line and caught a whiff of his masculine cologne. "Can I help you, Officer?"

She noticed his cheeks rise in a smile.

"Uh, do you know why I pulled you over?" His tone indicated she should.

Lily shrugged her shoulders and shook her head. "No, Officer. I don't." She then glanced at the phone in her hand. "Oh, is it illegal to talk on the phone in Michigan? I'm sorry, I'm from Illinois so I didn't know. I'll put it away."

Officer Spencer leaned his head to the side. "It's not illegal, but maybe it should be. I stopped you because you were driving like Danica Patrick in the Indy Five-Hundred. Did you see the speed limit sign when you got off the highway?"

Lily winced. She couldn't recall seeing much of anything after she exited the interstate. There were some trees and a billboard, she at least remembered that much. A quick glance at the officer revealed he was pulling a notepad and a pen from his chest pocket. She wondered if she should roll out the waterworks. The last thing she needed was a ticket on her first day in town. Officer Spencer didn't let her answer.

"From Illinois, huh?"

Well, duh, Sherlock. I just said I was. "Yeah."

She could feel the officer take a step back and look at the backseat. "You got a lot of stuff packed in there."

Lily sighed, her right foot tapping against the floor mat. *How much longer is this going to take?* "It's not illegal, is it?"

"No, not at all. You heading to Huron Cove?"

Lily squeezed her eyes shut and then opened them. Her head was beginning to throb. She didn't even want to be here. A part of her wanted to throw the car into gear, stand on the gas, and make like Danica back to Illinois—back where she belonged. She kept telling herself that she was only going to be in Huron Cove for a short period of time. Then she could return to civilization and never look back. "I'm just passing through, Officer." She gave him a little sniffle and a wipe of her eye in hopes of garnering a bit of sympathy.

Officer Spencer held out his hand. "License and registration, please."

CHAPTER 2

The Saturday morning commute didn't have the same gut-wrenching questions for Luke as the previous day, but that was only because Kayla stayed all night at Emma's house. The silence in his home gave Luke some peace and quiet to think. Unfortunately, he wasn't able to come up with any answers that would satisfy him or his daughter. He was alone, and he didn't think there was anything he could do about it.

"Morning, Luke," Arlene said from behind the counter of The Coffee Cove.

Clad in his police uniform, he strode to the counter, nodding at a few locals on the way. "Morning, Arlene. The usual, please."

Arlene filled up a large cup of The Coffee Cove's strongest brew and handed it over. "And how is one of Huron Cove's finest doing today?"

"The streets are quiet and calm this morning, Arlene. Just as everyone likes it." The lack of a smile indicated his heart wasn't into it today.

Arlene wiped down the counter with a towel. "So why so glum?"

It is that obvious? He shook his head and looked away, disgusted that he couldn't mask his problems. He tried never to bring his personal business to work, but with his daughter's comments from the previous morning, it was hard not to. "I just have a lot on my mind, Arlene. Something that Kayla said yesterday has got me all out of sorts."

Arlene folded the towel and placed it on the counter behind her. "Come on," she said, pointing toward the front window. She started in that direction as if she expected Luke to follow.

"Let's step into my office and you can tell me what's wrong."

Having grown up in Huron Cove and been a member of the ten-officer police force for almost ten years now, Luke Spencer was well aware that Arlene had become the unofficial therapist around the town square. If anyone was having a problem at home or at work, sometimes all it took to clear one's mind was a cup of coffee and a heart-to-heart talk with Arlene.

Luke took a seat at the table after Arlene sat down with her own cup of coffee. The August sunshine warmed them as the tourists walked by.

"So, what's going on with Kayla?"

Luke gripped his cup and gritted his teeth. He really didn't want to have this conversation, but he didn't have anyone else to talk to. His parents had passed away. Although he had no shortage of friends, most of them were married with children and too busy to get together. All Luke had was Kayla, and he was okay with that.

But apparently Kayla wasn't.

"She wants to know when I'm getting married again."

Arlene nodded like she expected to hear it. She knew Luke's life story. Most people in town did. It seemed like the entire county came to his wife's funeral, and it was a good bet every woman in Huron Cove had fixed a casserole or a coffee cake to take over to him and Kayla in the aftermath. "How long has Maria been gone now?"

Luke looked down at his cup. He could still see his wife's face like it was yesterday—her shoulder length blonde hair, her blue eyes, her effervescent smile. Kayla had been the beneficiary of her mother's genes.

"More than five years."

"You still miss her, don't you?"

Luke nodded. "Not a day goes by that I don't think about Maria. She was my whole life." He shook his head trying to scramble the sadness from taking hold again. "Now Kayla is my whole life. We got along okay for the first two or three years because it was just us. I think we took turns taking care of each other. But in the last year, things have changed. She hangs out with Emma a lot, which is great, don't get me wrong. Emma has helped Kayla come out of her shell and put the smile back on her face. But I think Kayla sees Olivia and Ethan being Emma's mom and dad, and . . ."

When Luke couldn't finish his thought, Arlene sat back in her chair and gave the comments a chance to simmer in her mind before she came up with a diagnosis. The man across the table from her was a young-looking thirty-five, in great shape, and would be the most sought-after bachelor in Huron Cove if he ever pronounced himself available. But the shield around his heart was up in full force. To get him to open his heart to love again was going to take a lot of work. And someone special.

"You know, Luke, it wouldn't hurt for you to get out on the town and meet someone."

Luke felt his shoulders grow heavier at the thought. He had spent two years wooing Maria and then poured his heart and soul into loving her during their marriage. *And now Arlene wants me to go out and find someone else to love just as much?* "I don't know if I can do it, Arlene. Losing Maria broke my heart. I don't know whether I'm able to love another woman after losing her."

"But don't you miss having someone?"

Luke took an extra few seconds to think of an answer. He looked at Arlene and then down at his coffee. "Well, to be honest, I guess I do miss having someone to talk to, to confide in, to lean on when life gets a little difficult. It's hard not to feel the emptiness of the house when Kayla's over at Emma's."

Arlene took a sip of her coffee and focused her thoughts. "Have you ever thought of what it's like from Kayla's perspective? She could use a mom, you know."

Luke's eyes narrowed, his gaze zeroing in on Arlene as the statement rattled around in his brain. "Kayla said something similar to me yesterday when I was dropping her off at Emma's." A thought hit him. "Did she say something to you?

Have those two been in here plotting another one of their crazy schemes?"

Arlene laughed. "Oh boy, those two darlings are in here every day chatting up a storm. They ought to have their own TV show." She slapped her hand on the table and then pointed at him. "Now that would be entertaining to watch."

Luke frowned. "You're deflecting, Arlene."

Arlene started to speak but then stopped, her cheeks blushing. "I'm what?"

"Deflecting. Changing the subject. Stalling. Whatever you want to call it, you didn't answer my question."

A smile began to form in the corner of her mouth, and she placed a hand over her heart. "Luke, you know I can't divulge the secrets of my clients. People come in here and know that they can talk to me in confidence." She thought better of it and held out her hands. "Within reason, of course. Sometimes matters of the heart are too important to keep under wraps and I have to take action." Then she reached over and placed her hand on top of Luke's. "But it's time, Luke. You need to find someone to share your life with. I know you still have a lot of love to give in that big heart of yours. Find someone to share that love with. It will be good for you and for Kayla."

Luke was beginning to realize he had no choice. He was going to have to consider opening his heart to love again—for his sake and for his daughter's.

Hoping to move Luke along, Arlene gestured a finger at him. "When's the last time you talked to a woman?" She thought better of it and added, "I mean a woman you didn't know."

Luke looked out the window as he racked his brain. *How long had it been?* The number of seconds that passed began to worry him so he grasped for any answer he could think of. "Yesterday. I talked to a woman yesterday."

"Okay. What was her name?"

Luke could tell Arlene didn't believe him and he looked down at his hands as he tried to come up with someone, anyone.

All the women he remembered from yesterday were local and married, and Arlene would know every one of them. His mind snapped to attention. There was one woman. He had never met her before and, since she said she was just passing through, it was a safe bet that Arlene wouldn't know her either. He decided to go with it. "Her name was Lily. Lily O'Leary. I talked to her yesterday morning." He hoped she'd drop the subject until he was ready to discuss it, which would probably be never.

"Oh, Lily. That's a nice name. I don't recognize it, though. What's she look like?"

So much for dropping the subject. His mind went back to yesterday morning. Even belted in her seat behind the wheel of her Camry, Luke could tell Lily O'Leary was an attractive woman. "Dark brown hair, brown eyes, five-eight, twenty-eight years old."

Arlene's eyes widened. "Wow! You must have really been checking her out."

Luke sighed and shook his head, having a hard time believing the only single woman he could remember talking to in the recent past was a scofflaw. A pretty scofflaw, but a lawbreaker nonetheless. Given how rumors could spread like wildfire in Huron Cove, he came clean to set the record straight from the get-go. "It was on her driver's license, Arlene. I pulled her over for speeding."

Arlene tried not to laugh. "Oh no! That's not the best way to meet women, Luke. You didn't give her a ticket, did you?"

"Well, yeah."

Arlene's jaw dropped. "Luke! How could you do that? Why couldn't you let her off with a warning?"

Luke shrugged. "She was fifteen miles per hour over the limit. It was like she was trying to set the land speed record or something. If she would have been within five, I probably would have given her a break. But I was in a bad mood. And she was kind of rude, too. A bit snippy if you ask me—like I was an inconvenience to her." When Luke saw Arlene's head shaking in disappointment, he added, "I can't turn a blind eye to excessive speeding just because a woman's pretty. That wouldn't be fair."

Arlene sighed, her head still shaking. "Well, I don't know whether that counts as meeting a woman. You're going to have to try harder. I'm sure you can find someone. Better yet, I'll put the word out that you're looking for someone special."

Luke cocked his head to the side and held out his hand. He wasn't jumping on board just yet. "Discretely, Arlene. Why don't we try and keep this quiet to start with. I don't want hot-pink flyers with my face on them posted on every telephone pole in the county."

The smile couldn't get any wider on Arlene's face. "Wouldn't have it any other way, Luke."

"And it doesn't mean I have to fall in love with the first person who happens to show some interest."

"Of course not," she said, her smile still growing wider.

"And she has to be right for Kayla. We're a package deal. Otherwise, it's a no-go."

"I wouldn't expect you to settle for second best, Luke."

He shook his head, like he didn't know what he had just gotten himself into or how he had been roped into doing so. He could feel the hairs standing up on the back of his neck. *Dating?* He was going to have to start all over at thirty-five. He looked thirty, worked out regularly, and had yet to see any gray hairs. *But dating? A night out on the town? Flirting?* That thought alone made him break out in a cold sweat. Not to mention the flowers, chocolates, and candlelight dinners. It had been so long he wondered if he could get back up on the horse. *I guess I'm going to have to find out.* He offered a smile like he knew his time on Arlene's "couch" was over. *Now the hard part begins.* "I had better get to work, Arlene. Thanks for the coffee and for listening." He stopped and shook his head at what might be in store for him. "I think."

* * *

"Morning, Rose," Lily said into the phone. From the top step of the post office in downtown Huron Cove, she surveyed the town that she would call home for the foreseeable future. The sun was shining, which Lily was thankful for because she forgot her umbrella in Chicago. She wondered if they even had a place to buy an umbrella in Huron Cove. She looked to her left and saw a pizzeria, an antique store, a greeting card shop, and a bakery. She decided to worry about the umbrella later because she needed food first.

"Hey, sis, how was your first night in the middle of nowhere?"

Lily walked down the steps and turned right. There were a handful of people walking, a couple of them with cups of coffee in their hands. Two others were walking their dogs. They all smiled and mouthed "good morning" to her. She nodded and returned her focus to her sister.

"Not good. That bed was stiff as a board, and now my back is paying the price."

"Oh, you poor thing."

"It was a quiet night, though." She stopped at the intersection and looked around. "It was so quiet I couldn't sleep. It's totally different than Chicago. I don't think I heard one jet overhead the entire night. For a while I thought there might be something wrong with my hearing."

She waited for a car to pass before she crossed the street.

"What are you doing now?"

"I dropped my resumes in the mailbox for a couple of potential jobs back home. One is in Plainfield and the other is in Bolingbrook. They are good schools, so I thought I'd get my name on the list before a vacancy opens."

"That's smart, Lil. I hope you get some good news. I feel so bad for you being so far away from home."

"I'll be fine." She said it just to soothe her sister's feelings. She didn't like being far away from home either. "All I need to do is keep busy and the school year will be over before I know it."

"So what else is new?"

Lily entered the Food Mart and yanked a cart from the corral. She tried to think of something "new" that happened since she talked with Rose the day before. The seventy-five-dollar speeding ticket was left unsaid for the time being. "The town is so small that practically everything you need is found right around the courthouse square. The post office, the bookstore, the coffee shop, the movie theater, the grocery store. It's like one-stop shopping. And there's hardly any traffic either. So at least that's something good about the place."

"Sounds boring to me."

Lily could hear her sister thumbing the pages of a magazine, her Saturday morning ritual. She was probably sitting on the couch in her condo resting up for a night on the town. Lily sighed. Nightlife. Restaurants. Handsome males around every corner. *Not going to find any of that around here! Oh, I can't wait to get back to the big city.*

She wheeled the cart through the produce section with one hand as the other held her phone. A hand drawn sign promoting a special on blueberries caught her attention. *Made in Michigan!* the sign blared. She picked up the container, looked it over, and put it in her cart.

"What do you have going on today?" Rose asked.

"I'm probably going to work on my lesson plans this afternoon. They said I can get into my classroom and have a look around. I should probably get things squared away in there before the start of school on Monday."

She packed her cart full of soup and cereal, some bread and cheese, and some milk and orange juice. She added a variety of canned vegetables—peas, carrots, green beans—all of the generic brand. While she was there, she figured she might as well stock up on the essentials and found the mustard, ketchup, butter, and some sugar. Starting to feel the loneliness of the place, she threw in a quart of strawberry ice cream—and then a bag of animal crackers just in case the loneliness lasted into next week.

"I should probably go, Rose. I'm about ready to check out and then I need to get the groceries back to the house. I'll call you later."

"Morning," the man in the blue apron at the cash register said.

Lily put her phone in her back pocket and then hurried to place her items on the conveyor belt. "Morning."

"You're not from around here."

After grabbing the ice cream, Lily looked around and saw no one. She guessed it was obvious. "I'm . . . uh . . . I just moved in yesterday." She didn't know what to say. People in Chicago didn't ask questions of strangers. She reminded herself to come up with an answer that would satisfy the questioner but keep him or her at a distance—because she didn't have any desire to meet people when she'd be leaving as soon as a new teaching position opened.

The man started waving cans of soup across the scanner. "Well, welcome to Huron Cove. I'm George Butler. I own the Food Mart. We're glad to have you in town. If there's anything you need, let me know."

Lily almost started laughing at the man's friendliness. *Am I dreaming?* "Thanks."

"What's brought you to Huron Cove?"

After emptying her cart, Lily fumbled around in her purse, pulling back the divider between compartments. She knew her credit card was in there somewhere. "I . . . um . . . I'm going to be teaching at Saint Peter's." Another quick search of the far corners of her purse caused a shiver in her spine. She wanted to curse but held her tongue.

"That's great to hear. I have a couple granddaughters starting kindergarten this year. It's nice to have new teachers in town." Mr. Butler looked at the total on the screen. "That'll be forty-five dollars and sixty-seven cents."

Lily felt her stomach drop. She hadn't even been in Huron Cove for twenty-four hours and she got a speeding ticket and now she couldn't find her plastic. "I can't seem to find my credit card. I thought I put my wallet in here this morning." She rallied a bit when she found her travel wallet. There was always something in there for emergencies. She yanked it open and flinched. Two twenties. She looked at Mr. Butler. "I only have forty dollars. Could you take off a few items? I'm really sorry."

Mr. Butler smiled and waved off her request. "That's not necessary, young lady. Forty will do."

Lily smiled, the old man's kindness touching her heart. "I appreciate it. I can pay you back when I get my wallet."

"Really, it's not necessary. Welcome to Huron Cove."

Lily thanked him, although her mind was too busy wondering what she had done with her wallet. *It's this cursed town!* she told herself. She knew she wasn't going to like it here, and if her first twenty-four hours were any indication, it was going to be a long, long school year.

With another customer in line, Lily hurried to help Mr. Butler pack the groceries into the plastic bags. She dumped as many cans of soup and vegetables in the bag as she could and threw it in the cart.

"Thank you so much."

When she had everything packed, Mr. Butler said, "Enjoy your time teaching. Come again."

Not wanting to push the cart down the street, she grabbed the five bags and started walking. Mumbling to herself, she remembered she had gone through her wallet the night before and laid it on her dresser. She opened the trunk of her car and dumped in the bags. *How else can I make a fool of myself in this town?*

She thought about calling Rose but decided to save it for later. Slamming down the trunk lid didn't make her feel any better. She got behind the wheel and fastened her belt. *Things can't get any worse.* She turned the key, put the car into *Reverse*, and backed out until she heard a crunch and felt a jolt. She gasped, her right hand covering her mouth.

No, she was wrong. Things could get worse.

"Oh, no," she said, her eyes darting to the rearview mirror. "You have got to be kidding me."

And the future wasn't looking any better because she looked out the driver's side window and saw a police officer heading right for her. Her stomach dropped. It was the same officer who gave her the ticket yesterday. She finally reached her breaking point. Her hands shot up to her face and the tears started to flow. This wouldn't have happened if she hadn't lost her job. Now she was in the small town of Huron Cove, Michigan, and nothing in life seemed to be going right. She sobbed to herself.

Then that dreaded yet familiar knock on the window came.

Through her teary eyes, she saw the officer motion with his hand to lower the window. She did, readying for her bad day to get even worse.

"Morning," Luke said. "We meet again, Miss O'Leary."

Lily wiped her tear-streaked cheeks. She saw the nametag said Spencer. *Yep, same guy from yesterday.* She wondered if she was going to see the inside of the Huron Cove jail. Her voice quaking, she said, "I'm sorry, Officer, I didn't." She looked in her mirror. "I didn't see whatever it was I hit."

"Why don't you pull forward and step out of the car for a second."

Lily did as she was told and dreaded the thought of what she was about to see. *Oh no! I don't have my license!* For a split second, she thought about making a run for it. The thoughts of fleeing from the law were interrupted by the sight of the officer in her mirror.

Figuring she was in enough trouble already, Lily stepped out and walked to the back of her car to look at the damage. With the sound of the impact, she expected to see her bumper dragging on the ground. Being new to the area, she had completely forgotten about the median intersecting the two lanes. Her tires had hit the curbing and her bumper crunched the giant plastic apple decoration that promoted the upcoming Apple Festival. The apple was currently resting in the gutter across the street, its green leaf, now three pieces instead of one, strewn in the roadway.

Luke walked over to the gutter to corral the apple, the obvious crack indicating it would no longer be appropriate for further display.

Lily rubbed her hand across her face and mumbled something to herself. When Luke walked back, she threw her hands up in disbelief. "I'm sorry, Officer. I didn't see it. I thought I had plenty of room."

Luke put the apple back in the grassy median for the time being. Then they stood looking at each other. "Well, you're not the first person to back into one of these things. They should probably do a better job of placement. Doesn't look like it did any damage to your bumper, though. Might have scraped the underside on the curb."

Lily looked at the back of her car and breathed a sigh of relief. The last thing she needed was a car repair bill. She then turned her attention to the officer. In the sunshine, Luke's blond hair was cut short, and she recognized the strong jaw line. But now, with his sunglasses on top of his head, she noticed the man had eyes as blue as the ocean. She had never seen such a brilliant shade of blue. *And my is he handsome.* He looked like one of those hot cops from TV. She had to shake herself to stop from staring. *The guy's a cop! You better hope he doesn't ask for your license again!*

"Again, I'm really sorry. I'll pay for the apple." Her heart sank when Luke reached for his notepad.

"I'm afraid I'll have to write it up," he said, clicking his pen.

After a flash of heat hit her cheeks, Lily sighed. *Could this guy be any more of a jerk?* "Is that really necessary? I said I'd pay for it," she snapped.

Luke's eyes narrowed, and she could tell he was thinking how to respond. "Ma'am, I have to write it up just in case the town wants to know what happened to its apple. I wouldn't worry about it, though. The apples don't cost much. Could I get your driver's license again?"

Lily's eyes closed and her shoulders sank. *How many laws have I broken in the last twenty-four hours?* She had to struggle to keep it together. *Let me out of this town!* "I'm sorry, Officer. I . . . uh. . . I forgot my wallet at the house."

Luke cocked his head as his blue eyes glared down at her. "Now you're driving without a license?"

Lily shook her head. It was all she could do. "I forgot my wallet this morning and then I didn't have enough money to pay for all of my groceries. Mr. Butler was so nice, he let it slide. With the speeding ticket and this," she said, pointing at the damaged apple, "it's been an awful couple of days." She held out her hands and lowered her head, waiting for him to slap on the cuffs and haul her off to jail.

She never saw the hint of a smile cross his face.

Luke clicked shut his pen. "I'll give you a break on your driving without a license, Miss O'Leary. I can use the info from yesterday's ticket to write up the damage report. Like I said, I wouldn't worry about it. Accidents happen."

"Thank you," she said softly.

Their eyes locked. She thought he was going to say something, but he looked like he changed his mind. Then she noticed he smiled at her before he nodded and pulled down his sunglasses. "Drive safely, Miss O'Leary. Try not to cause any more trouble during your time in Huron Cove."

CHAPTER 3

The home Lily rented was located only a mile north of downtown Huron Cove where the houses were outnumbered by the trees. Off to the east beyond the nature preserve sat Lake Huron, its tranquil blue waters enticing swimmers and boaters on the warm August morning. The house was painted blue with white shutters, and it had been well maintained over the years. Mrs. Fossan, the little old lady who had rented the place ever since her husband passed away twenty years ago, was very choosy in selecting her tenants. There would be no smoking, partying, or any illegal activity whatsoever. No loud music either. It was a quiet neighborhood, and Mrs. Fossan wanted it to stay that way.

Lily drove up the slight incline of a driveway and parked in front of the detached garage. She had only lived in an apartment since entering the working world, so the space was welcome. She liked the idea of having a garage, although it had no automatic door opener, so she'd have to get out and raise it herself.

"Try not to cause any more trouble," she muttered to herself as she jammed the shifter into *Park. What a jerk.* She could tell Officer Spencer Something-or-Other enjoyed mocking her.

She shut off the engine and took a breath. She had made it back to her temporary home without speeding, backing into anything, or committing any other violations of the Michigan Vehicle Code. She decided she needed to be extra vigilant because the cops probably had her picture tacked to the bulletin board next to a motley crew of felons and fugitives.

Another deep breath. She was hoping her bad luck had run dry so now she could focus on getting ready for school. She got out of her car and gave the door a good slam to release some of the tension. After walking up the front steps to unlock her front door, she went back to the car to retrieve her groceries.

She felt a trickle of perspiration slide down her cheek. "Better get that ice cream inside before it melts."

She looped her right arm through two plastic bags and then worked to put two more on her left. She was beginning to think she could get it all inside in one trip.

With four bags weighing her arms down, Lily had to heft her right arm high in the air to pull down the trunk lid. When she slammed it shut, two of the bags met their breaking point and lost their loads. The sound of plastic ripping and steel thumping on the concrete filled her ears. Cans of soup and vegetables started racing down the driveway toward the gutter, the tub of butter rolling off to the side until it hit the grass.

With her shoulders slumped, Lily stood there and looked at the carnage. She wanted to cry. No, she wanted to flee this town as fast as possible and go back home. Back to where she was meant to be with friends and family nearby. She closed her eyes and wished it would happen.

"Butter!"

With her hands and arms still full of what was left of her morning purchases, she opened her eyes and looked around wondering what in the world she just heard.

"Butter!"

There it was again! She thought it sounded like a young girl's voice. For a split second, she had the crazy thought that someone was selling butter door to door. *Do they do that in this crazy town?* Her tub of butter was currently warming itself on her front lawn.

She put what was left in her arms on the front porch and went to gather her cans of soup and veggies in the gutter.

"Butter!"

Lily bent down and began picking up her cans of chicken noodle. From behind, she heard footsteps and finally figured out what she was hearing. Two girls were walking on the sidewalk in her direction. They were both dressed in red shorts with pink tank tops. Both had a pink bow in their hair. Maybe they were twins with mismatched hair. Lily stood up, a can in each hand, and waited for them to approach.

The girl on the left spoke first. “Have you seen Mr. Butterlickens?”

Lily’s eyes narrowed. *What? Mr. Butterlickens? What kind of a name is that?* She shook her head and then glanced at the mailbox next door. It said Barnes, not Butterlickens. *This is one weird place.* “Who?”

The girl on the left spoke again. “Mr. Butterlickens.”

“I’m sorry, I don’t know anyone by that name.”

“No, Mr. Butterlickens is my dog.”

Lily chuckled, thankful to finally get some answers. She noticed the leash in the girl’s hand. The two looked like they must be ten or eleven. One had blonde hair, the other dark.

“We just call him Butter. He’s a goldie. Sometimes he gets out and we have to go looking for him. We usually find him over at Marvin’s house . . . That’s Miss Julia’s border collie. They’re best friends. But we have to find him because it’s supposed to storm this afternoon, and Butter doesn’t like storms.”

Lily smiled at the two but shook her head. “I’m afraid I haven’t seen any dogs. I got home a couple minutes ago and was about to carry in my groceries. I just moved in yesterday.”

The girl on the right with the dark hair finally spoke. “What’s your name?”

“My name’s Lily. Lily O’Leary.”

The girl’s eyes widened. “Oh! You must be our new teacher!” She grasped the arm of her friend. “This must be our new teacher! They said her name was Miss O’Leary. I’m Emma, and this is Kayla.”

Emma Lynn Grayson Stone, adopted daughter of Ethan and Olivia Stone, had come to Huron Cove only a handful of years earlier, but she already made a name for herself as a kindhearted, intelligent ray of sunshine with a particular fondness for matchmaking. She had befriended most of the townsfolk, but none more so than her best friend Kayla.

The two girls took turns giving their new teacher a hug and then the barrage of talking began.

"We're so happy to meet you," Emma said. "We didn't think we'd be able to meet you until school starts on Monday. We thought you'd be older, kinda like Mrs. Hardy. She has gray hair. She was supposed to be our teacher this year, but she decided to retire because she just became a grandmother. We haven't met her granddaughter yet, but we hope to soon. The Hardys live up the road just around the bend. Mrs. Hardy was a good teacher. We can't wait for classes to begin."

Kayla took over when Emma stopped for a breath. "Oh, yes. We're very excited for classes to start. We love to learn and read. We spent the whole summer reading. We read all of the *Anne of Green Gables* books. We had already read them, but they're so good we read 'em again. School is so much fun. There's so much to learn."

Hearing a slight pause, Emma looked at the soup cans lined up in the driveway and the bags behind the car and asked, "Do you need some help with your groceries, Miss O'Leary?"

The sweet whirlwind that had become known in Huron Cove as the *Emma & Kayla Show* had blessedly descended on the life of Lily O'Leary. For the short time she had known them, they had completely taken her mind off all her problems. And to think these two darlings were going to be in her sixth-grade class.

Lily looked around. Given her day so far, she came to the conclusion that, yes indeed, she could use a few extra hands. "Do you think it would be okay with your parents if you help me get my stuff inside?"

"Oh, yes," Emma said, reaching for a can of tomato soup. "They won't mind. Anybody who lives in Mrs. Fossan's house is a good person."

Kayla agreed. "Mrs. Fossan doesn't let ne'er-do-wells live in her house. That's what Dad says. No smoking, no partying, and no illegal activity whatsoever."

"No loud music either," Emma added.

Lily smiled, thankful again at the break in an otherwise forgettable morning. "Okay, then. Why don't you two grab the soup and vegetable cans, and I'll get the milk and ice cream."

Lily held the front door open as the two girls, their arms full of cans, walked inside. "The kitchen is straight back."

The living room had a faux leather couch, a recliner, a coffee table, and a TV. Lily hadn't used any of them yet. After hanging up her clothes and unpacking what little she had, she had spent most of yesterday afternoon in bed working on a lesson plan. She was thankful the house came furnished. It would save her a ton of time when she moved out.

Kayla looked around the living room before they reached the kitchen. "You don't have much stuff, Miss O'Leary."

For a split second, Lily had a thought to tell them that she wouldn't be in town very long and didn't need to bring a lot of possessions. This was a short-term gig, and there was no sense in hauling all her stuff to Michigan only to pack it up again in a year. Even though she realized the two girls would only be in her class one year, she decided to keep her intentions to herself.

"I don't need a lot." She set a box of kitchen towels on the floor. "A bed, a fridge, a microwave, and a TV are all I really need. And a washer and dryer, too. At any rate, I'll probably be so busy with my work at school to notice much."

Emma and Kayla put the soup and vegetable cans on the counter as Lily placed the softened ice cream in the freezer and then the milk in the fridge. She opened a cupboard, found it completely empty, and held out her hands as Emma and Kayla took turns filling them with cans—soup on the left and vegetables on the right. She noticed how the girls worked together, like they had been doing so since the day they were born. She wondered if they were twin sisters. Or what it was going to be like with them in her class.

Once the cans filled the cupboard, the girls helped unpack the rest of the bags. "Oh, you bought blueberries!" Emma said.

"We love 'em. My grandma makes a great blueberry coffee cake. Michigan is famous for its blueberries. A lot of them come from the Lake Michigan side. That's known as the fruit belt part of the state."

Lily smiled. "Is that so?"

"Yep. And Michigan is famous for its apples, too. We love apples."

Kayla agreed and handed over the butter. "Are you going to the Apple Festival, Miss O'Leary?"

"Well, I don't know. I haven't been here long enough to think about it."

"It's in the fall and it's always a good time. Everybody goes to it and has a lot of fun."

Lily closed the fridge with the last of the groceries put away. "I'll have to put it on the calendar then. Thanks a lot for your help, girls. I really appreciate it."

She walked the girls back outside, both of them talking up a storm. Lily smiled at their exuberance, laughing like their lives were overflowing with joy. Once in the driveway, both girls gave her hugs, the simple act warming her heart. She was so preoccupied that she never saw what came up behind her.

"Butter!" Kayla yelled at the golden retriever, whose dirty front paws were now printing the back of Lily's jeans. "Butter! Get down! Get down!" It took both girls to grab Butter's collar and pull him away. "I'm so sorry, Miss O'Leary. Butter's very friendly."

When Kayla was able to get the leash on, Lily bent down and gave the dog a good rubbing. "That's okay. I don't mind. You're a good boy, aren't you?" she said, a smile on her face. "Such a handsome dog."

"We got him at the shelter. He looked lonely so Dad said we could give him a home."

With Butter safely corralled with his leash, Lily stood up. "Stop by anytime, girls. It was nice meeting you both."

Emma and Kayla walked down the sidewalk, Butter leading the way. The two girls waved like they had been friends with their new teacher for years.

Lily's day had been brightened like a thousand suns were shining on her. She was reminded of why she wanted to become a teacher—to nurture young minds as they grow in body and spirit.

She waved back. "Bye, girls. I'll see you at school on Monday."

CHAPTER 4

On Monday morning, Luke woke up early, showered and shaved, put on his police uniform, and headed to the kitchen. Hearing Kayla getting ready, he opened the fridge to start making her breakfast and her lunch. As a single parent, he had gotten used to the routine. It was a part of his life. Thinking about his conversation with Arlene, he couldn't help but wonder what it would be like to have a spouse to share his life with. Eating breakfast together in the morning, coming home to her at night, thinking about her throughout the day. He was warming to the idea of finding someone. But who could he find in Huron Cove?

As much as he tried not to, his mind kept coming back to Lily O'Leary. He had spoken to her two days in row, although she might say not under the best of circumstances. He hadn't seen her on Sunday but figured she was long gone from Huron Cove and would never be seen again.

But with the lack of available females in town, she was all he had to go on at the present time. She came off as independent—a determined woman with a plan. Sure she was a bit feisty, but there's nothing wrong with that. Nothing wrong with being beautiful either. The brown eyes were what he remembered. Big brown eyes that could cause a single man to get lost in. He shook himself, trying to scramble the thoughts of a woman he didn't know other than her unfortunate habit of committing minor traffic violations.

He liked the thoughts, but . . .

He rolled his neck. While the thought of having someone in his life was appealing, the actual act of finding that special woman was giving him a good size headache. And he scolded himself that he shouldn't be thinking about someone who was just "passing through" anyway. He needed to get a grip and get serious. He was going to have to start thinking about places to meet single women. *The bar? The grocery store? Church?* He sighed and muttered something under his breath. He wasn't a fan of the bars and he liked to zip in and out of the store as fast as possible. And he hadn't been to church since Maria died. He didn't have a clue where to start. Thankfully, for now at least, he had a major distraction, and her name was Kayla Ann Spencer.

"Good morning, beautiful," he said, planting a kiss on the top of her forehead. He gave a scratch behind the ears to Mr. Butterlickens as the dog followed Kayla to the kitchen counter. "Are you all ready for your first day of school?"

Kayla took a seat on a stool. Mr. Butterlickens laid down next to her and buried his face between his two front paws. Luke thought the dog looked particularly dour that morning. He didn't think golden retrievers could frown but this one sure looked like he could.

Kayla said softly, "Yeah, I'm ready."

Luke put a bowl of Frosted Flakes in front of her and added a glass of orange juice on the side. "You don't seem too thrilled."

Kayla shrugged and spooned some flakes around in her bowl.

Man, is it going to be like this until she turns eighteen? "Everything okay?"

Kayla took a bite but kept her head down. She nodded as she crunched a mouthful. Mr. Butterlickens remained still, his eyes the only part of him moving as they went back and forth between Kayla and her father.

Luke felt the hollowness in his stomach starting to form again. His daughter could brighten any room she entered, but he was beginning to wonder if the cloud hanging over their heads would be detrimental to her well-being. He leaned on the counter across from her. With nothing to go on in the parenting department, he tried to do his best.

"I've been giving a lot of thought to what we talked about the other day in the car, Kayla."

He noticed the flinch and then the slight widening of her eyes. He had been a police officer long enough to notice "the tells" when he had exposed a lie or struck a nerve. She tried to cover herself by shrugging again and spooning out some more flakes.

"I'm . . . uh . . . willing to . . . uh . . ." He could tell she was desperately waiting for what he had to say because she stopped chewing. "I'm going to try and find someone who might want to hang out with me." He noticed the corner of her mouth begin to rise. "Hang out with *us*, I mean."

She gulped down the last bite. "Really?"

"Yeah."

The smile that ran from one ear to the other warmed his broken heart. She jumped off the stool and wrapped her arms around his midsection. "Thank you, Dad. Thank you."

Luke wrapped his arms tighter around her. He didn't want to let go, in part so she wouldn't see the tears pooling in his eyes. All he wanted was for his daughter to be happy. But he had to temper her enthusiasm or risk big problems down the road. "Now you have to be patient, sweetie. It's not something that I can just snap my fingers and make happen in an instant. These things take time, sometimes a lot of time."

"I understand, Dad. Thank you."

With his tail wagging at a furious pace, Mr. Butterlickens tried to nuzzle his wet nose in between the both of them, his mood apparently brightening as well. Kayla took her seat again and gobbled up the rest of her cereal. She gulped down her juice and took her bowl to the sink.

Luke smiled at the transformation. "Peanut butter and jelly okay for your lunch?"

"Oh, yes. That'll be great. Come on, Butter." Then she was off with the dog right behind her. "Thanks, Dad."

Well, at least I made someone happy today. Luke washed the bowl and the glass and let them dry on the counter. He wiped his hands and wondered what was next. *Now I'm going to have to produce some results.*

* * *

The alarm clock had her out of bed before the sun rose. The first day of school always brought a handful of jitters, not only for students but for teachers as well. There were big jitters for Lily this year, however. Unlike in past years, she didn't have the indirect knowledge of knowing who was entering her class. She oftentimes relied on her fellow teachers to give her a heads-up on certain students who might need a little extra help or encouragement. Now it was a blank slate, other than her newfound friends Kayla and Emma.

After a shower, she combed through her closet for her first-day attire. She decided on conservative—black slacks with a short-sleeved white blouse. It was professional, yet comfortable. She added a pair of shoes that would keep her feet from hurting after a whole day of standing. She ate a bowl of cereal and had a glass of orange juice.

When she went back to her bedroom to finish getting ready, she reached into her dresser drawer for the countdown calendar she had made up the day before. She grabbed the red marker on the top of the dresser and drew an X through the box for Sunday, August 20th. According to her calculations, there were 280 days between Monday and May 27 of next year when she would be able to pack up and never look back. Only 280 more days until her life could really start. That meant there were only 6,720 more hours, 403,200 more minutes, or 24,192,000 more seconds to go. *Give or take. But who's counting?*

After a restful Sunday evening, she had slept well, the open window bringing in some cool breezes off the lake. She decided that was one characteristic of summer in Huron Cove she could get used to. That and the short drive to work. At that early hour, the streets of Huron Cove were slowly beginning to spring to life, but it was nothing like the bumper-to-bumper madness she had to endure during her morning commute in and around Chicago.

She turned on the lights to her classroom that she had spent the previous day putting on the final touches. In the sixth grade at St. Peter's Christian School, she had twenty students, split evenly between boys and girls. She arranged the desks into four rows of five and placed name tags on each of them. To start the year, she decided to seat the kids in alphabetical order in hopes of getting to know them by way of her seating chart. Given their last names of Spencer and Stone, Kayla and Emma were in the back row on the right side of the room.

She straightened her blouse and swiped a speck of paper off her slacks. Everything seemed ready to go. All she needed now was a roomful of kids and she could officially start a new school year—and be that much closer to going home. She glanced at the clock on the wall and wondered how many seconds she had knocked off her grand total.

* * *

After leaving the house in the care of Mr. Butterlickens, Kayla hopped in the front passenger seat of her dad's police SUV and placed her Wonder Woman backpack and lunch box on the floorboard in front of her.

From their house on the north edge of town, the drive to school would take less than five minutes. They passed in front of the police station across from the courthouse. Two intersections later, Luke turned right and then made a left into the parking lot of St. Peter's Christian School.

"I know you're getting big and everything, but is it okay if I walk you to your classroom? I think they finally found a new teacher for you. Kind of a last-minute deal. Anyway, I'd like to meet her. See what she's like."

Kayla unbuckled her seat belt. "Sure. She's nice."

Luke did a double take. "You've met her? Where?"

"Emma and I met her on Saturday when we were looking for Butter. She lives two doors down."

Luke turned off the engine. "In Mrs. Fossan's house?"

"Yep. We helped bring in her groceries."

Luke nodded and smiled. That sounded like something Kayla and Emma would do. They'd been known to help little old ladies cross the street so why not a gray-haired lady who was called out of retirement to teach sixth grade. At least that's what he heard through the grapevine. He wondered why she would be renting Mrs. Fossan's house, though. Maybe she was from out of town.

Luke held the door for his daughter. She wore a pink dress with white polka dots with a matching bow in her hair. He reminded himself to thank Olivia for picking out some nice outfits for Kayla, grateful he didn't have to figure out what she should or shouldn't wear.

Speaking of Olivia, as Luke and Kayla neared the classroom, Olivia's husband, Ethan, walked out. Luke extended a hand while Kayla continued inside.

"Ethan, good to see you. Another school year begins."

Ethan shook his head like he couldn't believe it. "Seems like they go by so fast. Pretty soon they'll be off to high school and before you and I know it, they'll be getting their drivers' licenses."

Luke shivered at the thought. "Oh, let's not get too far ahead of ourselves. I'd like to keep Kayla out of her teen years as long as I can. If you talk to Olivia before I see her, please thank her for me for taking Kayla shopping. I appreciate it."

"No problem. Olivia loves doing it, and I know Kayla and Emma always have a good time."

Luke checked his watch. "If it's okay with you, I can drop off Emma and Kayla at your house after school. Kayla mentioned something about working together on a project."

"Sure, no problem. See you then."

Luke let another father walk into the classroom with his son before he entered. In doing so, he missed the colorful hand drawn sign next to the door that said *Miss O'Leary. Sixth Grade.*

Once inside, Luke looked around the room for his daughter. He found her and her best friend Emma giving hugs to the only adult woman in the room. The woman had her back to him, but he realized she wasn't a gray-haired lady called out of retirement like he expected. His eyes scanned the room again. *Am I in the right place?* The woman stood about five-eight and had shoulder-length brown hair. He couldn't help but notice the slacks fit her athletic lower half and the white blouse accentuated her hourglass figure. *Is it a student's mother that I don't know? Maybe a teacher's aide?*

Luke walked closer but stopped when he heard the woman laugh. When she spoke, he thought the voice sounded familiar. He felt a jolt in his chest. The name written in black marker on the whiteboard confirmed that "Miss O'Leary" was not only a scofflaw but a sixth-grade teacher. Luke sucked in a breath. *Oh boy.*

Lily told Kayla and Emma they had better put their backpacks and lunch boxes in the closet, and the two hurried to comply. When Lily made a half turn, she caught a glimpse of the police officer standing and staring at her. She flinched and then her eyes narrowed. The smile turned upside down in an instant. She fronted him and placed her hands on her hips. Luke could tell the fire was lit and, by the flare in her nostrils, it looked like Miss O'Leary was ready to charge.

"Oh, great, it's you again."

CHAPTER 5

Everything had been going so well. Her kids had started filtering into the classroom, and their parents introduced themselves and welcomed her to Huron Cove. Everyone seemed so nice and glad to see her. Smiles abounded as friendships were reconnected after the summer away from school. The arrival of Kayla and Emma gave Lily an extra shot of joy and she couldn't wait for the bell to ring so she could start class.

But then.

The long arm of the law decided to invade her classroom. She wondered if he was going to cuff her and haul her out in front of the kids. *The nerve of the man! Doing his business in a packed classroom! He's probably here to give me another ticket!* She gritted her teeth, her eyes drawn to the name tag on his uniform. Spencer. Spencer something. She didn't know his last name and didn't want to know. Unless it was to file a complaint for harassment. She just wanted him gone. A part of her considered thrusting her finger toward the door and giving him an order to hit the bricks. She had a class to teach, and she thought it would be a great opportunity to show the kids who was the boss in this classroom. For now, she decided against it, forcibly removing police officers from her presence not being in her DNA.

But that didn't mean she couldn't be direct with the man.

"What did I do wrong now? Park in front of a fire hydrant?"

Luke stepped forward, a smile beginning to form. "Miss O'Leary. We meet again. So nice to see you this fine morning."

The smile was not reciprocated on Lily's face. She glanced up at the clock, still ten minutes from the bell ringing to start the day. She took her hands off her hips and crossed her arms across her chest. She wasn't moving. The staredown gave her a chance to finally size up the officer on her turf. He stood about six-two, the uniform perfectly pressed, his upper body filling out his shirt. The sunglasses were on top of his head and it gave Lily a chance to take in his ocean blue eyes again. *Man, this guy is handsome. But he's also my one and only nemesis in this place, which means no matter how handsome he is, he has got to take a hike.*

At some point, someone was going to have to break this logjam, so Lily took the lead. "I wish I could say the same thing, Officer." She was waiting for him to whip out his notepad and click his pen. Maybe give her another ticket or a summons to appear in court. She didn't like how he kept smiling at her. She thought he was mocking her. "Is this about the apple?"

Luke took another step closer and stopped within arm's length, but Lily didn't budge. The only thing she did was raise her head to meet his eyes.

"No, Miss O'Leary, it's not about the apple. That's been taken care of. Anyway, I am not here for police business. I'm . . . uh . . . "

For some reason, Luke didn't finish his thought. Lily was beginning to think she was missing something, and she didn't really want to spend the time to figure it out. "So, what then?"

The smile on Luke's face grew wider. "I'm here for my daughter." He threw a thumb over his shoulder to where Kayla had taken her seat.

"Your daughter?" Lily leaned to the side and saw the blonde-haired girl chatting with Emma. Kayla Spencer. Then she remembered the name tag. Her eyes widened and she stifled a gasp. *Did things just get better or worse?* "Kayla's your daughter?"

"Yes she is. She's my pride and joy."

Lily shook her head to try and make sense of things. The man had done nothing but cause her angst since the minute she sped into town. Now, his daughter was in her class. *This is great. He'll probably be one of those parents who does nothing but complain about my teaching, badger me the whole year, and do everything he can to ruin my reputation. Well, let me tell you something, Buster. I'm no pushover.* "I'm sorry, I guess I didn't put two and two together with your name and all."

As the time for the bell to ring drew closer, the students began settling down without being told. Perhaps because their new teacher was talking with a police officer in the middle of their classroom.

Luke opened a chest pocket, pulled out his department-issued business card, and handed it to Lily. "I have to confess that I hadn't put two and two together either. I was expecting someone else to be the new teacher." He shrugged like he wasn't disappointed in his mistake. "Anyway, I just wanted to meet Kayla's new teacher and introduce myself. Although, technically, we've already become acquainted outside the classroom."

Lily's cheeks rose and blushed. "Yes, you could say that. I appreciate you coming in Officer Spencer—"

"Please, call me Luke."

The redness in Lily's cheeks darkened and she nodded. "Fine. It was nice meeting you, Luke." She looked at the clock. "I should probably get ready."

"Sure," he said, offering a nod and a parting wink. "Have a good day."

"You, too."

Lily watched as Luke turned and headed down the aisle. He gave a fist bump to his little buddy Chase and then stopped in the back to hug Kayla. He then patted Emma on the shoulder and left the room.

But not before taking one last look at his daughter's new teacher.

* * *

Luke walked down the hallway toward the exit, but he saw nothing of the colorful bulletin boards welcoming the kids back to school. Lily O'Leary had made an appearance in his life for three of the last four days. This was the same woman he told Arlene about on Saturday, but he never thought he would see her again after her run-in with the apple. *It's just a coincidence. Don't make it out to be more than it is.*

With each step, his mind replayed what just happened. Her brown eyes kept flashing in his brain, like they were drawing him closer to her.

No! She's not the one for me. Did you see how standoffish she was? The scowl on her face said it all. It's clear she hates me and doesn't want anything to do with me. Fine by me. I'll find someone, and I'm not going to fall for the first woman I happen to bump into. All I know is, she better not take her frustrations out on Kayla.

His face felt flush and he stopped in his tracks. Feeling slightly dizzy, he put a hand against the wall and tried to catch the breath he had lost since he left Lily's classroom. He could feel his heart beating in his chest as it thumped against his bulletproof vest.

He took a deep breath. He didn't need a doctor to tell him what was wrong. It was an overload of anxiety that finally bubbled over. He had told Kayla he was open to having a new woman in his life. Lily just happened to be the first one (and, recently, the only one) who came into his life. *Be patient. There will be others.* He smiled at his next thought. *And they might even like me, too.*

Releasing the breath cleared his mind. He was about to head out the door when Pastor Carlton walked through the doorway.

"Luke," he said, reaching out his hand. "So good to see you. Dropping off Kayla?"

Luke stiffened but gripped the man's hand. "Yes. Another first day of school in the books." He then waited for the inevitable question that he had been asked a thousand times in the past five years.

"How have you been?"

Make that a thousand and one. Ever since Maria's death, he had been asked that very same question. He understood the concern, but he never felt he gave an answer that satisfied the questioner. He started out with "we're doing okay" and then moved on to "we're doing fine." In the last year or two, he hoped "we're doing well" might keep people from asking again. But, in reality, he didn't really know how he and Kayla were doing. They took life one day at a time and hoped for the best. Some days were good, some days were bad. But they kept plugging along. That is, until recently, when the thought of finding someone special came front and center in their lives.

"We're doing well, Pastor. Thanks for asking." Luke made a move to his left, but Pastor Carlton didn't budge.

"That's good to hear, Luke. I hope to see you in church sometime. It's been a while."

Luke's jaw clenched and he swallowed a helping of guilt down his throat. A blind man could have seen those two "tells." He hadn't been to church since Maria's funeral. At first, it was because of his hope to avoid the questions of "how are you doing?" from all the parishioners. A year became two and then three.

But there was a deeper reason. He had gone to church most of his life, enjoyed it even. But then Maria got sick. He had prayed and prayed for her to get better and look what that got him—a dead wife and a daughter without her mother. What was the point?

He tried to change the subject. "I'm on duty most Sundays. It gives the guys a chance to have time with their families."

Pastor Carlton nodded and smiled. "I'm sure Kayla would like some time with her dad."

"I make sure she goes to church and Sunday School every week. She and Emma are always there." *What more do you want from me, Pastor? Isn't sending Kayla good enough?*

Pastor Carlton reached out an arm. "It sure would be nice to see you there too, Luke. I know Kayla would like it when her dad's there to enjoy her singing with the Sunday School choir."

The bell rang and broke the uncomfortable silence that had overtaken them. Luke looked at his watch and then reached for the door. “I should get to the station, Pastor.”

“God’s arms are always open to welcome you back, Luke. Think about it.”

Luke walked away. “Thanks, Pastor. I will.”

CHAPTER 6

The first day had flown by so fast Lily didn't know where it had gone. She had only looked at the clock on the wall once, and that was five minutes ago when she realized there were only fifteen minutes left before the final bell was set to ring.

She was pleasantly surprised with her students. They were all well-behaved. And she only once had to say "let's settle down," but that was expected on the first day. They were attentive and respectful, and no one spoke up without first raising their hand. She half expected a bevy of moans when she told the students to take out their books on math, her specialty, but they all seemed eager to learn.

At lunch, she sat with Beth Duncan, who taught fifth grade, and Jessica Knight, who taught fourth grade, and they traded email addresses, phone numbers, and a handful of war stories. Beth and Jessica both told Lily she had a good crop of kids, and Lily remarked that the students must have had a good crop of teachers prior to reaching sixth grade. Beth and Jessica also invited Lily out for pizza and iced tea at the pizzeria on Friday night, calling it a tradition that "must be adhered to."

At recess, she kept an eye on the kids and even showed her athleticism by taking a turn at the plate in kickball. It had been an enjoyable first day.

With the kids running out of energy and the last class of the day winding down, she decided to end on a high note and get to know her students a little better. *Nothing could go wrong with that idea. Could it?*

"Remember to start your reading tonight so we can discuss it tomorrow. Now, I usually like to take some time to get to know my students. I'll do my best to get your names right as soon as I can. Does anyone have any questions for me? Or about me? You can ask anything."

Without any more prodding, two hands shot straight to the ceiling in the back row.

"Emma."

"Where are you from?"

"I'm from Illinois, just outside of Chicago."

"Kayla."

"How old are you?"

"I'm twenty-eight."

"Emma."

"I like your hairstyle."

Lily grinned. More of a comment than a question, but she wasn't going to get technical. "Why thank you." She smiled at the hand in the air. "Kayla."

"Do you have any brothers or sisters?"

"I have an older sister named Rose." She pointed at Emma.

"What does she do?"

"She's a nurse."

Kayla: "What's your favorite color?"

"Red."

Emma: "What's your favorite flower?"

"What else? Lilies."

Kayla: "Do you like dogs or cats?"

"Dogs."

Emma: "What do you like to do in your spare time?"

"I like to read and run."

Kayla: "Do you like baseball?"

"Yes."

Emma: "Who's your favorite team?"

"The Cubs."

Along with the smiles vanishing from their faces, Lily noticed the two girls crinkle their noses and look at each other like the answer she gave produced a foul odor.

Kayla: "When's your birthday?"

"February fourteenth."

Emma: "Oh, that's Valentine's Day. What's your favorite food?"

"Pizza."

Emma had a follow-up: "What kind of toppings?"

"Italian sausage and green peppers."

Kayla: "Do you like long walks on the beach?"

"Of course."

Emma: "What about candlelight dinners?"

Lily shrugged. "I guess."

It went on and on. It was like the two cuties with pink bows in their hair were a tag-team of prosecutors grilling a mob boss on the witness stand. Perhaps the rapid-fire Q&A session wasn't the best idea in the world. Lily didn't even have time to object. Kayla was, of course, next.

"Do you like Huron Cove?"

Lily gave the question an extra second of thought. Given that her first impression of the town had been colored by Kayla's father ticketing her for speeding and reporting her for destroying one of the town's decorative apples, she would be forgiven if she took a dim view of the place at that juncture. But she was diplomatic. "It's a nice little town." She then glanced at the clock hoping the bell would ring.

The girls in the back row weren't finished with their cross-examination, however.

"Are you married?" Emma asked.

"No."

Emma looked at Kayla and Kayla looked at Emma. Emma nodded to her friend like it was her turn.

Kayla licked her lips and cleared her throat. "Do you have a boyfriend?"

"No."

The two girls looked at each other, and Emma waggled her eyebrows. Their cheeks then rose in unison. They had extracted all the information they needed from the witness. They kept their hands on the desk and smiled at their teacher.

No further questions, Your Honor.

* * *

Luke sat in his police SUV at the end of the parking lot hoping not to be noticed. He didn't want Miss O'Leary to think he was there looking to catch her committing another traffic violation. He figured she'd stay after the students were let out for the day and work on tomorrow's lesson plans. All he wanted to do was pick up Kayla and Emma and get them over to Emma's house so he could finish his shift.

"Afternoon, ladies," Luke said as the girls got in the back seat.

"Hi, Dad."

"Hi, Mr. Luke."

Once the seatbelts were securely fastened, Luke put the SUV into gear. "How was your first day of school?"

Emma took the lead. "Oh, Mr. Luke, it was so much fun. We got to play kickball and then we wrote essays on what we did for summer vacation. We can't wait to go back tomorrow."

Luke smiled and looked in the rearview mirror. Kayla was nodding in agreement with her best friend. "We get to paint tomorrow in art class. It'll be so much fun."

Luke flicked on his turn signal and turned left out of the parking lot. He waved to one of the other parents and then stopped at the intersection.

"Mr. Luke, can we turn on the siren?"

Luke laughed. Emma always asked that when she rode with him. "I don't know if the Chief would go for that, Emma." He looked in the mirror and saw Kayla shrug to her friend. He hated to disappoint them. "Maybe when we get out to your house we can turn it on."

That brought a smile to the girls' faces.

"Cool, Mr. Luke."

As they drove by the courthouse, Luke asked, "Do you girls have any homework?"

"Just some reading for history class."

"Do you have any new classmates?"

"No," Kayla said. "The only new person is Miss O'Leary."

The two friends giggled and whispered in each other's ears. Luke kept one eye on the road and the other in the mirror. He had dubbed the two girls as Giggles and Wiggles for the last year, although he wasn't entirely sure who was Giggles and who was Wiggles. But the two were particularly rambunctious today. Maybe it was just the euphoria of the first day of school. Now they probably needed to blow off some steam from being cooped up in a classroom for the first time in three months.

That must be it. Surely they're not thinking what he thought they might be thinking. *The woman hates me. There was no chance of getting together with her. I need to set my sights elsewhere. But where? The bar? The coffee shop? Maybe Arlene has someone in mind for me.*

He picked up speed as they hit the outskirts of town for the two-mile drive to the Stone residence on the shores of Lake Huron. The giggles and the whispers continued for the entire drive, along with a couple glances at their notebooks.

Maybe it was about a boy. That had to be it. Maybe there was a boy in class and they think he's cute or something. A bit early in life to do so, but it's probably harmless. As long as it's not something involving me. Or a certain someone who loathes me with a passion.

"Miss O'Leary's really nice," Kayla said just before another round of giggles.

Luke's smile brought on by two pretty eleven-year olds quickly turned upside down at the mention of Lily O'Leary. *So much for thinking they were talking about a cute boy in class.* The last thing he wanted was Kayla trying to fix him up with someone who had no desire to even talk to him. Talk about a dead end. If he was going to find someone, he was going to have to get on it pretty quickly. Otherwise, Kayla could get ideas in her head that would only lead to heartbreak in the end. That was out of the question. He needed to change the subject and fast.

Approaching the Stones' driveway, he knew what to do. "How about we turn on that siren?"

That got their attention off Miss O'Leary. "Yeah, Mr. Luke!"

Luke flipped the switch that sent the lights flashing and siren wailing. The girls' laughed and looked to see if Emma's parents were outside.

"Can we use the loudspeaker, Mr. Luke?"

Luke turned off the siren and handed the mic back to Emma.

She cleared her throat and pressed the button. "Now hear this, now hear this," she said before being unable to continue due to her laughing so hard.

She handed the mic to Kayla, whose sweet voice echoed out across the waters of Lake Huron. "Attention Kmart shoppers, attention Kmart shoppers. We have a blue light special on aisle three."

Luke pulled to a stop in front of the Stone house and watched as Olivia came outside to watch the spectacle with a smile and a shake of her head.

Emma took the mic for the last go-round and lowered her voice as best she could. "Now batting for the Tigers, number twenty-five, Jordan Foster."

Emma kept the mic open long enough to broadcast the two girls' laughter to anyone within earshot. Luke's worry that they would bring up Miss O'Leary again was no longer a concern. All it took was a siren and a loudspeaker. He filed that away for future use.

"Thanks for the ride, Mr. Luke."

"Okay, you're welcome," he said turning around in his seat. "Kayla, I'll pick you up at six. Be good."

Kayla unbuckled and threw open the door. "Bye, Dad. See you later."

Luke waved to Olivia and watched Kayla and Emma hurry inside, jabbering all the way about something. *As long as it's not about me I'm okay with that.*

CHAPTER 7

The first two days of the school year were great for Lily. The kids were well behaved, the lesson plans were taking shape, the sun was shining, and the days were warm but comfortable. Then Wednesday came around, and the euphoria of the first two days of school abruptly ended. Lily woke up with a terrible headache, she had to call the landlord about the kitchen faucet not working right, a heat wave made her sweat as soon as she stepped out of the house, and her students were bouncing off the walls.

At the end of the day, Lily stumbled into the teachers' lounge and collapsed in a heap on the couch. She laid her head back and closed her eyes hoping for a moment's peace. The throbbing of her head seemed to subside, but only if she remained completely still. She heard movement in the room.

"You feeling it, too?" Beth Duncan asked her.

Beth had been a fifth-grade teacher at St. Peter's for twelve years now. At forty years of age, she had seen it all—temper tantrums, playground fights, and even the occasional but unfortunate bout of projectile vomiting. Plus, her students were just coming to the age when boys start to notice girls, and the girls start to notice the boys are noticing them, which only brings about more drama to the classroom. And don't even get her started on parent-teacher conferences.

Beth plopped down on the couch and the jostling caused Lily to wince. "Sorry."

"That's okay," Lily said with little energy.

The two sat and enjoyed the silence for a minute. After a deep breath, Lily opened her eyes and slowly leaned forward, careful not to unleash another bout of her migraine. She rotated her neck to the right and then toward Beth, who had her forearm over her eyes.

"Are you bleeding!?"

Beth looked down at the red splotches on the side of her white blouse. Although it looked like she might have been the victim of a stabbing, she shook her head like it was nothing. "Art class got a little out of hand this afternoon. What about you?"

Lily ticked off the litany of other classroom abuses that she had to endure that day. With her six years of experience, she had finally concluded the blame should be placed squarely on the warm weather and the full moon—two of a grade-school teacher's worst nightmares. Teachers across the fruited plain would no doubt agree that the mixture of warm sunny days and the night's full moon meant nothing but wild-eyed and out-of-control kids who couldn't concentrate, sit still, or listen. She thought the administrators ought to just keep the kids home from school on full-moon days like they do during a blizzard.

"The boys can't keep from looking out the window and wanting to go out and goof around. They were bouncing off the walls like it was Halloween." The very thought of the candy-filled and sugar-laden festivities sent a cold shiver up the two teachers' spines. "And half the girls are just as bad. It's like something is wired in their brains that makes all of them want to become Chatty Cathys all day long. Yack-yack-yack."

Beth smiled and tried to stifle a laugh. "That doesn't sound like the kids that I had last year. They were angels when they left my classroom."

"Sorry. I didn't mean it that way." Lily folded her hands and rolled her neck. "I guess I've had a lot on my mind lately with the move and the start of the year. I think I just need to get to the weekend and catch my breath."

"You can always talk to one of us. We'll give it to you straight. We might even have a few tricks up our sleeves that you could use."

"Thanks, I appreciate that."

Beth leaned forward, her recharge complete. "Say, it wasn't Kayla and Emma giving you problems, was it?"

Lily looked over and thought what she should say. "No, they're great girls." She smiled for the first time that day. "Talkative, but great girls."

"They are wise beyond their years. I learned that after spending last year with them. What I came to realize was that if the class needs a little redirection, whisper it in their ears, and you'll be surprised how fast the order goes forth to the other students."

"I'll be sure to keep that in mind."

Beth stood and grabbed a bottled water from the fridge. "You're still planning on coming out with us on Friday night, aren't you? Only two more days and then we celebrate the end of the first week."

"Sure. I can't wait to get this week over with." Lily got up as well, but she had to stop part way to make sure the headache didn't return with a vengeance. "I should probably get home to see if the landlord sent someone to fix my faucet."

Lily winced at her first step outside into the sunshine, her hand shooting to her forehead to keep the piercing rays out of her eyes. She was looking forward to some of the cool Michigan days she had been hearing about, but the blistering hot August afternoon made her feel uncomfortable. When she got into her car, the furnace-like heat of the interior didn't help any. She had a thought to hightail it to the house, crank up the air conditioner, and crawl into bed. She groaned as she closed her car door. She remembered she had her first batch of homework to grade that night.

She drove north through downtown Huron Cove, wanting to floor it as fast as she could to get home. But, as she passed the police station, she reminded herself that she had gone two days in a row without being accosted by a certain police officer who was probably lying in wait to write her another ticket. And she hoped to keep Luke Spencer as far away from her as possible.

She parked her car in the driveway, not even wanting to take the time to raise the garage door. She thought she might do it later. Or maybe she'd just leave it out all night. All she wanted to do was get inside, throw off her shoes, and remain still for the rest of the day.

She grabbed her purse, shut the door, and walked up onto the porch.

It was then that she stopped in her tracks.

The thoughts of a pounding headache and unruly students vanished from her mind.

The front door was ajar.

Her eyes darted around for the plumber's truck, but she didn't see anything or anyone. Maybe the repairman had forgotten to close the door.

Her senses on high alert, she crept forward and pushed open the front door. She took a step inside and then another. She decided to leave the door open in case she had to make a run for it. Her hand grabbed the phone out of her purse. A part of her thought about calling the police, but the last thing she needed was to have Officer Spencer come over and mock her for being scared and thinking the worst.

She took another step and froze. She thought she heard something. She put the phone in the back pocket of her slacks and grabbed the can of Mace from her purse. She put it in her front pocket. For good measure, she grabbed her brand-new pink umbrella resting next to the door.

There was another bump. She heard it clearly this time. It was coming from the kitchen. She held the umbrella in both hands like a baseball bat, readying to go all Babe Ruth on anyone unfortunate enough to cross her path. She wished she had a Louisville Slugger, but the umbrella would have to do. She took a breath and then a step, the blood rushing through her veins like a locomotive.

Another bump followed by grunt. *There's somebody in my house!* She told herself to run but she was too close to the kitchen now. She didn't want to run and be on defense. She figured it was best to go on offense and then run. She gripped the umbrella so hard her knuckles were turning white. *Wasn't Huron Cove supposed to be a safe place to live?*

She inched a step closer but came to an abrupt halt when she saw a man's shadow on the kitchen wall. He was coming for her. When she saw the first bit of flesh make an appearance in the doorway to the kitchen, she let loose a week's worth of frustration on the intruder.

"Get out of my house!" she yelled as she smacked the man across the face. The man staggered a few steps, tripped over a toolbox, fell backwards, and landed hard on the tile floor. The loud crash of tools added to the chaos. Lily pounced and started raining umbrella blows on him with every bit of force she could muster. In between her yelling insults at the man, the thwack-thwack-thwack of umbrella on flesh echoed off the kitchen walls.

Once the man was down on his backside and covering his face with his hands, she had half a mind to give him a swift kick to the head to finish him off. Maybe an extra kick to the groin to make him think twice about breaking into a woman's house again. She was about to draw back her leg when she thought she heard her name.

"Miss O'Leary, it's me."

She could barely hear the man because his hands and arms were still covering his face. The adrenaline pumping through every square inch of her body kept her on edge. She moved her umbrella to her left hand and grabbed her Mace with the right. "Don't move or I'll Mace you."

"It's me, Miss O'Leary." What the man said next took her breath away. "Luke Spencer. Kayla's dad."

He took his hands away from his face and dared to look at the enraged woman standing over him. Her nostrils flaring, she had enough of the man and she was going to take control of her life. "Police officers are not allowed to break into people's homes!"

"I'm not a police officer!"

"What!? Now you're a liar!" She bopped him over the head once more with her umbrella.

"I mean I'm off-duty, Miss O'Leary. I'm not here on police business."

"That still doesn't give you the right to break into my house!" When he struggled to his feet, Lily stood her ground and readied her Mace. "Stay back! I'm not afraid to use it."

Luke held up both hands in surrender. "Please, Miss O'Leary. Didn't Mrs. Fossan tell you Luke Spencer was going to stop by to fix your faucet?"

Her eyes still ablaze and her chest heaving, she offered her answer. "No, she said it was a handyman who lived two houses up the street."

Luke took a breath and tried to explain. "That's me, Miss O'Leary. I'm the handyman she calls first to see if it's an easy fix. And I live two houses up the street." He pointed to the north. "The white house on the corner with the fenced backyard."

Lily's chest heaved again but she said nothing. There was a red toolbox on the floor. But did the man live two houses up the street? *It's possible. Kayla was out looking for their dog the other day. Maybe he's telling the truth.*

"Why don't you put down the Mace, okay?" He backed to the wall but kept his hands up. "Try the faucet."

Lily took three steps to the side, not once taking her eyes off him. She kept her finger on the Mace in case he made any sudden movements. She put the umbrella on the counter and then raised the handle on the faucet. The water flowed freely like it was brand new. She shut off the water and lowered the Mace.

"You should've put a note on the door or something! I didn't see a car in the driveway and then the door's open and I hear things going bump in the kitchen."

Luke nodded. "You're right. I should have made you aware of my presence. I'm sorry. I thought Mrs. Fossan would have told you. And I guess I thought it would be an easy fix and I'd be in and out in no time." He pointed at the faucet. "It took me a little longer than I thought it would. All I needed to do was clean the aerator screen and then tighten the bolts underneath. You should be good to go for now."

Lily's eyes widened once more. "Oh my gosh, you're bleeding."

Luke raised his hand to his right eyebrow and then took it away. A healthy dose of red coated his fingers.

Lily set the Mace on the counter and ripped off a paper towel. "I am so sorry. I didn't mean to hurt you."

She hurried over and reached up to dab the blood with the towel. The kitchen fell silent as Lily stood on her tiptoes to keep the towel in place. Luke was bloodied, and she was shaking. But they experienced a closeness they had never felt before. Her eyes had nowhere to go but to look into his blue eyes. They weren't mocking her or looking to lecture her on following the law. They were soft and caring. She kept her hand on the side of his forehead, her palm resting on his strong cheekbone. She could feel the heat radiated throughout her body.

"I'm really sorry," she whispered up to him.

Her breath caught when Luke reached up and took hold of her hand and kept it pressed to his forehead.

"It's okay. I'll be all right."

"I didn't mean to hurt you."

Luke kept his hand on hers. Then he broke into a smile. "Sure you did. You thought I was an intruder. I'd expect you to want to hurt me." He grabbed her hand and took the towel away. "It'll be fine."

When their heart rates had returned to normal, Lily took a step back. She noticed it was the first time she had seen Luke out of his police uniform. He wore a pair of blue jeans that hugged his thighs and a white T-shirt that clung to his pectorals after having worked up a sweat in the hot kitchen. He didn't look like he had an ounce of fat on him, just muscles that rippled in his chest and arms.

Lily shook herself from staring. "Um . . . can I at least get you something cold to drink?"

She noticed he licked his lips and blew out a breath. She could also tell he was giving the offer a thought. But then he looked away and shook his head.

"No, thank you. I should probably get home to check on Kayla."

CHAPTER 8

Lily lost count of the number of times she shook her head trying to erase the memory of seeing the handsome Luke Spencer in her kitchen the other afternoon. It happened every time she turned on the kitchen faucet that evening and the next morning when she was fixing breakfast. She scolded herself for her thoughts. The guy's married. *Isn't he?* She hadn't met Kayla's mother yet, but he had to be married. Plus, even if he were single or divorced, he's got a kid. With the dangers of stepmotherhood well known, she was smart enough to steer clear of that minefield. At any rate, Lily wasn't interested in finding a man in Huron Cove.

That's what she kept telling herself. Luckily, it didn't matter. At the end of the day, she'd have one week under her belt at school and she'd be one week closer to moving on. She grabbed the red marker on the dresser and put an X through the Thursday box. It wouldn't be long before she could fill the remaining squares in August and start the countdown through the month of September.

She packed a lunch and reminded herself she was supposed to head out for pizza with her fellow teachers after school. All she had to do was get through the day and she could finally catch her breath and relax over the weekend.

The fifth and sixth graders had a combined recess after lunch, and the warm sunshine brought the students outdoors. Beth Duncan supervised the kickball game, and Lily watched over the students on the playground. Sitting on the bench gave Lily a chance to enjoy the sun's rays and get some outdoor time for herself for the first time since she arrived in Huron Cove.

While keeping her eyes on the children gave her a moment to relax, she was not without company.

Emma sat on her right side and Kayla sat on her left. The two girls apparently felt talking provided all the exercise they would need that afternoon.

"Have you ladies been studying for your Michigan quiz?"

"Oh, yes," Emma said. "But we didn't have to study much. We love all things Michigan."

Kayla agreed. "Michigan is the Mitten State or the Wolverine State. And the state flower is the apple blossom."

Emma went next. "And the state bird is the robin, although I wish it was the cardinal or maybe a sandhill crane or a common loon or the great blue heron. Or a pileated woodpecker! Wouldn't it be fun to have a pet woodpecker?"

Kayla laughed and then said, "The state mammal is the white-tailed deer. I'd like to have a pet deer, but I don't think Mr. Butterlickens would like it."

Lily smiled at the mention of Butter. "It's too bad Michigan doesn't have a state dog. It could be a golden retriever."

Kayla chuckled. "Butter would like that. I don't know what they'd have for the state cat, though."

"Oh!" Emma leaned forward. "Maybe they could make it the Mishebeshu."

Lily looked to her right. "The what?"

"Mishebeshu. It's a giant lynx that lives in the water near the Serpent River in the northern part of Lake Huron. It's a Native American legend or something." She reached out, touched Lily on the arm, and gave her a wink. "But don't worry, we're not afraid of going in the water."

Kayla shook her head like she agreed they weren't afraid. "Butter would probably bark at it." They all laughed.

"Have you enjoyed your first week of school, Miss O'Leary?" Emma asked.

"It's been an interesting week to say the least."

Kayla got up to retrieve a wayward rubber ball and kicked it back to the boys. Then she twirled around in place, her red skirt flaring outward. "It's too bad Michigan doesn't have a state dance. Some states have the square dance, but Michigan doesn't have anything."

"Maybe we could try to petition the state to have an official dance," Emma said.

Kayla continued twirling in place, content to spin around as they talked. Lily watched Kayla, nimble as a ballerina. She was such a joy to be around, unlike her by-the-book dad who seemed to take great joy in finding something wrong with everything she did.

"Kayla, I guess it's probably not your dad, so it must be your mom who has such great taste in clothes."

Kayla's spinning stopped in an instant, her flowing skirt wrapping around her as it came to an abrupt halt. She looked at Lily, her eyes moistening at the mention of her late mother. Without a word, she ran off to the edge of the playground. Lily watched her flee, wondering what was going on. She then looked to Emma for an explanation.

Emma cleared her throat. "Um, Miss O'Leary. Kayla's mom died a few years ago."

As soon as Emma said the words, Lily felt like a ton of bricks fell on top of her. *Kayla's mother died a few years ago.* The thought never crossed her mind, but now she could feel the hole in her stomach expanding like a mushroom cloud. *How could I be so stupid?* She thought she had read through Kayla's records. Maybe it was wrong. Maybe it hadn't been updated. She scolded herself. *Never make a comment about someone's parent until you've met them!* The blank stare on Lily's face remained until Emma started in again.

"I guess that might be why we get along so well. My parents were killed in a car accident when I was little, so I can relate somewhat. Kayla remembers her mom, even though it's been several years. I found a new mom and dad, but Kayla hasn't found a new mom yet. So it's tough for her."

Lily felt like a total heel. She had caused pain to one of her students, partly because she was taking a shot at the girl's father who happened to have caused her so much angst since she arrived in town. But no matter how much the man aggravated her, his daughter didn't deserve to be on the receiving end of any potshots toward her father.

After collecting her thoughts, Lily found Kayla standing on the edge of the playground next to the school garden. She approached quietly, praying to find the right words to salve the girl's aching heart.

"Kayla," she said, putting her arm around the girl's shoulder. "I'm so sorry about mentioning your mom. Emma tells me she passed away a few years ago."

Kayla sniffled and then nodded.

"I want to apologize for bringing her up and for making you sad. I didn't mean to, and I really do like your outfit. It's very stylish."

Kayla didn't respond, her eyes staying focused on the flowerbed and the butterflies fluttering about. Lily rubbed Kayla's back, hoping she would say something or at least give her a smile.

"Was your mom pretty like you?"

Kayla's cheeks rose slightly as she glanced toward Lily. She nodded.

"You have pretty blonde hair, like an angel." This brought a smile to Kayla's face, and Lily tried to keep it going. "And so you and your dad live up the street from me, don't you?"

"Yep."

"With Mr. Butterlickens."

Kayla's eyes widened, like she was impressed Lily thought to bring up the dog's name. "Yeah, it's just me, my dad, and Butter."

The sweetness of the girl touched Lily's heart. She bent down and looked Kayla in her blue eyes. "I want you to know that if you ever need someone to talk to, you can talk to me. Or if you need some time to yourself in class, let me know and I'll help you in any way I can, okay?"

Before Kayla could answer, the bell rang and kids started

heading for the door. Lily felt she had made peace with her, and when she opened her arms, Kayla fell into them.

With the embrace, Lily felt a tug she had never experienced before. It was almost a clinging sensation like Kayla didn't want to let go. Or that she had been deprived of the touch for so long she wanted to hold on to it for as long as she could. Lily thought she might be dreaming it. Perhaps she was mistaken. When Kayla finally let go, Lily saw something in her blue eyes. There was water around the edges, but a spark in the middle. She acted like she wanted to say something but couldn't. The girl smiled and blinked, and then she was off to join her classmates.

* * *

Officer Luke took his usual spot in the parking lot as he waited for the girls to be dismissed. The police chief didn't mind Luke taking some time to pick up his daughter, figuring it would be beneficial to have an officer looking after the students as they made their way home at the end of the school day.

He hadn't seen Miss O'Leary since she tried to bash his head in with an umbrella. The thought brought a smile to his face, although he did hope the guys down at the station didn't catch wind of it. But now, maybe he could move on and get back to finding someone special to share his life with. He had plans to go to dinner with some of the guys tonight and get the lay of the land in terms of finding a single woman in Huron Cove. This would be his first night out on the town in a long time. He had spent half the day trying to think of things to say if he were to meet someone. He could tell them his age, his occupation, his hobbies. *Maybe she'd be interested in me.* In the end, he decided to make it known right away that he was the proud father to an eleven-year-old daughter. If the woman had any qualms about him being a single dad, it was best to put his cards on the table as soon as possible.

What if she has a kid? What then? And what if she smokes?

Or doesn't like dogs? What if she's mean? Or bossy?

Luke sighed. So many questions, and so few answers. The dreaded thought of dating again made him close his eyes and hope it would magically go away. He didn't want to do this. Maybe it would be okay to grow old without having someone to share his life with. But when he opened his eyes, he realized why he had to force himself out of his comfort zone. Kayla and Emma were walking toward him. He had to take the chance at loving again, and tonight was the night to start. At the very least, he could tell Kayla he went out and took the first step toward finding someone.

"Hi, Dad," Kayla said as she opened the back door.

"Hey, baby doll."

"Hi, Mr. Luke," Emma said as she buckled herself in next to Kayla.

"You ladies have a good day?"

"Oh, yes," Emma said. "It was a great day. We didn't want it to end."

Since Luke had plans that evening, he was to take Kayla over to Emma's so they could have a sleepover. The giggles and whispers started before he turned on the engine, and the sound never got old. As long as his daughter was smiling and happy, he was happy. After glancing in the rearview mirror, he shook his head as the two girls laughed at something he didn't hear.

Luke stopped at the intersection at the northeast corner of the courthouse square and had a thought. "Ladies, how about some ice cream to celebrate the end of your first week at school?"

"Yeah, that would be great, Dad."

"Emma, you don't think it will spoil your dinner or anything, will it?"

"Oh, no, Mr. Luke. Ice cream never spoils dinner."

Luke turned right and pulled the SUV to a stop in an open space outside of Lighthouse Creamery.

"Good afternoon, Officer Spencer," Bill Tucker, owner of the store, said behind the counter as the trio entered.

"Afternoon, Bill. We thought we'd celebrate the first week of school with some ice cream."

"Can't beat that. What can I get you?"

Kayla ordered a cup of strawberry ice cream and Emma went with the chocolate. Luke decided on the rocky road. They took a seat at the table by the window looking west toward the courthouse. The two girls continued with their giggling and their whispering in between bites of ice cream.

Luke was hoping for a little father/daughter plus friend interaction while they ate. He figured in another couple years or so the girls would be so interested in boys and fashion and whatever else it is that they are interested in that dear old dad would have to take a backseat. "What are you two girls giggling about?"

Kayla looked at Emma and Emma looked at Kayla. Then they started laughing before thrusting their hands in front of their mouths.

Luke smiled and gestured with his hand to give it up. It was clear they were up to something. "Come on, girls, out with it."

Emma nodded to Kayla like she should take the lead. "Dad, we think we've found someone perfect for you."

Luke nearly choked on his rocky road. *I should've known.* "I didn't realize you two were on the lookout for someone."

Emma shrugged. "Oh, Mr. Luke, you know me. I can't help myself. And Kayla's just as bad. When we see people in need of love in their lives, we have to do something." She smiled sweetly. "It's kinda what we do."

Luke set his cup of ice cream on the table and gave a quick glance around the shop. Had anyone heard he was in need of love in his life? The last thing he needed was for names to be thrown around that would catch the winds of the rumor mill. He shook his head and drummed his fingers on the table as the two girls sat ready to burst.

"I hope you two aren't going to get me in trouble."

Kayla smiled. "No, she's perfect. It's Miss O'Leary."

Luke frowned. He was afraid their new teacher was the

target. Lily was the only single woman the girls had been around for the entire week. But the woman was obviously not a fan of Luke Spencer. He wondered if he should divulge his short history with Miss O'Leary and maybe add that she seemed to take a healthy dose of satisfaction in smacking him over the head with her umbrella. The small bump under his eyebrow constantly reminded him of her feelings for him. He tried to nip their little plot in the bud. "I don't think so, girls. I can't see her being interested in a guy like me."

He could tell by the looks on their faces that Kayla and Emma were having none of his claims.

"Oh, no, Dad, she's perfect for you. She's smart and funny and beautiful." She stopped to gather one last thought, like it might be the most important of all. "And she's really kind, too."

Luke held out his hands and tried to be gentle. "Well, if she's smart and funny and beautiful and really kind, I'm sure she already has someone special in her life." He smiled and nodded like the girls should drop the matter once and for all.

Emma would have none of it. "Oh, Mr. Luke, she doesn't have someone. She's single and doesn't have a boyfriend."

Luke's eyes went from Emma to his daughter in search of clarification. *It was the first week of school. Shouldn't they have been busy learning?* "How do you know that?"

Kayla smiled. "We asked her."

Luke gave his daughter the look that said a lecture was about to be given. "Kayla, you're at school to learn. You shouldn't be asking personal questions of your teachers."

Emma shook her head. "Oh, but Mr. Luke, Miss O'Leary said we could ask her anything." She shrugged like it was no big deal. "So we did."

The girls were too sweet to lecture further. They were just trying to help. But Luke knew things about Lily O'Leary that would be a strong indication of her dislike for the man. He did his best to throw cold water on their plans.

"I'm probably too old for her anyway."

Kayla disagreed. "Oh, no, she's twenty-eight and you're

thirty-five. That's not much of a difference at all."

Do these girls have a comeback for everything!

Emma took the reins and offered a few morsels. "She's from Illinois and she has an older sister named Rose. And she runs in her spare time and she likes baseball."

Kayla leaned forward over the table, covered one side of her mouth, and whispered like what she had to say could be deemed offensive if said too loudly. "She's a Cubs fan, though."

Luke winced at that unfortunate tidbit, a frown crossing his face. He would have thought differently if Kayla had said Lily rooted for the Tigers, but he offered a mild defense. "Well, nobody's perfect."

Knowing the two girls like he did, Luke realized they could sing Miss O'Leary's praises until the sun set. He just couldn't see things working out between them. They had gotten off on a bad foot, and she didn't appear too keen on forgiving and forgetting. He wasn't going to settle for the first single woman he came across anyway. He reminded himself that these things take time.

He made a show of looking at his watch and feigned surprise at the time. "We probably better get you two over to Emma's house."

CHAPTER 9

Although she was glad the day was over and her first week at school had come to an end, a part of her was sad she wouldn't see her students again until Monday. It had only taken a week to grow attached to them. And the one she would miss the most was Kayla Spencer, the daughter of the man who had been the recipient of a multitude of less than kind thoughts in the last week. But she still felt bad about what happened with Kayla. She prided herself on being a kind and nurturing teacher, but her one wisecrack sent Kayla off in tears. She wished she had more time to make sure the girl's heart was mended.

But she would have to wait until Monday. And she would also have to hope Kayla's father didn't report her to the school board for being a teacher insensitive to a student's wellbeing.

After taking a shower, she put on her favorite pair of jeans and a short-sleeve red top. Since she had been wearing her regular shoes the entire week, she slipped on a pair of boots. She grabbed her purse, a red-and-white windbreaker, and headed to the car, hoping a night out with her fellow teachers would help clear her mind and decompress.

When she backed the car out of the drive, she decided to go north to the end of the block. She drove slowly by the Spencer house. It was the first time she got a good look at it. It was a two-story white house with black shutters. She noticed the fenced backyard and wondered if Mr. Butterlickens was out running around. Luke's police SUV was sitting in the driveway, and she had a thought to stop and let him know what happened with Kayla earlier that day. She decided she would take a walk sometime this weekend and make sure to talk with Luke and check on Kayla.

After the short drive into town, Lily was surprised at the number of cars in downtown Huron Cove on a Friday night. She half expected it to be deserted, but as she passed the bookstore, the coffee shop, and the movie theater, there were plenty of people on the sidewalks enjoying the cool August evening.

She found a parking spot out front of the Cut & Curl and grabbed her purse. As she walked east down the sidewalk toward Rose's Italian Pizzeria, she was stopped by a couple whose son was a student in her class. They welcomed her to Huron Cove and said Michael was happy to have her as a teacher. Their kindness warmed her heart, reminding her that she hadn't been a complete failure this week.

"Lily! Over here!"

Once inside the pizzeria, Lily turned to see Beth Duncan waving her hand from the three tables bunched together in the corner. Seated around the tables were Lily's fellow teachers, including Marcie Lincoln (first grade), Tara Carpenter (second grade), and Kendra Anders (third grade), Jessica, and Beth. Marcie, Tara, and Kendra were all in their thirties, married, with one child each. Jessica and Beth were in their early forties, married, and the mothers of two boys each. Bonnie Sutherland, grade seven, and Nancy Smith, grade eight, were the dean of the teachers, both in their fifties, but they were out of town for the evening.

"Hey, everyone," Lily said, as Beth pulled out a chair next to her.

"We're glad you could make it," Jessica said from across the table. "We were afraid you might have collapsed from exhaustion after your first week."

Lily smiled. "It was a good first week, but I'm looking forward to sleeping in a little bit tomorrow."

Beth handed a menu to Lily and said everything was great. "Rose's has become famous for its flavored iced teas over the last few years. They have strawberry, peach, raspberry, and blueberry. Regular too, of course. But we usually don't leave until we each have the four fruited teas."

"That sounds good," Lily said. When the waitress came over to take her order, she ordered a blueberry iced tea and a small bowl of ravioli. "It smells so good in here." She looked around. "And it's busy too. There are a lot of people out tonight."

"The biggest town nearby is Jasper. So unless you want to drive thirty miles, downtown Huron Cove is the place to be on Friday nights." Beth flipped through the menu. "The ravioli is great by the way, and the fresh bread is served right out of the oven."

The women chatted amongst themselves as the restaurant filled up. Some of the locals stopped by the table and introduced themselves to Lily and said they were glad she was in town. She would have to give Huron Cove high marks for friendliness, even though it might not have everything that Chicago offered.

When the waitress brought the first round of iced tea, the women toasted their new colleague and wished her well. The laughter and conversation that followed helped Lily feel at home in her new school, and she was thankful to have her new friends.

"So, Lily," Jessica said. "Any siblings?"

"I have a sister who lives in Chicago. She's an ER nurse."

"Are you two close?"

"Very close. I talk with my sister almost every day. It's been hard being away from her because we used to hang out all the time."

Beth mentioned she had a sister who lived in Ann Arbor, but they don't get together as much as she would like. "You have a boyfriend back home?"

Lily shook her head like she wasn't upset about it. "No, no one special at the moment."

Jessica leaned over to Beth. "We should fix her up with someone."

The statements caused a buzz in the group, but Lily was

shaking her head before Jessica opened her mouth. "That's okay," she said, waving off the offer. "I'm really not interested in finding someone right now. I'd like to focus on my work at school."

Jessica gave Beth the look that said it couldn't hurt to see what's out there.

Beth pointed to Jessica. "Jess and I each found our husbands in high school. So it didn't require much looking on our part. Marcie and Tara found their husbands during college, and Kendra fell for her doctor hubby after one trip to the emergency room for a sprained ankle."

Kendra raised her glass of tea and shrugged.

Beth continued. "So I guess we're lucky. But there are a handful of single men here in Huron Cove that might catch your eye. You never know what the Lord has in store for you."

Apparently Jessica didn't hear Lily's stated desire not to be looking for a man because she tapped her index finger on her lips before saying, "Okay, ladies, let's put our heads together and think of the perfect guy for Lily." Glances were exchanged as images of single men filled their minds. Jessica piped up with the first candidate. "You know, there's Jake over at the fire department. He's hot." She fanned herself to accentuate the man's purported hotness.

But Beth frowned and shook her head like it was a no-go. "He's going out with Lacey. I think there might be something going on between them. Put an asterisk by his name, just in case it doesn't work out."

When Lily tried to butt in once again to say that she really wasn't interested, Jessica tapped Beth on the arm. "How about Pete over at the Oil-&-Go?"

Beth gave it thought and then shrugged like it was a possibility. "Once he cleans the grease and oil off him, he's a decent guy." She rubbed her chin in deep thought. "Of course there's Bubba."

Is everyone in here hard of hearing? Lily wondered if the women, and Beth in particular, could see her eyes widening.

Bubba? Didn't she say she wasn't interested in finding someone? *I said it out loud, didn't I?*

Beth might have seen the look of fear on Lily's face because she tapped her on the arm. "But don't worry, his real name's not Bubba. It's Butch. Butch Nutting, but everybody just calls him Bubba Nuts."

What!? Bubba Nuts! Am I dreaming? Is she serious? Does she really want to fix me up with a man known as Bubba Nuts? And do the women around the table actually expect me to consider someday becoming Mrs. Bubba Nuts? My goodness what would Rose say!?

"Funniest guy you'll ever meet. My husband saw him in the big and tall section at Ballantyne's Clothing Store last weekend. Bubba said he broke it off with his girlfriend, so I think he's probably available if you're interested in meeting him."

With her hands sweating, Lily almost dropped the glass of tea as she picked it up to get some moisture back in her dry mouth. "Like I said, I'm not looking to find anyone right now. I want to focus on my schoolwork." *Isn't anyone listening to me!?*

Beth smiled at Lily, but apparently didn't hear what she said or figured she was being overly modest. "Don't worry. We'll find someone for you. Just give us some time."

Before Lily could object, Beth pointed toward a group of men walking in the door. "That's Ethan, Noah, and Alex," she said, ticking off each one. "They're great guys. All married, though. That guy pulling up the rear is my hunk of a husband. He's a police officer. I'll introduce you to Mike once he finds his way over here. So you see, with all those handsome gentlemen around Huron Cove, there has to be more of them. And one of them could be yours."

Lily was thankful when the waitress placed the round of peach iced tea in front of them. She didn't need to be thinking about finding a man, especially since she had no plans on staying in Huron Cove beyond the end of the school year. A part of her thought she should say something to her colleagues, but she couldn't bring herself to do it. They were so nice to her and had taken her under their wings. The last thing she wanted to do was tell them at the end of the first week that she couldn't wait to skedaddle out of Huron Cove and get back to Chicago. As she took a sip, she told herself to beg off any more Friday night gatherings. It would be best to keep to herself. That way it wouldn't hurt so bad when she left town for good.

Her thoughts were interrupted by Beth excitedly tapping her on the arm before pointing toward the door.

"Hey look! It's Bubba Nuts!"

CHAPTER 10

Luke parked his SUV in the lot behind the police station and sat in the driver's seat. For some reason, he didn't let go of the wheel. He wondered if he should go back home and call it an evening. Kayla wouldn't know, although she and Emma did have their spies around the square who might rat him out.

Could he really find someone willing to be a loving mother to Kayla? Would anyone want to join a family in progress and become a cop's wife? He groaned in the silence of the vehicle. *What am I getting myself into?*

He turned off the engine and unbuckled his seat belt. He had only been with one woman in his life, and that was Maria. He wasn't a player and, truth be told, he was shy around women. He had been lucky to find Maria during high school when blossoming love was a lot different than when one turns thirty-five.

His mind ran through the list of single locals he thought he might run into that evening. Ava Pearson was probably waiting tables at The Cellar. She was single and, according to some, always available. She was cute, although she did have a mouth on her. But that could be the product of working at the bar. Was she the only one he could think of? *Oh boy.* He decided he might call it an early evening if the guys suggested they grab a beer.

He took a deep breath and tried to calm himself. *I don't have to propose tonight. I'm simply going to see who might be out there. Maybe I'll introduce myself to a couple of women. That's all I have to do tonight. And then I can report to Kayla that I took the first step.* He figured the steps thereafter would be easier once he got the hang of things.

Grabbing the towel in the console, he wiped the sweat pooling on his forehead. He had gone with the dark blue button-down shirt, and he was glad he did. Anything lighter might show off the perspiration he was starting to feel on his lower back. He decided he had better get out there or he would have to go home, take another shower, and change clothes.

He got out, thankful the evening had turned cooler, grabbed his blue jacket, and draped it over his arm. He glanced at himself in the reflection of the window and forced himself to smile. He'd probably have to force himself to do that all night long. With one last shake of the head, he locked his SUV with the fob and headed for the square.

Let's get this over with.

He crossed the street on the south side of the square and walked into the pizzeria. The warmth of the place hit him and set off a worry that he'd start sweating again. But then the aroma of spaghetti sauce and fresh warm bread filtered into his nose. At least the smell of the place was pleasing. If nothing else, he thought he could have a nice meal.

He waved when he saw Ethan motioning him to a table near the back of the restaurant.

Luke shook hands with Noah Thorne, Alex Armstrong, and Mike Duncan and then sat next to Ethan. When Rose came over to take his order, he decided to start with a large iced tea, hoping it would cool him off. He took a menu to decide what he was hungry for.

After the guys made small talk about their week, Ethan leaned toward Luke and spoke as quietly as he could but loud enough for him to hear over the din of the crowd.

"I just wanted to warn you that I think there's a plot afoot."

Luke wondered if he heard correctly. "A plot?"

"Yeah, a plot. And it involves you."

"Me? Who would want to plot against me?"

Ethan raised his eyebrows and looked at him like it was obvious who the culprits had to be. "I think you might know them by their street names—Giggles and Wiggles."

Luke frowned and rolled his eyes. "What did you hear?"

"When I was getting ready, I heard those two jabbering away in the kitchen with Olivia. Something about they had found the perfect someone for you." While Ethan had been lighthearted in his talk about a plot, he grew serious. "I didn't hear a name, but they started talking about you falling in love and getting married again."

"Oh, geez." Luke rubbed his hand over his forehead. He realized he still hadn't done a very good job at cautioning Kayla about the time it would take to find someone. He didn't want her to get her hopes up, only to be dashed because it didn't work out in the end.

"I thought you might want to know what they're up to."

"I do. And thank you. I know they're trying to help, but I worry about Kayla. I should probably have another father-daughter talk with her to make sure we're on the same page. The last thing I need is for her to get her hopes up." *Or my hopes up, too.*

Rose brought Luke his iced tea, but he decided he would wait on ordering dinner. His mind was swimming in uncertainty, and now he had lost his appetite.

"Listen up, guys," Ethan said leaning closer to the middle of the table. Noah, Alex, and Mike all leaned in and turned an ear toward Ethan. "Luke here is open to finding a new woman."

Luke winced at the announcement, although he appreciated Ethan keeping his voice down.

"Any ideas?"

Alex, Noah, and Mike looked at each other and then at Ethan. Alex's wife owned Turn the Page Books, Noah's wife ran CupKate's Confectionery, and Mike's wife taught fifth grade at St. Peter's. None of the women had any sisters. Ethan's wife, Olivia, had two sisters, one of whom was married and the other a recent college graduate.

Alex's eyes widened after a thought struck him. "What about Lacey over at the Cut and Curl?"

Mike shook his head. "She's going out with Jake. Beth says

it might be getting serious."

The guys were mostly drawing a blank. Alex mentioned Janice down at the mini-mart, but Luke politely declined, having arrested her twice for stealing over the years. He was kind enough to keep her criminal record out of the discussion. All of the names of the women thrown out around the table brought blank stares and shakes of the head from Luke. He was ready to give up and tell Kayla it was a lost cause.

Maybe I should try a dating site on the Internet.

Thinking it might be a good idea to call it an evening and head for home, he turned to the entrance just in time to see Ava walking in. His stomach dropped at the sight. The patrons parted on each side as Ava sashayed through the crowd, her hips swinging left and right like a metronome as they cleared a path for her. The skirt was black leather and looked only an inch longer than the waitresses' aprons. The white top had more holes than Swiss cheese, which allowed everyone to see her colorful collection of tattooed butterflies and roses on her back and stomach, not to mention put her ample bosom on full display.

When Luke saw her heading straight for him, he looked down at the floor and closed his eyes. *My goodness, is she here for me? Oh, please, don't let her be here for me.* With Ava fast approaching and locked in on her latest target, he could feel the hole in his stomach growing larger by the second. *And now it begins.*

"Hey, Luke," she cooed, stroking his shoulder. "How's it going?" Seeing no chair available, she took a seat on his lap.

Luke choked slightly at the perfume that hit him in the face, a wave of something flowery with the distinctive scent of cheap beer and stale cigarettes mixed in. He kept the gag inside him for fear of coughing into her breasts.

"You are looking mighty handsome tonight, although I kind of like it better when you're wearing your badge and gun." She smacked her gum and smiled. "I heard it through the grapevine that you're on the market."

"I . . . uh . . . I . . . um . . ." he stuttered, desperately trying to find something to dissuade her from any thoughts of going out with him.

She smacked her gum again and ran her red fingernails around his collar. "I bet we could have some fun together. I have to go to work at eight, but I get off at two. Maybe you could swing by the bar later and have a few drinks. Then we could go back to my place."

Although he was glad the restaurant was crowded and hoped the customers were too busy chatting amongst themselves to notice, the last thing he wanted was for people to start talking about the voluptuous Ava Pearson sitting on his lap. He decided to tell a little white lie. "I don't think I can make it tonight. I really need to get home to Kayla." *Kayla.* Just saying her name focused his mind. *What would Kayla think?* He had a quick hope that mentioning Kayla would send Ava running for the exit. The thought of bringing Ava home to his daughter about made him wretch. He wondered if his buddies had left him. Or maybe they were laughing so hard they couldn't offer assistance to help him out of this jam.

Too polite to throw her off, Luke squirmed in his seat, which did nothing but sink Ava deeper into his lap. He could feel the sweat starting to run down his forehead and he feared Ava might take the initiative and mop it up with the remnants of her shirt. His mind was going a million miles an hour. *Maybe I should tell her I have to use the restroom.* A part of him worried she'd follow him in there. Without a way out, he did the only thing he could think of.

He hoped for a miracle—a call for a police officer or someone rushing in to say there was a cow loose on the streets of Huron Cove. Anything. He wished he could make his phone ring. He'd talk the ear off a telemarketer if only he'd get the call. With the passage of every second, his heart felt like it was about to beat out of his chest. And if he licked his lips one more time, he worried Ava might take it as an invitation to kiss him.

He sucked in a breath when the miracle appeared like an

apparition right before him. In all the sights and sounds of the restaurant, and even with the buxom, beer-scented barmaid on his lap, his eyes somehow focused on a woman on the other side of the room. With her wide eyes and constant fidgeting, she looked like she was in distress. And right then and there, Luke thought he was the only person in the world who could save her.

Luke put his hands around Ava's hips to pick her off him. "I'm sorry, Ava, but I really need to get going."

Before he could extract her from his lap, Ava blew a bubble, popped it, and then frowned like she was thoroughly disappointed that he had rebuffed her advances. "Okay, maybe some other time. The offer still stands though." As one last parting offer, she leaned in to whisper in Luke's ear. "Just make sure you bring your handcuffs."

CHAPTER 11

"Bubba! Over here!"

Lily cringed when she heard those ominous three words. She couldn't believe Beth would do this to her. *I thought we were friends. Didn't I just say I'm not looking to meet anyone?* She was afraid to look, but there was no chance of missing the hulking mass of humanity sauntering her way. With only a quick glance, she figured the man in the blue bib overalls probably tipped the scales at three-twenty. The bushy brown beard looked like he had two squirrels wrapped under his chin. She felt like crawling under the table. No, she would rather throw herself through the plate glass window and run back to Chicago.

Beth stood, leaned toward the man, and gestured to Lily. "Bubba, this is Lily, she's teaching sixth grade at St. Peter's. Lily, this is Bubba."

"Nice to meet you, Lily," he said. His hands were so large that when he shook Lily's, she could feel his fingers wrapping around her wrist.

Please, Beth, don't say what I think you're about to say.

"Pull up a chair, Bubba."

You cannot be serious!

Bubba did so, although he really could have used two chairs to support his massive back side. Lily noticed the man's overalls had a white patch on the front with the words *Bubba Nuts* stitched in red. The pocket on the right had a black pen, the one on the left had a stick of beef jerky.

"So, you're a teacher?" he bellowed loudly over the noise of the restaurant.

Lily, looking like a small child amongst the massive mountain of flesh sitting next to her, said "Yes" so softly that no one could have heard her. She added a nod and then looked down at her plate of half-eaten ravioli.

Bubba's eyes went back to Beth, and the two chatted like they were lifelong friends. "I had the day off today, so I was working out in the fields helping my dad."

That would explain the red lobster skin tone, Lily thought to herself.

Beth leaned toward Lily. "Besides farming, Bubba drives the potato chip truck here in town."

"Yep, been doing that for ten years now. I stock all the gas stations and grocery stores within fifty miles. If you ever need some chips, I'll hook you up. Little donuts, too!"

Lily couldn't even bring herself to respond. All she could think about was bolting from the restaurant and never looking back. If she had a superpower, it would be to melt away and transport herself back to the Windy City.

"Bubba, are you hungry?" Beth asked.

Lily almost choked. *Was the man hungry? Given his girth, the man probably never stopped eating.* She reached out for her glass, thankful she had some raspberry tea left. She held the glass in front of her mouth and tried not to laugh.

"You gonna eat that piece of bread?"

When Lily realized the man was talking to her, she quickly shook her head and gestured that he could help himself. *What would he do if I said yes?* She then watched as the man slathered a pat of butter on the slice before turning it over and smearing another pat on the other side. He then thrust the whole piece in his mouth. The act brought a smile to the big man's face.

"It's good," he mumbled with a mouthful. "Best bread in town."

"I'm sorry to hear about you and Tracy," Beth said loudly across the table.

Bubba scarfed down the bread with giant gulp. Then he shook his head and held up his hands. "It didn't work out. We're still friends, though."

Lily could feel a cold sweat coming on. She could sense things about to spin out of control. She had to find a way to leave. Right now. Because it could only get worse. Especially if Beth kept going down that dead-end road of finding Lily a man.

Don't do it, Beth. I'm begging you, please don't do it.

Beth pointed to the frightened woman sitting next to her. "Lily's single."

Are you drunk, woman!? How can you say that with a smile on your face?

Lily didn't even try to hide the deer-in-the-headlights look in her eyes. She just stared across the room, her body shaking at the thought of having to hurt people's feelings. Her mind froze, she couldn't think of anything to say. There was so much noise, but she could still hear her heart pounding in her chest. She felt like she was drowning. She wanted to reach out to something, someone, anyone who could save her.

Please help me!

Her head twitched as her eyes saw a flash of blue in the distance. A few seconds later, she felt a strong presence beside her, and then she heard a man's voice that sounded familiar.

"Hey, Bubba, how's it going?"

"It's good, Luke." He rubbed the front of his overalls to wipe the crumbs off his hand and then extended it toward Luke. "Spent the day out in the fields helping my dad."

"That's great." Luke put his hand on Lily's shoulder and looked at those gathered around the table. "You all wouldn't mind if I had a word with Miss O'Leary here, would you? It's about Kayla."

Lily didn't care if anyone did mind because she was scrambling for her purse under the table.

"Maybe we could talk outside where it's a little quieter?"

"Absolutely," Lily said. She grabbed a twenty from her purse and laid it next to Beth. "Just in case the bill comes." She excused herself from the table. "It was nice meeting you, Bubba. Feel free to eat the rest of my ravioli."

"Hey, thanks, Lily," he said as his big left paw swiped the bowl closer to him. "It was nice meeting you, too."

Luke and Lily wormed their way through the crowded tables and the people standing in line as the two made their way to the door. When they stepped out of the restaurant onto the sidewalk, the quietness was the first thing that hit them, then the coolness of the evening. It was a welcome relief on both fronts. Lily sucked in the first breath she had taken in what seemed like ten minutes. She exhaled and closed her eyes.

"From the looks of things, I thought you might have needed a little fresh air."

Lily opened her eyes, looked up at him, and broke into a grin. Her uncomfortable state had at least been obvious to someone. "You have no idea. I can't thank you enough. I didn't know how I was going to get out of that. I'll tell you one thing, Beth has some crazy ideas."

"I think I know how you feel." Luke looked across the square. "Care to take a walk?"

It's the least I can do to thank my rescuer. And I sure don't want to go back inside to give Beth any other wild ideas. "Yeah, that sounds great."

They walked like they weren't in any hurry to get anywhere. They headed west, passing Grandma's Closet, Cards Galore, and CupKate's Confectionery, until they reached the corner and turned north. They crossed the street and walked on the sidewalk closest to the courthouse.

"You didn't bring your Mace, did you?" Luke asked with a smile and lean away from her.

"Of course I did." Lily patted her purse. "I'm always packing."

Luke laughed. "Good to know. I'll be sure to be on my best behavior."

Through the front windows of The Coffee Cove, the two could see the place doing a brisk business. With a handful of women congregating on the couches at Turn the Page Books, it looked like the bookstore was doing okay as well. A line of people snaked around the corner waiting to get into the movie theater. Luke checked his watch. Fifteen minutes before the eight o'clock showing.

With the fresh air, Lily felt emboldened to try and mend a few fences. "Um . . . I wanted to apologize for the way I've acted since the first time we met. You know, the speeding ticket—"

Luke waved it off like she shouldn't give it another thought. "It happens. Nobody likes being pulled over by the cops. It's been known to put a person in a bad mood."

"Well, that's true, but it wasn't very professional of me. Then there was the apple incident. And I'm sorry for beating you over the head with my umbrella."

Luke laughed again before reaching up and touching his eyebrow. "You're forgiven. The headaches and the blurred vision have subsided."

Lily gasped. *Did I do lasting damage?*

He reached out and gave her a pat on the arm. "I'm kidding. I think the cut has almost fully healed."

The two continued on with smiles on their faces.

"Say, I really didn't have anything particular I wanted to ask about Kayla by the way," Luke said. "It was just something I said to get us out of there. Anyway, is everything going okay with Kayla at school?"

Lily put her hands in her coat pocket. She felt like a weight had been lifted off her shoulders after enduring the dating game at the pizzeria. The guy walking next to her was the father of one of her students. She knew him, had interacted with him, albeit in less than ideal circumstances, and felt comfortable in his company. For the time being, at least.

"I did want to discuss something that happened today with Kayla."

Luke pointed to his right when they reached the end of the block and they turned east. "What happened?"

Lily took a breath. She hadn't had time to prepare what she was going to say. "I was talking with Kayla and Emma at recess this afternoon and . . . um . . . I made a comment about how nice she looked in her outfit." She turned to look at him. "And I mentioned something to the effect that I thought Kayla's mom must have good taste in clothes because it couldn't have been you that picked them out." Lily's stomach dropped. Saying it again made it feel even worse the second time around.

Luke kept his eyes focused forward and then he put his hands in his jacket pockets.

"I'm terribly sorry. Kayla got upset and ran off, and Emma told me your wife passed away a few years ago. I went to talk to Kayla, and she had tears in her eyes." Lily shook her head. "I'm so disgusted with myself. I should have been more careful."

They turned the corner and headed south. Luke still hadn't said anything, and his poker face didn't indicate how he was feeling.

"I really am sorry. I promise you it won't happen again."

Luke took a breath, and Lily couldn't tell whether he was going to explode or not. She didn't know the man and she didn't know what Kayla had told him. She gulped and readied herself for any fury he might unleash on her.

He turned his head to look at her. "So you don't think I have good taste in clothes?"

She could tell the shocked look on her face must have registered with him and she struggled to keep her smile from growing wider. She took a second to glance at what he was wearing. It was the attire of a handsome man, crisp pants, blue shirt covered by a matching jacket. And even in the fading daylight, the blue shirt highlighted the ocean blue eyes. She had to look away to keep from staring. "It's not that. . . it's—"

He held out his hand to stop her. "It's okay, Miss O'Leary. I—"

She reached over to him and interrupted him herself. "Please, it's Lily."

He smiled and they turned the corner to start their second lap. "Alright, Lily. Um . . . being a single dad of an eleven-year-old girl does present its challenges, especially when it comes to clothes. I can imagine it's only going to get more difficult in the next few years. Luckily, Emma's mom keeps me from buying something Kayla would be embarrassed to wear. At any rate, to be honest with you, Kayla didn't say anything to me after school. And she didn't seem to be upset, so I wouldn't worry about it."

"Well, that's a relief. If you don't mind me asking, how long have you been a single dad?"

"It's been five years since we lost Maria." He looked at her and sighed like he was about to say the dreaded six-letter word for the thousandth time. "Cancer." He focused forward again. "It was hard on both of us, but we've endured and somehow made it work so far."

"Kayla is a wonderful girl. Smart, sweet, and a smile that could brighten the darkest cave."

They went back north. "Thank you. I've had a lot of help. Everyone around town pitched in when it looked like we needed an extra hand. It wasn't easy in the first year or two, but I've been able to get Kayla to open up more. Mr. Butterlickens was actually a big help." He took his hand out of his pocket and placed it on her arm. "That's our dog."

Lily laughed. "Oh, I know. I've met Butter. He's a nice dog, and Kayla and Emma love him."

"Emma has helped a lot, too. She's like a sister to Kayla. After her mom died, Kayla didn't want to leave my side, never wanted to go over to anyone's house. I think Kayla thought if she didn't hold on to me, she might lose me, too. I hated that Kayla couldn't be a normal child to go out and have fun, but Emma has given her that opportunity. They hang out a lot and it gives Kayla someone to talk to. Although recently Kayla's been asking about . . ."

They reached the corner and turned east. Lily couldn't tell whether Luke was going to finish his thought or if she should try to draw it out of him. A couple walked past and said hello. As Luke and Lily finished their second lap, they stood at the corner. Lily didn't know whether Luke was going to say something or if the walk was over. Luke looked at the pizzeria and then gave her a mischievous grin.

"You know, Bubba's single, if you're interested."

Lily blushed and buried her head in her right hand.

"I could put a good word in for you. Funniest guy you'll ever meet."

Lily shook her head and then looked at Luke. "So I've heard. I think I'll pass."

Luke shrugged. "Suit yourself. Don't blame me if you come to regret it. Along with a large farm, his family runs the local snack food distributorship. He'll probably wind up with more money than all of us someday." He pointed at the pizzeria. "I don't know about you, but I didn't get much to eat in there." He then pointed west to the end of the block at CupKate's Confectionery. "Could I buy you a cupcake or a brownie for dessert?"

Lily couldn't wipe the smile off her face even if she tried. She didn't even have to think about the question. She was hungry, but more importantly, she realized she wasn't ready to end the night yet.

"Sure, I'd like that."

CHAPTER 12

Lily woke to the sounds of birds chirping outside her window. She had finally made it to Saturday, and it had been an eventful first week in Huron Cove to say the least. Although it took her awhile to fall asleep, she slept peacefully when her eyes closed for the final time. Luke Spencer had invaded her thoughts ever since she last saw him the previous evening. And her dreams were no exception.

After enjoying a couple chocolate brownies from CupKate's Confectionery, Luke had walked her to her car, and she offered to give him a ride to his SUV at the police station. He accepted and then followed her home. She parked in the driveway, and he waited until she was safely inside. They exchanged waves to end the evening.

And from that moment on, she couldn't stop thinking about him.

Once in bed, she stared at the ceiling for what seemed like an hour. With the window open and the cool breezes allowing her to snuggle under the covers, she replayed the entire night. Well, she fast-forwarded through most of the pizzeria matchmaking talk until she came to the part where she was rescued by the handsome police officer who saved her from an unknown host of relationship calamities. In the darkness of her bedroom, she smiled when she heard a dog barking from the north. Knowing Mr. Butterlickens was outside patrolling the grounds and keeping an eye on the neighborhood comforted her.

As did the thought of Luke Spencer. He was handsome, confident, strong, not to mention a decent, honorable man and a loving father. Try as she might, she could not keep herself from wondering what life would be like with Luke. She was nowhere near the point of doodling Mrs. Lily Spencer in her notebook, but she didn't think it would hurt to dream. He had forgiven her for her rudeness and slip-up with Kayla, and it made her want to get to know him even more.

She sat up, stretched her arms, and looked out the window on the north side of her house. She wondered what Luke was doing. Her thoughts were interrupted by her phone buzzing on the nightstand.

Lily grabbed the phone and saw the picture of a red rose on the screen. It was time for some Saturday morning sister talk. "Hey, Rosebud."

"Hey, Lilybean, happy Saturday."

"Finally." Lily could hear her sister flip the page of one of her fashion magazines, probably *Cosmo* or *Vogue*.

Four years older than Lily, Rose O'Leary was the outgoing flirt of the two, the one to suggest a night of karaoke and dancing. Talking was her main hobby. The younger Lily, more of a bookish introvert, preferred to listen and learn. They complemented each other perfectly. Rose had been her sister's mentor, protector, and confidante since the day Lily came into the world. From life to books to clothes to men, Rose was always willing to give her baby sister sage advice and words of wisdom.

"How was your first week?"

Lily looked out the window again. She remembered the classroom activities, her kids, and the man with the blue eyes.

"It was good. I have a class of twenty. Ten boys, ten girls."

"That's good. Do you have any bad apples?"

"Not really. A couple of talkers but everyone has been well-behaved." She remembered the full moon from the past week. "For the most part."

Another snap turn of the magazine page. "You haven't met any men, have you?"

Lily couldn't respond truthfully, and she knew full well the lack of an immediate and honest answer would set off alarm bells that could be heard ringing all the way from Chicago. She readied herself for a lecture.

There were no more pages being turned. Her sister's voice sharpened. "You haven't, have you?"

"Um . . ."

"Lily Ann O'Leary! What have you done?"

Lily could hear her sister get up from the couch to start pacing the floor of her condo. She sighed loud enough for Rose to calm down. "I mean, it's uh . . . It's just a guy I met."

"You've only been there a week and now this. You didn't get picked up in a bar last night, did you?"

Lily sighed again and rolled her eyes. "No, I did not get picked up in a bar last night. You know I don't care for the bar scene anyway. The guy helped me out of a jam and then we talked a bit. We even had some brownies at the bakery."

"Brownies at the bakery! Oh, Lilybean, what are you doing? I thought we talked about this. You don't want to find a guy right now, especially a guy from Michigan."

Lily threw off the covers, jumped out of bed, and started pacing herself. "What's wrong with guys from Michigan?"

"They're Michiganders."

Oh, well, that clears things up. "So?"

"I read in one of my magazines that men from Michigan are colossal bores. I think they're rated number one in that department." Having considered herself a relationship guru, what with all the women's magazines she had read at the hospital, she claimed to know all the love tips, romance tricks, and warning signs. And in Rose's mind, men from Michigan sent up giant red flags. "You're never going to find your Prince Charming in Michigan. You need to find yourself a good Illinoisan." Apparently men from the Land of Lincoln were high enough on the list to meet Rose's strict criteria.

"It will be kind of hard for me to find a guy from Illinois when I'm living in Huron Cove, Michigan."

"That's why you need to come back home!" Rose pleaded.

Lily stopped pacing and put a hand on her hip. "I can take care of myself, Rosebud."

"Have you heard anything from those schools you applied to?"

"It's only been a week. I don't expect to hear anything until early next year."

In her mind, Lily could see her sister shaking her head in disgust and trying to keep Lily from making a huge mistake in life. Whatever that was—apparently anything that Rose didn't authorize or give her stamp of approval. The silence told her Rose was thinking long and hard about her next question.

"What's his name?"

Lily stopped pacing and sat at the edge of her bed. Through the parted curtain, she could see the police SUV sitting in the driveway two doors up the street. Her mind raced from the first time she ever met Luke to the last. From the speeding ticket to the busted apple to the first day of school. Then, of course, when she found him all hot and sweaty in her kitchen. *Is this really happening? Had it gotten that far already?* She realized she was about to say the name of the man who caught her eye for the first time. She wondered if she should. She didn't wonder if she wanted to.

"Come on, Lilybean, out with it. What's his name?"

"His name is Luke." She felt her skin tingle at the first mention of his name.

"What's he look like?"

Lily flashed back to the previous evening and the walk around the courthouse square. "He's about six-two, blond hair, and blue eyes." She sucked in a breath when she thought of those gorgeous blue eyes again. "He's really nice."

Rose huffed like she needed more to go on. "Nice guys are a dime a dozen, Lily. How old is he?"

Lily started pacing again, biting her lip with every step. "I'm not entirely for sure." She was being honest. She didn't know Luke's exact age.

"Ballpark."

Lily took a deep breath. "My friend Beth, you know the one who teaches fifth grade, she said her husband and Luke are the same age. Her husband is thirty-five."

"Thirty-five!"

Hearing the exclamation, Lily jerked the phone away from her ear. She thought she might have felt the ground shake, like Rose had come close to hitting the ceiling in disbelief. She also wondered if the neighbors could hear the outburst.

"Thirty-five!"

"Thirty-five is not that old, Rose."

"He's almost five years older than me!"

Lily smiled and shook her head. *Nice try, sis.* "Um, Rosebud, you're thirty-two."

"Hush, child. You know full well my birth certificate has a margin of error of a couple years." Rose grew silent, obviously pacing back and forth. "Do I have to remind you, young lady, that you are twenty-eight years old?"

Lily straightened a picture of her and her sister on the dresser. "No, Rose, I'm well aware that I'm an adult woman."

"What does he do for a living besides collect Social Security?"

"He's not that old!" Lily laughed.

"He's a fossil. You'll probably have to carbon date him just to get an accurate age of this dinosaur."

"He doesn't have a gray hair on his head."

"Uh-huh. Gray hairs can pop up like a thief in the night. One day he looks like he's thirty, the next day he'll be buying stock in hair-dye companies. That's if it doesn't fall out before then. Does he even have a job or does he just hang out at the old-folks' home all day long and play shuffleboard?"

Like when guessing Luke's age, Lily knew his employment would bring a stern talking-to from Rose. She thought she should drop the subject altogether. It's not like they were dating. Why should she go down that road just to listen to Rose lecture her on everything that she found wrong with the situation? But Luke had rescued her last night, and she felt compelled to stand up for him this morning. She took a deep breath and prepared for Rose's onslaught. "He's a police officer."

Lily could hear the head slap all the way from northern Illinois. "A police officer! Really? Oh, Lilybean, what has happened to you? Haven't I warned you about these things?"

"By 'things,' you mean men?"

Rose didn't like the back talk. "Yes, I mean men. They're nothing but trouble. All of them. Especially old policemen from Michigan. You can't go out with him."

The decision had been made. The case had been closed. The foot had been put down. And Rose expected her baby sister to comply if she knew what was good for her.

"What's wrong with police officers?"

"They're notorious drunks, cheaters, and liars. They eat donuts all day long and get fat. I saw it on an episode of *Law & Order*. He's probably dumb as a box of rocks, too."

"He is articulate and kind, Rose. He has treated me like a gentleman ever since I got into town."

"Uh-huh," Rose responded, like she didn't believe her sister one bit. "That's how those old farts get you. It's like giving candy to little kids."

Lily rolled her eyes. "Whatever."

"Have you been over to his place?"

Lily shook her head. She didn't feel the need to tell her that Luke only lived two houses away. "No, I haven't been over to his place."

"Don't. Under any circumstance. He'll probably have a shrine to you. That's what those crazy old weirdos do. Pictures and candles and freaky voodoo stuff."

Lily couldn't take much more of this. "Really, Rose. He's a nice guy. His daughter's in my class."

The shriek nearly blew up Lily's phone. "He's got a kid!? Have you gone mad!?"

Lily sat on the bed again, the exhaustion of her sister's riot act starting to wear her down. She rested her head in her hand.

Yes, he has a kid. And she's the sweetest little girl you'd ever want to meet.

"I can't believe this. Run, Lily. Run and don't look back. A man with a kid is nothing but bad news. You don't want any part of that. Have you not listened to anything I've taught you?"

Lily figured Rose must be right. Her sister had never led her astray in the past. And she was just trying to keep Lily from making decisions she'd come to regret. Her mind went back to the countdown calendar on her dresser. She had been so distracted with her walk with Luke last night that she hadn't marked off Friday when she returned home. *I'm not going to be in Huron Cove very long so I can't be getting involved. That's the way it has to be.*

"I have been listening, Rose. There's nothing between me and Luke, so you don't have to worry. Plus, it's his daughter that I'm concerned about, and my main focus is to make sure I can do everything possible to help her be the best student she can be."

Lily thought the explanation seemed to soothe any thoughts Rose might have to make a run to Huron Cove to kidnap her sister and drag her back home.

"Well, okay then. Just make sure your focus is on the daughter and not him. You don't want to get involved with a single dad."

"I know, Rose," Lily sighed. She rolled her neck a few times. The talk had made her tense, and she thought some exercise might do some good. "I should probably get going. I want to get a run in before it gets too hot." She walked over to her closet. "But you don't have to worry. I have no plans to get involved with anyone, and I'm one week closer to moving back home."

* * *

A startled Luke sat up straight in bed. *I forgot to fix breakfast for Kayla.* He threw off the covers and planted his feet on the floor. He was about to spring into action but stopped cold when he saw Butter raise his head and give him a quizzical look.

Once the realization kicked in, it took a few seconds for his heart rate to return to normal. He forgot Kayla was staying all night at Emma's, thus the reason for Butter sleeping on the floor of his bedroom. He still wasn't used to Kayla being gone overnight, although he was glad she was getting out and having fun. He wondered if he would ever have any fun. The dog figured it was time for his morning rubbing so he ambled over to the side of the bed.

"Hey, buddy. You miss her, too, don't you?" He gave the dog a good scratch behind both ears.

Once the thoughts of the two most important things in his life—Kayla and Butter—receded, he went back to what he had been dreaming about most of last night. Lily O'Leary. The memory of walking around the courthouse square with her made him smile. It was the most enjoyable time he spent with a woman in a long time. There was no pressure, no jitters, nothing that would make him break out in a cold sweat. It was just two people walking and talking and then enjoying some chocolate brownies.

Lily had a wonderful smile. That's what he remembered most about sitting across the table from her. Whenever she smiled, it reddened her cheeks and made her eyes twinkle like stars. Surprisingly, they had CupKate's Confectionery mostly to themselves for the time they were there. They stayed long enough that owner Allie refilled their coffee cups twice.

She told him she was from Illinois, twenty-eight, and had an older sister named Rose. She loved to read in her spare time and was an avid runner. Of course, he knew all that courtesy of Giggles and Wiggles. He found her to be caring and kindhearted. And that smile! If only he could make her smile again.

What am I doing?

He leaned forward and folded his hands. *She's Kayla's teacher. And she's young. Not too young, but still. Why would she want to get involved with me—a single father? She could go out with any guy she wanted. And she doesn't seem to be someone looking to settle down with an older man and his eleven-year-old daughter.*

But what were his other choices at the moment? Ava? He wondered if he was going to have to go to the bar tonight to find someone who might want to start a relationship. He sighed and rolled his neck. That's the last thing he wanted to do. What he really wanted was to see Lily again. Maybe he was the one for her. And maybe she was the one meant for him and for Kayla.

His thoughts were interrupted when Butter rubbed his wet nose against his hand. Luke gave him a good scratch and then had an idea. "How about we go for a run, bud?"

Butter barked and wagged his tail. Luke hustled to take a quick shower and then threw on a pair of shorts and a white T-shirt. He found Butter by the door, and after attaching the leash to his collar, they hit the sidewalk to get some exercise.

And maybe catch a glimpse of the woman he couldn't stop thinking about.

CHAPTER 13

Lily let the warm Michigan air envelop her as she stepped out the front door. She noticed the peaceful quiet that Huron Cove had to offer. It was so unlike what she was used to growing up in the suburbs outside of Chicago—the constant roar of jets overhead and the never-ending din of vehicle traffic on the interstates. Now she was lucky to hear two or three cars pass by every hour, and the clear blue sky offered nothing more than a smattering of wispy white clouds and gulls heading to the lake.

Despite the countdown calendar on top of her dresser, she had no desire to hide inside her house from now until the end of the school year. Sure, she didn't want to get close to anyone, but that didn't mean she couldn't get out and enjoy some fresh air and sunshine. So, she thought she would use the morning to explore her new home for the next 275 days—*give or take, but who's counting?*

With her pink shorts and matching running shoes, she wore her white running top. She had tied her hair in the back with a rubber band and added her running sunglasses. There had been talk about a nature preserve east of town on the way to the lake, and she hoped to check it out on her run. She headed south to start. She had thought about going north by the Spencer residence but decided it best not to. If she changed her mind, she could always run north on her way back and come down the street to her house. Rose's words about Luke echoed in her ears. *He's a cop with a kid, and you don't want to get involved with anyone in Huron Cove. Come back home so you can find yourself a good Illinoisan.*

She picked up the pace, but with every step she took, she

couldn't help but think about him—his muscular chest, his strong jaw line, his intoxicating blue eyes. If she ever wanted to imagine his eyes, all she had to do was look up to the Huron Cove sky.

"Morning," a man walking his dog said from the opposite sidewalk.

He acted like he knew Lily, but, even with her short period of time in town, she was coming to the realization that there were no strangers in Huron Cove.

She waved and smiled. "Hi," she said without breaking stride. *Such nice people in this place.*

She hit the northeast corner of the courthouse square and continued south. Several cars were parked outside the Food Mart and a handful of locals were out enjoying the sunshine with a morning walk. Hard as she tried not to, her thoughts returned to Luke. Just over twelve hours before, she had walked these same sidewalks with him. She felt so at ease with him, like they had known each other for longer than a week. She crossed the street and kept going on the east side of the pizzeria. She couldn't hold back the smile that flashed across her face when she remembered being introduced to Butch Nutting. *Bubba Nuts!* It didn't take her long to recall the strong hand of Luke Spencer on her shoulder as he rescued her from Beth's attempts at fixing her up with every guy who walked in the door.

She turned right at the intersection and watched a couple cars pull into the lot at St. Peter's. She remembered seeing something about a rummage sale fundraiser that started at nine. She thought she might come back into town after her run and check it out. She turned north at the next street and headed back toward the square. She caught a glimpse of the sign for CupKate's Confectionery and smiled again. That place had some great brownies, and the man she enjoyed it with was pretty great himself.

Stop it! You cannot keep thinking about him!

She crossed the street and ran past The Coffee Cove.

Through the big picture window she could see most of the tables were full. With the front door open, she caught a whiff of fresh roasted coffee beans and cinnamon. She reminded herself to bring some money next time in case she got hungry. She crossed the street and made a final right turn at the movie theater. If she headed straight east for another half mile, she would hit the nature preserve and then Lake Huron. She decided she'd run out there before heading back home. She'd keep herself busy the rest of the day by focusing on schoolwork.

And all she would have to do to focus on her work would be to stop thinking about the man she couldn't get out of her mind.

* * *

Luke pulled his running hat down an inch, the sun bright even with his shades. He and Butter had gone north from his house. He had thought about going past Lily's, but decided against it. She might think he was checking up on her, or maybe stalking her. But that didn't mean he couldn't stop and walk near her house once the run was over. They turned left at the corner, ran to the next intersection, and then headed south on the next street. Once a block south of Lily's house, they went back east and then south, which would take them straight into downtown Huron Cove.

Luke usually ran with the dog for a mile or so before bringing him back home. Then Luke would go out and finish a few more miles. Butter led the way today with a quick pace, as if he was determined to catch whatever scent he had sniffed out of the air. He kept his focus forward, not even distracted by the squirrel that darted across their path and then up a tree.

"Morning, Luke," the man walking his dog said.

Luke recognized him as Joe Cantrall, who used to run the machine shop two blocks west of the courthouse square. "Morning, Joe."

"If you hurry, you might catch her," he yelled back at Luke

as he and Butter ran by him.

Luke waved, not knowing what the old man was talking about. Perhaps there was a dog up ahead that Butter would like to play with.

He imagined running with Lily. He remembered the girls saying she liked to run and, given her athletic figure, he didn't doubt it. He wondered if she played any sports when she was younger. It would be great if she did because Kayla was very active. They could be an active family.

You need to stop thinking about her. Lily is Kayla's teacher. Nothing more. The only reason you're thinking about her is because last night it was either her or Ava. Find someone who likes you. And find someone who will be a good mom to Kayla.

His thoughts about finding someone vanished in an instant. In the blink of an eye, he never saw it coming. It happened at the northeast corner of the square, just outside the Food Mart.

Luke was about to give a tug on Butter's leash when the dog sped up like he had somewhere to be. Luke saw a flash of pink and white. There was a gasp and then a yelp. And the next thing he knew he ran smack dab into the woman he couldn't stop thinking about. With Lily running east, her forward progress screeched to a halt with the leash blocking her path. Luke couldn't stop his momentum, and the two crashed into each other. Luke let go of the leash and his arms suddenly wrapped around the most beautiful woman currently in Huron Cove. Somehow, he was able to hold her in his right arm and break their fall with his left. Still, one minute they were running, the next minute, he's lying on top of her on the sidewalk. Their eyes met, their breathing out of control.

"I'm so sorry, Miss O'Leary, I didn't see you." His right arm was still underneath her, and he rolled slightly to the side to check on her. He couldn't help but notice the tan and toned legs. He knew right then and there that she wasn't a novice runner. He hurried to brush a pebble imbedded in her knee. "Are you okay?"

Lily's chest heaved as she tried to catch her breath. "I think I'm okay. I'm sorry, I didn't see you either."

With Lily wrapped in his right arm, he had the sudden urge to pull her closer and kiss her on her cherry red lips. He could feel her hands across his back holding on tight. She still hadn't let go. He wanted to pull her closer and kiss her right there on the sidewalk outside the Food Mart. He didn't care if anyone saw him or not.

Unfortunately, another male got there first and beat him to it. Mr. Butterlickens swooped in and gave her a lick on the cheek.

"Butter! Stop that!" Luke stood up with Lily still in his arm to rescue her from the slobbering dog. "I am so sorry, Miss O'Leary." He reached up and wiped her cheek with his finger.

Undeterred by his faux pas, Butter nuzzled his way in between the two. Luke and Lily looked down at the dog and broke into a laugh.

"Please, call me Lily," she said after finally catching her breath. "He sure is friendly."

Luke was still holding Lily close to him. He shook at the realization and released her from his embrace. "I'm so sorry again, Lily. I guess I kind of spaced out and wasn't paying attention to anyone coming down the sidewalk. Are you sure you're okay?"

Lily reached up and put her sunglasses on top of her head, her chocolate brown eyes sparkling. The sweat on her tanned face glistened in the sunlight. He had never seen her look more beautiful. The smile reddened her cheeks. She patted him on the arm. "Really, it's fine. I didn't hit my head or anything." Then she gave Butter a good rubbing, much to the dog's liking. "And Butter was just trying to make it all better."

Butter barked, apparently happy that Lily mentioned his name.

Luke looked her over as she swiped a trickle of sweat off her forehead. He wished he could brush her cheek again. He wished he could hold her again. Even with those two wishes out of the question for now, he did know he didn't want their meeting to end. "Um . . . were you heading back home?"

Lily pointed toward the east. "I was going to check out the nature preserve and then the lake. I haven't been out there yet."

Luke looked down at Butter. He wondered if his running buddy had anything left in the tank. The dog barked and then tugged at the leash. *Thanks, buddy. I owe you one.* He looked at Lily. "Care for some company?"

"Sure."

With Butter in the lead, Luke and Lily ran out east of town, the sidewalk ending at the entrance to the nature preserve. Once inside the gates, they had the blacktop mostly to themselves. Luke snuck glances out the side of his sunglasses. He could tell Lily was an experienced runner, and he was impressed when she would check her watch every so often to monitor her pace. She commented on how nice the surroundings were and said she would have to come out there more often. When they reached the end of the trees and the lake came into view, she gasped. They then slowed to a walk.

* * *

"Wow, it's beautiful," Lily said. She put her sunglasses on her head again as her eyes took in the shoreline, gazing from the north to the south.

"Want to walk on the beach?"

Lily didn't say anything, she just nodded and walked on. The tranquil blue waters of Lake Huron gently lapped at the shore. The only other sound was a gull flitting about overhead. A couple of boats could be seen in the distance.

Luke pointed to the north. "You can make out the lighthouse right up there."

"Yeah, I see it."

"That's near where Emma and her parents live. Kayla spends a lot of time out there."

"I can understand why. It's so pretty and peaceful out here."

They walked on as Butter sniffed something in the sand. "You're probably used to something similar living near Chicago. I'm sure Lake Michigan is pretty, too."

Lily glanced at him before looking out over the water again. "Lake Michigan is pretty but getting to it is a hassle. The traffic's a nightmare, and then there's the parking. You have to get pretty far north of the city before you can find a place like Huron Cove."

When Luke switched the leash from his right hand to his left, his hand brushed Lily's arm. She almost reached for his hand, wanting to interlock her fingers with his. She felt so comfortable with him— safe, secure. Her last boyfriend was an overgrown frat boy who lived to get drunk and watch sports. She could never get him to run with her. He said it was a waste of time. Apparently, Luke didn't agree. And given the muscles bulging out of his shirt, he wasn't wasting his life away sitting on the couch watching TV.

Lily realized she wanted a guy like Luke—a little older, wiser, with a good head on his shoulders. She also realized it couldn't be Luke. Not here. Not in Huron Cove. Because this wasn't home. This wasn't where she was meant to be.

"I should get going," she said barely over a whisper.

"We'll run back with you."

"No, that's okay, if you don't mind. I like to run alone. Gives me a chance to think." She started walking backwards, hoping he wouldn't protest or follow her. She hoped she didn't sound impolite, although with the look in his eyes, she worried he took her refusal as a slight. But she couldn't get close to him. It would make it so much harder to leave. And that was her plan. "Thanks for the tour, though. I'll see you later. Bye Butter."

CHAPTER 14

"Morning, Arlene."

Arlene picked up the two cups of coffee on the counter and headed straight for her "office" near the front window. Luke hadn't even ordered anything, but he had been there enough times that Arlene knew what he wanted. She didn't wait to see if he was on the job or had somewhere else to be either, and Luke knew full well she would hound him down the sidewalk if he didn't sit and chat for a few minutes.

He sat down at the table and fiddled with the lid on the cup. He was doing his best to appear preoccupied so it would give him some time to think of what in the world Arlene would want to talk about. He set the lid on the table and then took a sip of coffee. He caught a glimpse of her over the rim of his cup. Arlene sat there, smiling at him, not even touching her coffee. Luke put his cup on the table and raised his hands. "What?"

"How was your date?"

Luke's eyebrows scrunched together. "My date? I didn't go out on a date."

"That's not what I hear?"

Luke sighed and gave her the look. "Well, who did you *hear* that from?"

Arlene raised a hand to stop any further interrogation. "Luke, like I've told you before, I can't divulge my sources or the information I receive from them."

Luke's first thought was Emma and Kayla, but they had been at Emma's house when he ran into Lily. Hadn't they? It was too early in the morning for them to be in town. *Wasn't it? Who knows? I wouldn't be surprised if Arlene picked 'em up at the crack of dawn so they could commence their spying operation. But wait a minute, what if she's talking about Friday night when we were walking around the square? Two laps around the courthouse and then some brownies at CupKate's Confectionery could very well have set the tongues a-wagging.*

"So, how'd it go?" Her eyes told him it was time to spill the beans.

Luke decided to play hard ball. If she wasn't going to divulge what she knew, why should he? "I don't know what you're talking about, Arlene."

"Oh, come on, Luke. I heard you were hanging out with the very lovely Miss Lily O'Leary yesterday morning."

He did his best to remain stone-faced, trying not to exhibit one of the tells that would admit his guilt. *The run, not the walk around the square.* He crunched his teeth together and then, elbow on the table, rested his chin in his hand. "I don't remember 'hanging out' with Miss Lily O'Leary."

"I heard it from reputable sources that you were seen running with Lily out to the nature preserve and then walking along the beach."

Luke looked away. He didn't remember seeing many people when they were running. Maybe Arlene had a drone hovering in the skies of Huron Cove. He decided to come clean and hope she'd drop the subject. "Butter and I were out for a run, and I ran into her over by the Food Mart." He didn't tell her that he literally ran into her or that they ended up in each other's arms on the sidewalk. "We took a run out to the lake."

The smile on Arlene's face widened. "So it *was* a date."

"It wasn't a date, Arlene. We were out running separately and came across each other. She mentioned she wanted to go out to see the nature preserve, and since Butter and I weren't finished with our run, we decided to join her."

Arlene rested her chin in her hand, hoping for more details about how they gazed into each other's eyes and kissed on the beach. Or something like that. Luke could tell she wanted more info.

"That's about it."

"Did you two talk?"

Luke shrugged. "A little bit."

Arlene flashed him a look of anticipation. "So, will there be a second date?"

Luke shook his head. He was going to nip this obsession in the bud right then and there. It was obvious Lily wasn't interested in him, so he wasn't going to waste his time going down that dead-end road. "I don't see that happening. I offered to walk her home, but she declined. I think it's pretty clear that she doesn't want anything to do with me. It could be for a whole host of reasons. I'm older than she is. I'm a cop. I have an eleven-year-old daughter." He took another sip of coffee and then licked his lips. "So, not going to happen. I guess it's back to the drawing board."

"Well, I don't think you should give up so quickly, Luke. She could be the one."

Luke looked out the window. He'd be lying if he said he wasn't interested in Lily O'Leary. He went to bed thinking about her Friday night, and she was on his mind when he woke up the next morning. And he hadn't stopped thinking about her ever since she walked away from him. For the rest of the day, he replayed running into her, holding her in his arms on the sidewalk, and then walking on the beach. There was an obvious physical attraction—her beautiful brown eyes and athletic figure. But he knew there was even more beauty inside of her, if only he could draw it out. That, however, would require him to ask her out. And given the fact she wouldn't even let him walk her home, it was a good bet a date would not be in the cards. He could see things ending badly on so many fronts, and he didn't want to go down that road only to have his heart and Kayla's heart broken because he fell for the first woman he met.

"She's not interested in me, Arlene. I need to look elsewhere." He downed the rest of his coffee and stood up. "I should get going."

"Are you heading to church?"

"No, I'm covering Aaron's shift."

Arlene stood up and put a hand on his arm stopping his exit. "Think about what I said, Luke. Don't give up on Lily O'Leary before you know if there's a chance at something wonderful happening."

Luke nodded once. As much as he would like to get to know her better, he had to keep his distance. That's the way it had to be. "Thanks for the coffee, Arlene."

* * *

The Sunday morning sun had risen over Lake Huron and brightened the day. It looked like another beautiful day on the Sunrise Coast of Michigan. In her bathroom, Lily looked in the mirror as she blow-dried her hair. She could almost see the reflection wanting to ask her questions.

How'd your date with Luke go?

It wasn't a date.

You spent an hour with him on Friday night and he bought you a brownie and a coffee. That's a date.

It was not a date. It was two people enjoying a walk and then a little dessert.

That's called a date.

It was not a date.

You spent the next morning running with him and walking along the beach with him. Sooo . . . that's like two dates in less than twenty-four hours.

It was not a date.

Looks and sounds like a date to me.

Lily sighed. She felt like she was losing the argument with herself. Maybe the reason she didn't consider Friday night a date was that she felt so at ease with Luke, like they were two friends hanging out. The run with him was the same feeling. Just two friends enjoying each other's company. Nothing more. At least that's what she kept telling herself.

She had spent the rest of Saturday wondering why she declined his offer to walk her home. Probably because she was afraid, although she didn't want to admit it to herself. Afraid that she would want to spend more time with him. Maybe they would go out on a real date or get together for another run. Then it would be dinner and a movie. She closed her eyes.

You like him, don't you?

No, I don't like him.

You're lying to yourself.

Shut up.

It was like she was having an argument with her sister. She grabbed her brush and ran it through her hair. She needed to get to church, and perhaps the worship service would take her mind off the man she pretended not to want anything to do with. She wore her favorite yellow sundress and drove through downtown Huron Cove on her way to St. Peter's. Although she had gone to Wednesday chapel with the students, this would be her first Sunday morning service. With the parking lot half full, she found an open spot and parked.

Maybe Luke will be here.

She looked around for his police SUV but didn't see it. Maybe he was working or maybe he was on the way. *I don't care. I'm not here to see him.*

But you'd like to, wouldn't you?

Shut up.

Once inside the sanctuary, she took a seat on the end near the wall, three rows from the back. As many of the parishioners mingled before the start of the service, she recognized a few of the parents of her students. Ethan and Olivia were sitting on the right side near the front. The woman with the red hair that she met at the bakery the other night was sitting two rows behind them with her husband.

Lily was looking through her service folder when she heard a commotion of trampling feet coming down the carpeted aisle to her left.

"Hi, Miss O'Leary," Kayla whispered loudly.

Emma was right behind her. "Hi, Miss O'Leary." The two girls smiled and then giggled. "Are you sitting by yourself?"

"Yep, it's just me."

Emma looked at the empty row. "Can we sit next to you?"

"Of course." Lily scooted down the row as Kayla sat on her right and Emma on her left. She realized the girls wore matching red dresses. "You two look very fashionable today."

"Thanks," Kayla said. "And you look very nice, too."

Lily smiled and gave her a wink. The girl had blonde hair that cascaded down below her shoulders. With her tanned face and vibrant eyes, she looked like an angel in red. *Your dad's very blessed to have such a beautiful daughter* she wanted to say. She tried to shake away any thoughts of Luke.

"What did you two learn in Sunday School today?"

Emma took the lead. "Oh! We learned all about Saint Paul. He was Saul before he became Paul." She then proceeded to give her teacher the rundown on his life before Kayla took over.

"Next week we're supposed to learn about some of his famous Bible verses like 'I have fought the good fight, I have finished the race, I have kept the faith.' That's from Second Timothy, chapter four, verse seven."

"Speaking of races, did you know we're going to have a 5k race during the Apple Festival? Kayla and I are going to run it. They're going to give out medals and everything."

Lily saw Emma nod at Kayla like it was her turn to ask a question.

"Did you enjoy running with Dad and Butter?"

Lily flinched slightly, not expecting the question. How did they go from Saint Paul to running with Luke? And did Luke tell them about her running with him and Butter? Or had they seen them together?

"Did your dad say we went running?"

Kayla's eyes widened, and Lily thought she might have seen a hint of fear in the girl's eyes, like she said something she shouldn't have.

"No," she said, shaking her head. "Someone said they saw you running together with Butter."

Lily didn't want to upset Kayla for the second time in a

week. “I had a nice run. Huron Cove is very pretty, especially out by the lake.”

“My dad likes to run, and I get to run with him sometimes so we can train for the race.”

“Where is your dad this morning?”

Kayla’s smile turned upside down and she gave a disappointed shrug. “He had to work again.”

“Does he work a lot on Sundays?”

“Yeah. I wish he’d come with me, but he hasn’t come to church since my mom died.”

Lily clenched her teeth. There they were talking about Kayla’s deceased mother again. She scolded herself. It was obvious Kayla found her dad’s absence disappointing. By the look in her eyes, Lily feared the girl might run off in tears like she did on the playground. She had to do something. “Maybe you and Emma could run with me sometime.”

Kayla’s face brightened and so did Emma’s. “Oh! We would love that, Miss O’Leary. Maybe we could do that next weekend.”

Kayla tapped her teacher on the arm. “Are you going to the school carnival on Friday night?”

“Yep. I’m supposed to run one of the booths, but I don’t know which one yet. I’ll be there though.”

“That’s cool,” Kayla said, smiling. “It’s always a great time.”

The organist began the prelude and the clamor of the parishioners began to settle down. Lily looked forward, happy that Kayla had a smile on her face. Now all she wanted to do was make sure that smile never went away.

CHAPTER 15

Dinner in the Spencer household was noticeably quiet that Wednesday night. Mr. Butterlickens lay silent next to Kayla's chair at the dinner table. There was talk about Kayla's day at school and the upcoming school carnival on Friday, but she didn't have her normal amount of enthusiasm. Luke found it concerning enough that he asked his daughter if she was feeling okay. Kayla said she was fine, had already finished her homework, and planned on reading a book later that evening. Other than that, the clinking of forks and spoons on plates of spaghetti and bowls of corn and fruit salad were the only noises heard in the dining room.

And that all led Luke to conclude something was up.

"You sure everything's okay?"

Kayla nodded and ate a spoonful of fruit.

Great, we're back to the silent treatment again. He hadn't stopped thinking about Lily O'Leary since their run together on Saturday, but he kept telling himself she was a lost cause. His stomach grumbled, but not because he didn't get enough to eat. The thought of having to find another woman to go out with twisted his gut. He had only been trying to find someone for a week or so, and the only prospective candidates so far were Lily and Ava. Luke groaned silently. Would he have to ask Ava out on a date to see what she was really like? Maybe she was a sweet, caring woman who would be a wonderful wife for him and mother for Kayla.

Maybe.

"How about we watch a couple innings of the Tigers game?"

Kayla grabbed her plate and silverware from the table. "Okay."

After the table was cleared and the dishes put in the dishwasher, Luke turned on the TV and sat in the recliner. Kayla sat on the end of the couch with Butter's head resting on her leg.

The Yankees loaded the bases in the top of the first with two walks and a hit-by-pitch. Then the cleanup hitter promptly deposited the first pitch he saw into the left-field seats for a grand slam.

"Looks like it's going to be a long night for the Tigers, Kayla."

She nodded and stroked the dog's head.

Luke's cell phone buzzed on the end table next to him. He picked it up and looked at the screen filled with the picture of a smiling eleven-year-old girl known as Emma Lynn Grayson Stone. He held out the phone to Kayla.

"It's Emma."

Kayla smiled and bounded off the couch. She grabbed her dad's phone and answered it before rushing off to the kitchen so she could have some privacy. With her birthday coming up, Luke reminded himself that he promised to get Kayla her own phone. He lowered the volume of the TV and turned an ear toward the kitchen.

"Are you sure?" Kayla asked.

Luke noticed a hint of excitement in her voice, something that had been absent during their dinner conversation. He thought he made out the words "Should I?" and "How much longer?" Then, he definitely heard Kayla say, "I'll try to hurry."

Kayla rushed back to the living room and announced, "Dad, we have to go to the bookstore."

Luke muted the TV. "Right now?"

"Yes, we have to hurry."

"What for?"

Kayla stammered for a second but quickly recovered. "It's something for school."

"I thought you were done with your homework."

"It's something for school. It's very important. Please, Dad."

He could almost see water pooling in his daughter's eyes, like she was begging him to do her this one favor. Given the fact that this was the most conversation they had that night, he figured he better take the opportunity to make her happy.

"Alright," he said, getting up from the recliner. "Let me get my keys."

Kayla was already seated in the front passenger seat of the police SUV when Luke locked the front door. On the way, he noticed she took a good long look at Mrs. Fossan's house as they started the five-minute drive to downtown. Luke didn't see any lights on in the house. She tapped her foot on the floorboard, as if silently begging her dad to turn on the flashing lights and siren to get there quicker.

He found an empty spot in front of Armstrong Design Company, and Kayla had the door opened before he put the shifter into *Park*. She bounded across the sidewalk and into the store.

Luke turned off the engine and shook his head. "Well, let's see what this is all about."

* * *

After having to stay after school let out to grade papers and attend a meeting on the upcoming carnival, Lily decided a walk around town would give her some fresh air before she called it a night. Plus, she was still nursing a sore calf muscle after her Saturday run. She thought she might have overdone it running with Luke, but she hadn't wanted to show she couldn't hack it. The walk helped stretch her legs and gave her time to think.

She walked past Candy Junction and then the Cut & Curl. She stopped in front of the window of The Coffee Cove and looked inside. It seemed so warm and inviting, and the smells wafting out the open front door gave her the idea to stop and pick up a cup of coffee tomorrow before work. She continued on to Turn the Page Books and decided to check it out.

The bell over the door jingled when she entered. With its vintage light fixtures that reflected off the polished hardwood floors, she had never seen such a beautiful store. It looked like a mountain chalet with shelves of books enticing readers of all ages. There was a children's area over to her right. She walked over to the left side of the store where faux leather couches invited customers to sit and read for a while. The wall had a colorful array of paper announcing various events on the Huron Cove horizon—the St. Peter's School carnival, the Apple Festival, the lighthouse fundraiser.

Such a charming little town.

She was perusing the magazine rack when she heard a voice that sounded familiar. She thought she heard a girl say her name and "the bookstore" and "hurry." Seeing a couple of gray-haired ladies waiting to check out, she decided she must be hearing things. She flipped through a copy of *Elle* before she realized her sister had already told her most of what was in it.

"Miss O'Leary!"

She turned in time to see Emma, a wide smile on her face, walking out from behind one of the shelves. She gave her teacher a big hug.

"Hi, Emma, how are you?"

"Oh, Miss O'Leary, I'm fine. Do you like the bookstore?"

Lily looked to the ceiling and then around the store. "It really is beautiful. I think it's the prettiest bookstore I've ever been in."

Emma then proceeded to use the next five minutes to tell Lily how the store had been recently refurbished. Lily listened to it all, marveling at the excited storytelling from one of her favorite students. She noticed Emma's eyes kept glancing out the front window as she spoke excitedly about the store and how Julia, the store's owner, often lets her stack the shelves when new shipments of books come in.

"Are you excited about the carnival?"

Lily nodded. "I am. I'm going to be in charge of the milk-bottle knockdown. It should be lots of fun."

"Oh, it is. I can't wait." Emma then grabbed her hand. "Let me show you the checkout counter," she said, dragging Lily behind her. "It's in the shape of a compass."

The chatterbox Emma went on and on, barely taking a breath. She mentioned how a guy named Alex built the counter and started his own business next door. According to Emma, Alex and Julia were recently married and she even got to be part of the wedding. She acted like she was about to regale her teacher about the nuptials when her voice fell silent after the bell over the door clanged.

"Hey look, it's Kayla."

Kayla hurried toward them in a rush, her face red like she had run all the way from home. "Hi, Miss O'Leary, it's so nice to see you again." She threw her arms around her teacher.

Lily almost started laughing. It hadn't been three hours since she last saw the girls, but they acted like they were being reunited for the first time in ages. She wondered what they were up to.

* * *

Luke stepped out of the vehicle and saw Ethan walking out of The Coffee Cove with a sack of cookies.

"Hey, bud, you see the Tigers are down by four already?"

Luke shook his head. "Same old, same old. Maybe they'll turn it around one of these days."

"What's up?"

Luke gestured with his thumb toward the bookstore. "Kayla got a call from Emma and then there was apparently a school-related emergency that required us to drop everything and head downtown to the bookstore."

"Emma, huh?"

"Yeah, you know what's going on?"

Ethan grimaced like he was going to have to have an uncomfortable father-daughter chat later on this evening.

"Umm, I think I might." He nodded toward the bookstore window. "Have you been inside?"

Luke shook his head. "No, why?"

"Emma decided to stay at the store while I went to buy some cookies. On my way out, a certain sixth-grade teacher happened to walk in. I'd bet good money that she's been cornered in there by Giggles and Wiggles."

Luke ran his hand over his face and tried not to laugh out loud. *So that's what the big emergency was.*

Ethan held up his hands in defense. "I'm sorry. I didn't have any part in it."

Luke waved it off. "It's alright. Kayla was uncomfortably quiet during dinner, but she perked up when she got Emma's call."

The two men took a few steps toward the front door of the bookstore. Ethan lowered his voice. "I don't mean to pry, but have you thought about asking Lily out?"

Luke paused and then looked at Ethan. He hadn't stopped thinking about it.

Apparently, the truth was etched on Luke's face because Ethan said, "The reason I ask is that Emma can't stop talking about it. She has it in her mind that you and Lily would enjoy each other's company. For what it's worth, it can't hurt to ask. She seems nice. She might be good for you." He leaned in closer to Luke. "And she might be good for Kayla, too."

Luke nodded, his palms suddenly moist. He hadn't been expecting to ask a woman out on a date tonight, but apparently his daughter and her best friend had a desire to force his hand. He reminded himself that they had already spent time together at the bakery and running to the lake, so it wasn't anywhere near a blind date. But it would be a date. And he hadn't been on a date in years. A date meant something. It could lead to a whole host of things—love, marriage, children.

Just don't let it lead to a broken heart—yours or Kayla's.

He thanked Ethan and walked inside, the bell announcing his appearance. He caught a glimpse of Emma and Kayla before they suddenly found the need to hurry to the storage room in the back. That left a single person in the center of the store. Under the shine of the vintage lights and above the polished hardwood floors, Lily looked like an angel in blue jeans and a brown leather jacket. Their eyes met, and he could tell she knew the girls had something to do with them standing in the bookstore together on a Wednesday night.

Luke walked toward her. "Evening, Miss. . . I mean Lily."

"Evening. Fancy meeting you here."

Luke laughed. "Quite the coincidence if you ask me." He looked over her shoulder but couldn't find the two conspirators. He figured they were probably giggling with glee in the back. "I hope they haven't kept you."

Lily smiled and shook her head. "No, not at all. They're wonderful girls, and I love listening to their stories."

Luke tried to swallow but his mouth had suddenly gone dry. *Goodness, was asking a woman on a date always this hard?* When a customer approached the counter and the owner Julia prepared to ring the woman up, Luke gestured toward the side wall. "You got a second?"

"Sure."

When Luke was confident they were out of earshot of anyone, he asked the question he hadn't asked in years. "I was wondering if you're not busy or something." He had to pause to take a breath. "Could I take you out to dinner sometime?"

Then came the wince.

The lovely and beautiful Miss Lily O'Leary winced, like a jolt of electricity shocked her body. From his police training, as well as being a red-blooded American male, Luke had become highly attuned to female facial expressions and mannerisms—the shake of fright, the eye roll, the exhale, the "I'd really like to, but" response. This was a definite wince. Unmistakable. No doubt about it. Luke saw it with his own eyes, and it hit him like a punch to the solar plexus. For as long as he lived, he would never forget the wince that flashed across her sweet face.

In the silence that followed, Luke knew he had to make a quick adjustment. Calling an audible, he gave her a way out. "I know you're busy with school and everything, but maybe if you have some free time."

Lily looked down at the spotless hardwood floor to gather her thoughts. The wait was killing Luke. *Why did you have to ask her? You knew she didn't like you. Can I take it back? Can I run out the front door and hide?*

She looked at him again. "Can I think about it?"

CHAPTER 16

The crisp cool air of the early Friday evening indicated autumn had arrived and was here to stay. But that didn't keep hundreds of people from flocking to the parking lot of St. Peter's for the annual fall carnival. Food, fun, and games galore awaited kids and their families. There was the ring toss, the bushel basket toss, Tic-Tac-Toe, the duck pond, the balloon-dart game, the disk drop, and skee ball, just to name a few. The games were meant to be won, and local retailers donated prizes for the winners. There was even a dunk tank for donations and laughs, although with the cool evening, the victims, Mayor Linden and Principal Wheeler, were hoping most throws were high and wide. Hayrides and face painting added to the enjoyment. To fill everyone's stomachs, there were caramel apples, cotton candy, popcorn, hot dogs, funnel cakes, and elephant ears. Nothing put people in a good mood like the smell of deep-fried dough and hot buttered popcorn.

At the entrance to the parking lot, Luke handed over two tickets, one for him and one for Kayla. They had skipped dinner, figuring there would be no shortage of food to satisfy their hunger.

Confronted with a myriad of booths and what seemed like half the town walking around, Luke asked, "How about some cotton candy, Kayla?"

"Sure."

Kayla chose the pink and tore off a chunk. Luke even picked a couple fingerfuls for himself. He held it for her as she took a turn at the ring toss. Her three successful throws garnered her choice of small stuffed animals, and she chose the golden retriever because it "looked like Butter." It made her happy, and that made Luke happy.

But it didn't take more than five minutes of the carnival for Luke to feel like something was missing, that there was more happiness to be had in life. It hit him when he saw Olivia and Ethan enjoying the evening with Emma. They were a couple in love, holding hands and sharing knowing glances. They enjoyed each other's company as well as parenting the light of their lives. There would be another light pretty soon, and Luke could only chuckle about the little brother or sister that Emma was going to have a hand in raising.

But what about him? Would there ever be someone he could hold hands with, talk to, and grow old with? And what about Kayla? Would she ever have a new mom? Would she ever be a sister? The thought of Kayla imparting all the love and attention a sister could muster on her younger sibling warmed his heart. The thought quickly vanished when he realized getting to that point would take a monumental effort on his part.

And, even more so, it would take someone special. Someone willing to marry a single father and become a family. With a stuffed animal in one hand and a half-eaten mass of pink cotton candy in the other, he looked at the ground and sighed.

When he looked up and turned to the left, it was like the seas had parted and a solitary light over the milk-bottle-knockdown booth lit the woman underneath it like an angel. Luke let loose a "wow" under his breath at what he saw. Lily wore blue jeans and a red St. Peter's sweatshirt. Her hair was up and held in the back with a red bow. Her tennis shoes were red, too. Wow again. He watched her interact with the kids—smiling, encouraging, congratulating. She was breathtaking in every respect.

Could she be the one? *Do I want her to be the one?* She was educated, beautiful, great with kids, and athletic. Even having only known her for a short period of time, he knew she would be great with Kayla.

"She's single, you know," Mike Duncan whispered in his ear.

Luke had been so entranced with the sight of Lily O'Leary that he hadn't even seen his fellow officer standing next to him. He glanced out of the corner of his eye, knowing he had been caught red-handed staring at her.

"What are you waiting for?"

What am I waiting for? Luke looked down at the asphalt before saying, "I don't know. I did ask her out to dinner, but she said she'd have to think about it. She didn't seem too enthused, so I don't know."

"Well, you might want to try again because my wife might just try to fix her up with Bubba." Mike grinned. "And Lily might think Bubba is a better catch than you."

Luke snapped his head and was about to jab his friend in the ribs before he broke into a smile. Mike did have a point. If Luke didn't take the chance, some other guy might ask her. Then where would he be? Back to square one.

"Why don't you ask her out again? Maybe she's had time to think things over."

Luke nodded. Lily O'Leary was the only woman he had thought about since the whole search for someone special began. Kayla already loved her, and a large part of him was dying to get to know her better. And he realized the only way he was ever going to get the answer he was looking for was to keep asking.

Seeing Lily without any contestants in line, he took a deep breath and headed toward her. But then the thought hit him. *What am I going to ask her? Hey, have you thought about that question I asked you the other day? You know, the one that made you wince.* Luke's stomach twisted into knots, and the knots got tighter when he saw her looking at him. He grunted when he realized he was carrying a stuffed golden retriever and a cone of half-eaten pink cotton candy. He could tell she saw him so there was no turning back now.

* * *

Lily had seen Luke out of the corner of her eye when he was talking with Beth's husband. Even from a distance, she noticed how the blue jeans and the red checkerboard shirt made him look like a handsome lumberjack. He still looked young, too, and given the way he ran on Saturday, she knew the man kept in shape. She couldn't help having the thoughts. She had them since they walked around the courthouse square together and it only intensified when they ran into each other on the sidewalk the next morning. She had never felt so close to a man before, never been held like that before. She could still feel his strong arms protecting her from danger. She wished she had wrapped her arms around him and let him kiss her.

Stop thinking that way!

But she wanted to. She had boyfriends in the past but nothing remotely serious. She was getting to the age where she wanted to find the love of her life. Someone who would be with her in the good times and the bad. Someone she could kiss goodnight and raise a family with.

But not here! In Huron Cove! She could almost hear her sister's voice lecturing her.

The thoughts were flooding her brain. It was all happening so fast. She could feel her heart rate ticking up, and she had to try and not fan the flames on her blushing cheeks. She tried to take a breath but managed only a gasp. There was no mistaking it, he was coming right for her.

And she realized she didn't have an answer for him yet.

She won a reprieve when Pastor Carlton happened by and headed Luke off at the pass. They were close enough that Lily could hear them, and they were also close enough so she could see Luke didn't like the intrusion because it took his eyes away from her.

"Luke, so good to see you," Pastor Carlton said, patting him on the back. "You and Kayla enjoying the carnival?"

Luke smiled and held up the evening bounty so far. "Yeah, she's having fun. It's nice that the school puts this on."

Pastor Carlton nodded. "Anytime we can enjoy the fellowship of others is a blessing. And it looks like a record crowd this year. I'm just glad they didn't ask me to take a seat in the dunk tank." He shivered. "Poor Mayor Linden and Principal Wheeler. Hope the water's warm." He put a hand on Luke's arm. "And I hope to see you in church on Sunday."

"I'm afraid I'm working again on Sunday morning. But I'll make sure Kayla gets there, though."

"Alright, well, maybe next Sunday."

Once Pastor Carlton continued on, Luke stood still and made eye contact with Lily. She still didn't have any contestants at her booth. She was the one to break the silence.

"Looks like you've had a pretty successful night." She felt like her cheeks must have been as red as her sweatshirt.

"What?"

She pointed to his hands. "I like your dog. Did you win that at the ring toss?"

Luke looked down at the stuffed animal and laughed. He took two steps forward. "Kayla won it. She also won a pair of sunglasses and a glow necklace. So, she's making out pretty well tonight." He glanced to his left and right in a quick search for his daughter. "I lost her and Emma a while ago."

There was an awkward silence that followed. Lily silently hoped someone would show up to knock down some milk bottles. *Did everyone go home?* She brushed a strand of hair away from her face, and she could tell Luke was as uncomfortable as she was. She took the initiative again to break the ice.

"It's a nice night for the carnival."

"Yes, it is."

More silence followed and still no one showed up. Her shaking hands found a place to hide in the pockets of her jeans.

"I couldn't help overhearing what Pastor Carlton said. How come you always work on Sundays? I know Kayla would like to go to church with you. I'm sure Pastor Carlton would like it, too."

Luke shifted his feet, and Lily thought he was going to turn tail and walk off without answering her. He looked like he was trying to collect his thoughts.

"It's been hard to go back to church after Maria died. I know I should but it's difficult. We were married there, and her funeral was there. A lot of prayers were said there, but . . ."

Lily took a step closer and reached out her hand to touch his arm. "Life doesn't always work out the way we want it, Luke, but God is with you every step of the way. It says so high above the altar—Lo, I am with you always." She took a deep breath. "I hope I'm not out of line, but I can tell it breaks Kayla's heart that you're not there. She sees other families there and yet she's by herself. You said it has been tough for her to move on, but when she sees that her dad hasn't moved on, it makes it difficult for her to do the same. She needs you there."

Luke nodded and broke eye contact with her. "I'll think about it."

* * *

Luke hadn't been expecting Lily to mention his lack of church attendance, but she had obviously overheard his conversation with Pastor Carlton. He wasn't upset with her, and actually he was impressed she would broach the subject. He wanted to ask her out now more than ever. He was about to open his mouth when an eleven-year-old girl jumped to a stop next to him.

"Hi, Dad."

"There you are. I thought I lost you for a second."

"Emma and I were sharing a funnel cake. It was great."

He was reluctant to hand over the remaining cotton candy because it looked like Kayla was about ready to bounce off the walls. He decided to give it to her just so he didn't have to hold it any longer.

"Have you been having fun?"

Kayla smiled and nodded as she swiped the last bit of pink cotton candy into her mouth. She looked at her teacher, her eyes widening. "Are you going to play, Dad?"

"Me? Why don't you play?"

Kayla looked at her sticky pink fingers. "I've got cotton candy all over me, Dad. Won't you play please?" She glanced at the prizes. "Maybe you could win me another stuffed animal."

Having gone dry with her customers, Lily tossed the ball up in the air a couple of times. "Yeah, come on, Dad. Step right up. Knock down all the bottles and win a prize."

Luke held up his free hand and tried to decline the offer. *What if I miss and end up looking like a fool?* He hadn't thrown a baseball in a while, and it's not like he could go out and warm up in the bullpen. "I think the games are for the kids, Kayla."

Lily was having none of it. "Come on, the adults can play, too. Take a shot. You never know what you might win."

Luke locked eyes with Lily. Was she talking about the game or him asking her out? He had asked her out once, so it wouldn't be a surprise to her. *Is that what she wants? Does she want me to ask her right now?*

"Whattya say?" she asked, tossing the ball in the air again. "You want to take the chance?"

"Come on, Dad. Please."

Luke could hardly turn down two beautiful females at once. "Alright, I'll give it a try." He handed Lily one of the tickets, and she gave him the ball and arranged the bottles.

With a ball in his right hand and a plush golden retriever in his left, he stepped back to get some extra room. He thought he made the mistake of looking at Lily and saw her brown eyes fixed on him. Talk about a distraction! After a deep breath, he wound up and let it fly. The fastball hit the bottles square and they all crashed to the ground.

"Yay! Good job, Dad."

"Nice throw, Luke," Lily said, smiling. Luke accepted the congratulations and walked closer to her. "Well, what prize does the winner want? Pick a prize, pick a prize."

Luke looked down at Kayla. "Which one do you want, baby doll?"

A smiling Kayla surveyed the prize collection and settled on a friend for her golden retriever. "The basset hound."

"Awww," Lily said, picking it out for her. "He's so cute with his floppy ears. I used to have a basset hound just like it. His name was Barney."

Kayla looked at her still sticky fingers. "I really need to wash my hands."

Luke offered to take custody of the hound and now had a stuffed animal in each hand. Kayla took off to wash her hands, leaving Luke and Lily alone again.

"Not only are you a runner, you've got quite the pitching arm, too."

Luke shrugged. "I used to play."

"Your daughter is a sweetheart."

"Thank you. I think so, too."

A silence fell over them as Luke's mind kept telling him to ask Lily out. *Just do it! Just ask her!* Now was the time—the sports hero wins the day and asks the beautiful woman out on a date. Maybe it wasn't the big leagues, but it was the best that could be asked for on a Friday night on the Sunrise Coast of Michigan. Luke snuck in a deep breath. He waited until their eyes met.

"Would you like to get some ice cream after the carnival?"

This time it was a flinch instead of a wince. Well, maybe a little wince flashed across her face, but he couldn't be certain. All he knew was, it wasn't a smile of acceptance. He could tell her mind was thinking as fast as it could. *Not again!* He could also feel the hollowness in his stomach returning.

"Um . . .," her voice was soft and gentle. "I have to work until the end of the carnival and then it'll be pretty late."

The excuse rattled around in his brain. "That's okay, I understand. Maybe sometime this weekend."

This time it was a wince. A big one. She offered her next

excuse. “My sister is coming to town tomorrow, so that will take up most of the weekend. I’m sorry, but I don’t think I’ll be available.”

I guess it’s never going to happen. “No problem. Maybe some other time.”

Thankfully, a couple with their two children walked up hoping to knock down some bottles, and it gave Luke a chance not to embarrass himself any further. He felt like an idiot. He walked away, a stuffed animal in each hand, without saying goodbye. He wanted to get out of there as fast as he could. It was becoming glaringly obvious she didn’t want to go out with him. He wished she would come out and say she wasn’t interested. That would make it easier on both of them. But Luke had no desire to be strung along.

He decided right then and there that he would find someone else.

CHAPTER 17

On late Saturday afternoon, Rose O'Leary finally completed the six-hour trek from Chicago to Huron Cove, and she only got lost twice. She claimed the GPS unit in her car actually laughed at her when she typed in Huron Cove as her destination. Once off the interstate, she turned west when she should have turned east and then south "at the county road to nowhere" when she should have turned north. It's a wonder she didn't run into the lake. She was thankful the "hicks in the sticks" at least had decent cell service so Lily could guide her safely back to civilization and her house. That way Rose wouldn't have to suffer the indignity of stopping to ask "one of the local hillbillies" for help.

"There aren't any hillbillies in Huron Cove," Lily said, shaking her head.

"I don't know, Lilybean, it seems pretty far out in the middle of nowhere if you ask me. I haven't seen a Starbucks in a hundred miles." She looked at her sister with despair on her face. "A hundred miles!"

Lily rolled her eyes at Rose's plight and helped grab a bag from the trunk of her car. "Huron Cove is actually quite beautiful when you take the time to check it out. Lake Huron is gorgeous, and it's so peaceful and quiet. And they have a very nice coffee shop. You'll like it."

Once inside the house, they stopped to hug each other. The O'Leary sisters hadn't seen each other in over two weeks, which to them was fourteen days more than they would like. Although Rose was tired from the drive, they planned on staying up half the night to talk like they did in the good old days.

"I'll tell you one thing, if you blink once you can drive through this town and miss it. How did you ever find a job here?"

"Like I told you before, they had a last-minute opening. I didn't have a lot of other choices in the Midwest." She ushered Rose farther inside to look around. "I like it here so far."

"Well, don't start liking it too much."

Rose looked through the rooms. There wasn't much to see, as Lily had no desire to move all her possessions, which were currently gathering dust in her parents' basement back in Illinois. In the kitchen, Rose gawked at the rotary dial phone and the answering machine on the table. Lily shrugged, saying they came with the house and she could use the phone in emergencies.

Continuing through the place, Rose smiled at the framed pictures of the smiling sisters dotting the walls of Lily's bedroom. After the tour, Rose said the place looked "homey" and pronounced it habitable. When Rose said she was hungry, Lily said she would call for a pizza.

"You actually have pizza in this town?"

Lily looked up from her phone. "Yes, we have pizza in this town. It's not as desolate as you think."

"I'll make that decision once I get a good look at the place, which I guess won't take too long."

Once the pizza was on the coffee table, the two sisters dove in and commenced their chat session. They discussed their parents and everything that was going on back home. Lily quickly steered the conversation to Rose's handsome new beau.

"So, how's Doctor Nick doing?"

Rose giggled slightly, her cheeks blushing. They had been dating for almost three months now, and Rose had every intention of making it last. "He's good. We're good. Everything is good."

Lily smiled. "How old is he again?"

"He's twenty-seven."

"Cradle robber."

Rose almost spit out her iced tea. "I am not!"

Lily laid it on even thicker. "You're like one of those cougars."

"Stop that!" She continued when she saw Lily couldn't stop laughing. "It's been a little tough lately, though. It seems I only get to see him during my shift. We haven't gone out at night in a while."

"That's probably because it's past his bedtime."

"Funny," Rose said, not laughing. "I'm hoping to fix him dinner on Monday night."

"Are you going to make him beanie weenies?"

"Girl, where have you learned this sassy attitude? Are these Michiganders corrupting your pretty little mind?"

Lily laughed. "I'm just looking out for my big sister."

Rose picked up another slice and was about to take a bite when she said, "I'm sure Nick could find your knight in shining armor for you. There's always a bunch of new single doctors coming through the hospital. Maybe we can introduce you to some hot guys when you come home for Christmas. That way you can settle down once you move back to civilization."

Lily looked down at her empty plate and then set it on the coffee table. She took a sip of iced tea and held the glass between both hands. She didn't look at her sister when she offered to fix her up. *Is that really what I want? To find a man for when I move back to Chicago? What about Luke? Is he even part of the equation?* She took a deep breath, made eye contact with Rose, and then spilled the beans on what she knew would be big news.

"That guy asked me out again last night."

Rose about choked on her crust. "Guy? What guy? And what do you mean by 'again'?"

"I mean he's asked me out twice now."

Rose wiped her hands on her napkin and cleared her throat. "You mean that old man?"

Lily blew out a breath. "He's not that old, Rose. Like I told you before, he's been a gentleman since the day I met him."

"Sweetie, we've been through this before. Nothing good can come from going out with a cop with a kid. You can do so much better than that."

"You haven't even met him."

Rose dismissed it with a wave of the hand. "Don't need to. You don't know what you're getting into. Maybe there's a good reason he's a single father. Divorces are common when policemen are involved. Did he leave his wife or did she leave him?"

Lily cocked her head and frowned. "He's a widower, Rose. His wife died of cancer about five years ago."

"And now he's desperate to find someone to love and to be a mom for his kid." Rose shook her head like the warnings she was giving were so glaringly obvious that nothing more needed to be said.

Lily leaned her head back on the couch and closed her eyes. Rose had caused her not to go out with two guys in the past. One was in high school, the other in college. Lily lost track of the number of times Rose said a particular guy was "not right" for her. She knew Rose had her best interests at heart, but she was twenty-eight years old for crying out loud. How was she going to know whether a guy was "right" for her if she never went out with him because Rose said not to?

Even with her eyes closed, Lily could sense Rose studying her, as if weighing her next question.

Rose's voice softened. "You said he asked you out twice. What did you tell him?"

"I told him I'd think about it."

Rose considered the statement before giving her response. "That's good. You never want to say yes immediately."

Lily raised her head off the couch and opened her eyes. She looked directly at Rose. *It's my life and it's my decision.* She leaned forward and did her best to speak in a strong voice. "I'm going to say yes the next time he asks me." She didn't pause long enough to let Rose respond and made sure to let her know she had thought this through. "He's a nice guy and his daughter is wonderful. I don't plan on falling in love with him. I'll be up front with him that I'm not looking for a lasting relationship—just friends." She took a deep breath, proud that she finally got it out of her system. "But if I can help him and Kayla get through some of the things they're dealing with, my year in Huron Cove will have been well spent."

Rose gave her the look that said she wasn't happy but her little sister would have to learn on her own one of these days. But that didn't mean Rose couldn't impart some words of wisdom for what might arise in the future.

"*If* you go out with him." Rose paused, as if hoping Lily would come to her senses. "*If* you go out with him, don't let him pick you up. Meet in a public place. There are a lot of freaks out there, and I don't want to have to identify your body parts after the police find you stuffed in his garbage can." She pointed at her sister when Lily giggled. "Don't laugh. It's happened. Remember that lady out in Oregon?"

"Yes, I remember."

"Don't go if he has handcuffs on him either. He might have some kinky ideas in mind. Don't hold hands. Don't make eye contact. Don't let him kiss you. Don't kiss him. Don't wear anything too revealing. You've got a lot to show off so an oversized sweater would be good. No makeup or lipstick either." It was like she was reading from a prepared list. "And wear your pointy red pumps. That way if you have to kick him in the crotch, he'll feel it and get the message that you're not a girl to be messed with."

Lily's hand shot to her mouth to keep the laugh from escaping her lips. Given the beat down she had administered on Luke with her umbrella, she didn't think she'd end up having to kick him in the crotch.

"Do you still have that can of Mace I bought you?"

"Yes."

"Good, but think about getting some bear spray, too."

"Bear spray?" *What in the world?*

"Yes, Mace or bear spray. Either one should do the trick.

Call me before you go out. That way I can check up on you during your get-together."

"You mean my date?"

"No, no. Don't call it a date. Call it an evening meeting or a working dinner or whatever you want but don't call it a date. Dates turns into dating and dating turns into marrying and marrying turns into babying. You don't want to go there. You have to finish out this year and come back home so that the people who love you can take good care of you."

"Okay, whatever you say." Lily was starting to feel the weight of exhaustion overcome her. "Is there anything else I need to know?"

Rose cleared her throat. Gone was the joking and the sisterly lecturing. Now, she was dead serious. "Yeah, one last thing. Don't you dare let him break your heart, Lil."

CHAPTER 18

Three weeks later . . .

Luke sat behind the wheel of his SUV, his foot tapping the floor mat at a good clip. Most of the parking lot had cleared out of parents picking up their children after school let out. The only cars remaining that early evening were the teachers and the parents who were scheduled for parent-teacher conferences. Spaced at thirty-minute intervals, there were parents going in and out on a regular basis. They would keep coming and going until eight o'clock that night. Luke looked at his watch again. He still had fifteen minutes until his meeting with Lily.

It would be the first time he had spoken to her in three weeks.

Like some pimple-faced high school freshman, he had waited for her to call after he asked her out at the bookstore. The call never came. Then he asked her again at the carnival, but she gave him another excuse. Hadn't heard any inkling of a desire to get together since. There was also the time she didn't want him accompanying her home after their run. The brownies they had together didn't count because she was simply trying to avoid going back to the pizzeria to sit with Beth and Bubba. So, all told, he was zero for three, and he had no desire to strikeout for a fourth time.

He hated it that he had let himself think about having Lily in his life. From everything he had been able to come to know about her, she was intelligent, athletic, good with kids, and beautiful. But she wasn't interested in him, and he vowed not to fall for a woman unless he knew there was a chance at success. His disgust led him to pound the steering wheel with his fist.

Time to move on.

With gritted teeth, he reached into the breast pocket of his police uniform and pulled out a scrap of paper. It had been there for the better part of a week. He hadn't wanted to look at it but moving on required him to do so. He unfolded the paper and felt his stomach twist into knots at the words written in red ink.

Call me! Let's have some fun! Ava.

She had slipped it to him when he was escorting a drunk out of the bar one early evening. He looked at the number she scrawled on the paper and sighed. *At least she's interested.* Ever since he last saw her, he had tried to think positive thoughts about her. If he could get past the tattoos, the ever-present aroma of stale cigarettes, and her apparent love of profanity, she was probably a decent woman. Maybe there was even some love in that heart of hers. Could she be a mother to Kayla? Did he want her to be a mother to Kayla? He rubbed a hand down his face and grimaced.

He looked at the number again and then grabbed his phone from the console. *I guess it couldn't hurt to see what she's like.* He tried to push the nightmare of Kayla in the bar while Ava was slinging drinks and cursing up a storm as far from his mind as possible. *Kayla will not be going to the bar. I'll be clear on that.* He had typed out six digits of her number before his phone beeped reminding him that he had an appointment. He stopped typing, a part of him wondering if he had just been saved by the bell. Ava would have to wait until later because he had to think about Kayla and her schooling.

And somehow he had to try not to think about her teacher who wanted nothing to do with him.

* * *

It had been three weeks. Despite her sister's warnings, Lily had decided to go out with Luke Spencer. He was handsome, athletic, and a good father to Kayla. She couldn't think of any harm in getting to know him better, even if she was only going to be in Huron Cove until the end of the school year. And she might help Kayla in the process. That's what she kept telling herself. *Just be honest about your intentions and no one will get hurt.*

But it had been three weeks and Luke hadn't asked her out again. Was he mad? Was she supposed to get back to him? With school and preparing for parent-teacher conferences, she had been so busy she didn't know where they had left things. *Will he ask me tonight?*

She was about to find out because the man she couldn't stop thinking about was standing in the doorway to her classroom.

Lily looked at her watch and then at Luke. "Come on in, Luke, you're right on time."

The first thing she noticed was the hard frown etched on his face. It wasn't the normal "good to see you" smile she had seen in the past. The second thing she noticed was the rigid posture. Maybe that was a product of his police uniform, but he didn't look pleased to be there.

Luke nodded as he stepped inside. "Miss O'Leary."

That was the third thing. Hadn't she told him a thousand times to call her Lily? Given that his jaw was clenched tight, he did not appear to be in a talkative mood.

"Thanks for coming." She motioned to one of the two chairs next to her desk. "Have a seat."

Unlike most of the parents she had met with earlier that evening, Luke didn't act like he had any desire to engage in idle chit-chat. Nothing about the cooler temps or sports or local festivals. He just sat there with his arms crossed in front of his chest.

Lily moved some papers around on her desk and then began by saying how much she enjoyed having Kayla in her class. She stopped and let out a breath. Then she swiped a loose strand of hair off her forehead. She could feel her stomach muscles tightening when she prepared her next question. "Is everything going okay at home?"

She could see Luke's eyes narrow and then zero in on her, like her question struck a nerve and was really none of her business.

"Yeah, everything's fine."

She didn't believe him, although she wasn't surprised that he didn't open up to her. "Are you sure?"

Luke sighed, uncrossed his arms, and leaned forward. She thought he was going to storm out of the room. "What's this about, Miss O'Leary?"

Lily was taken aback by his abruptness. His tone hurt her. She held out her hands. "What's the matter? I just asked a question."

"And I gave you an answer."

Lily's shoulders slumped. *Could he be any more obstinate?* "What's wrong?"

Luke shrugged. "Nothing's wrong."

Ughh! She wondered if this was how she acted when they first met. *Is he mad at me? Why would he be mad at me? Is it about dinner? Or ice cream? Or running back home with me?* She was waiting for him to ask her out again for goodness sakes. "What's the matter with you?"

Luke shrugged again. "Nothing." He looked at his watch. "I thought I was here because of Kayla."

Lily gritted her teeth. *Fine, be that way.* "It is about Kayla," she snapped. Somehow she kept a few choice words from accompanying her statement. "The reason why I asked if everything was okay at home is because Kayla is having trouble with her math."

Looking like he had been punched in the stomach, she could immediately see the stone face of Luke Spencer melt into one of a concerned father.

"Trouble with math?"

Lily's tone softened. She could tell he was unaware of the development. "Yes. Didn't Kayla show you her last test?"

Luke's eyes widened but then squinted in search of an answer. He tried to swallow but came up empty. He shook his head. “No. I remember there was a test, but I guess I forgot to ask her how she did. What did she get?”

Lily pulled out a photocopy of Kayla’s most recent test. A large amount of marks darkened the page. Luke looked at the paper and then rubbed his forehead with his right hand. She could tell he was struggling to make sense of it all.

“That’s why I asked if everything is okay at home, Luke. Kayla’s doing okay in her other subjects, although I have no doubt that she could be doing better. She could be one of my top students, but she has taken a nosedive in math. She has shown some struggles in her math homework as well.”

Luke shook his head as he kept looking down at the paper. “I . . . uh . . . I don’t know what’s going on. I should have asked her about the test, but I’ve been busy. And she hasn’t said anything to me.” He looked at Lily and their eyes met. “I’m sorry. Math was never one of my strong suits, and now I . . . uh. . . I don’t know what to do.”

Lily looked at the man she had been thinking about for the last three weeks, actually more than three weeks. The stern demeanor had vanished, and she couldn’t help but feel the swell of her heart at his concern for his daughter.

“I can help, Luke,” she said softly. She shifted her chair closer to him. “I’d be happy to tutor Kayla in math. My degree in elementary education included an emphasis on math. I have no doubt in my mind that she can get better. She just needs a little help getting there.”

She caught the look in his eye, like he wanted to grasp the lifeline she was offering. She wondered if he would return to his obstinate ways and turn down her offer. Maybe he would tell her to butt out of his life and claim he could fix any problems Kayla might be having. She quickly realized she was wrong.

“I would very much appreciate your help.” He handed Kayla’s math test back to her. “Whatever you suggest, I’ll do it. Just tell me what I need to do.”

“I’d be happy to work with her after school. Maybe an hour

a day a couple of times per week. I'll give her some extra work that she can practice on and then we'll go over it."

Luke looked down at his folded hands. "I'd like that." He looked at her again. "I really would. I can't tell you how much I appreciate your willingness to help her. I'll talk to her tonight and get back to you, if that's okay."

"Not a problem." She reached for a pad of paper and then a pen. "I'll give you my phone number and email address. Whatever is best for you and Kayla, let me know and we'll figure something out."

Luke stood and took the paper. She caught the look of gratitude in his eyes. She felt it when he said, "Thank you again. I'll be in touch."

* * *

Luke left the classroom and saw the parents of Chase Power waiting in the hallway for their conference with Lily. He nodded at them. If they said something to him, he didn't hear it considering his mind was swirling with everything he learned in the last twenty minutes.

Have I failed my daughter? He thought he was a good father, but maybe he was missing something. Maybe he didn't see the problems Kayla was having because he was too busy with work. *Was it just math? Was she struggling in other areas of life as well? Would it get worse? How could he fix it?*

He needed to pick Kayla up from Emma's house. He'd have to fix dinner and then they could talk. *Be cool about it. She might be upset.* Before he reached the door to exit the school, Luke looked down at the piece of paper in his hand. He came in here not wanting much of anything to do with Lily O'Leary. She had made her intentions clear by her silence over the last three weeks. But her concern and willingness to help meant more to him than she would ever know. She was offering her assistance in caring for the one he loved more than anything else in the world.

And he realized he had to do everything he could do to

make sure Kayla received the help she needed.

Luke opened the breast pocket of his shirt. He realized it already contained the scrap of paper containing Ava's number. He looked at it and then Lily's number. He crumpled Ava's number into a ball and threw it in the trash. Lily's number took its place in his pocket.

After picking up Kayla and bringing her home, they shared a quiet dinner. She said little, and Luke wondered if she was worried that Miss O'Leary had told her how badly she did on the test. She barely looked at him, almost embarrassed. She excused herself to take a shower. Luke paced the floor of the living room, wondering how to broach the subject as delicately as possible. He obviously hadn't done a good job up to this point, and he didn't want to make it worse.

He turned off the TV and walked to Kayla's room. The door was open, and a quick check showed Mr. Butterlickens resting on the floor at the foot of the bed. Luke peeked his head inside. "Knock, knock," he said, tapping lightly on the door. He found his daughter seated at her desk in front of the mirror as she brushed her golden blonde hair. "Can I come in?"

"Yeah." She stopped brushing and looked down at her lap.

Luke sat at the corner of the bed and looked at his daughter in the mirror. "Give me the brush." She handed it over and he leaned forward to reach her. He took the brush and began brushing her hair that draped halfway down her back. He had been doing it since she was six years old, although she had been doing it mostly in the last year. "I haven't been able to brush your hair in a while." He saw her eyes look at him in the mirror before looking away. "You have hair just like your mom. Blonde and beautiful."

He could feel the tension in the air, like she was waiting for him to lecture her on her failings at school. Even Mr. Butterlickens looked a little worried about how things were going to play out. Luke tried a different approach.

"It's getting kind of long. If you want me to get you an appointment at the Cut and Curl, I can. I don't want you to trip over your hair when you're out running."

The mirror showed the smile that flashed across her face. The giggle that followed indicated the humor hit its mark. Luke continued brushing. He then did something he hadn't done in a while. He silently hoped to find the right words to help his daughter get through this difficult time. Their eyes met in the mirror.

"Miss O'Leary says you're having a little trouble in math." He noticed her eyes looked down and she gave a quick nod before hanging her head. "I used to have trouble in math, too. My favorite subject was recess." He felt the flinch of laughter in her body. "Miss O'Leary says she'd be willing to help you if you want."

Kayla raised her head, her eyes almost pleading for the help.

"I think she really knows a lot about math. More than I do. Would you be okay with staying after school a few days a week and doing some extra work with her?"

With tears pooling in her eyes, Kayla smiled and nodded.

Luke felt a wave of relief wash over him. He ran the brush through her hair a few more times before standing. "I'll let her know." He then bent down and wrapped his arm around her. He gave her a kiss on the top of her head. "You know I love you, don't you?"

Kayla nodded again. She whispered, "I love you, too, Dad."

CHAPTER 19

Luke pulled into the lot of the school just as the students were being let out for the day. He had emailed Lily as soon as he talked with Kayla, and it was agreed they would start the first tutoring session the following day after school. Luke decided to show up to make sure Kayla got to where she needed to be. And he also wanted to thank Lily once again for agreeing to help.

He walked inside the school and down the hall to the sixth-grade classroom. The sound of aspiring musicians warming up their instruments began filtering through the building. He took a peek through the glass next to the door of the classroom and saw Lily erasing the board of the day's history lesson.

She wore black slacks and a white shirt that showed her athletic figure. He realized he hadn't even noticed what she was wearing yesterday during the parent-teacher conference. But today her attire stood out. As did her hair. It fell to her shoulders and had a bit of a twist to it. *Was it like that yesterday? Was it always that beautiful?*

"Oh, hi," she said after turning around. "I didn't hear you come in."

He flinched, wondering if she realized he had been staring at her. He took another step inside the room. "Hi."

"Kayla had to run down to the art room to drop off some supplies that we were using. She'll be right back." Lily walked to her desk and grabbed a stack of papers. "Did you need something?"

Luke cleared his throat. "I just wanted to make sure Kayla was in the right place." He walked closer to Lily. "And I wanted to thank you again for agreeing to help her. It means a lot to me and to Kayla."

"Of course, it's my job." She then smiled. "And I think it's one of the best parts of what I do. I'm sure we'll see some progress before you know it."

They both smiled at each other, and Luke wasn't sure if he was supposed to say more or not. He was happy to stare at her in the silence. The standoffs and the staredowns of the past had gone away, and now both Luke and Lily had a common goal between them—to help Kayla do better in math. But Luke wondered if Lily could feel something else going on here, like a force was bringing them closer together. He had the sudden urge to wrap his arms around her. His dreams were interrupted by the girl walking in the door.

"Hi, Dad," Kayla said, giving him a side hug.

"Hey, baby doll. I just wanted to be sure you're ready for your time with Miss O'Leary."

She held up her backpack. "Yep, I'm all ready."

The screech of a clarinet rattled through the walls. Or maybe it was a flute. Or a wounded animal. No one could be sure. Then there was a rumble that sounded like rolling thunder followed by a crash of cymbals. Luke, Lily, and Kayla all looked to the wall on the south side of the classroom. The sound kept getting louder, and pretty soon the three were going to have to start covering their ears.

Lily grimaced. "I'm sorry. I forgot about the band practice." She looked at the clock on the wall. "They might be here for another hour. I think they're practicing for the lighthouse fundraiser."

After the first crescendo of the practice had subsided, Luke had a thought. He wasn't sure where the thought came from, but he didn't try to suppress it. He looked at Kayla and then at Lily. "Why don't you come over to the house?" He reached out a hand. "I mean, if it's not too much trouble. We have plenty of room so you two can spread out and work. It'll be quiet." The sound of a bass drum booming through the wall caused him to raise his voice. "At least it will be quieter than this."

Lily looked at the wall as the trumpets sounded. She smiled like she had no other choice. "I think that might be a good idea. I'm not sure how conducive to learning it would be if we stayed here."

* * *

Lily turned out the lights to her classroom and locked the door behind her. Luke and Kayla had left for their house and Lily told them she wouldn't be too far behind them. *I'm going over to Luke Spencer's house.* She wondered what Rose would think. Probably give her a boatload of warnings before she even stepped in the door. She tried to shake the thoughts of the handsome man she had just been staring at. He was lean and tall, and his blue eyes could make a suspect, and definitely a woman, wilt under the pressure of his gaze. She told herself she was going over there to help Kayla with her math. Nothing more, nothing less.

But that didn't really explain why she drove to her house and hurried inside to check her hair and give her neck a couple spritzes of perfume. A quick look in the mirror made her wonder what she was doing. Was there a dual purpose in going over to the Spencer house? To help Kayla and to get to know Luke? She straightened her shirt. *Is that wrong? Maybe I shouldn't have agreed to go over to Luke's house. We could've met at the park or the coffee shop. What am I getting myself into?* She left her purse in the house and grabbed her bag containing her materials, papers, and lesson plans from the car. *Don't do anything that would give the wrong impression.*

As she walked down the sidewalk, the image of her sister wagging her finger and lecturing her popped into her head. "Don't go over to his place under any circumstance. He'll probably have a shrine to you. That's what those crazy old weirdos do. Pictures and candles and freaky voodoo stuff."

Lily giggled to herself. *Well, I'm about to find out.*

She turned onto the sidewalk leading up to the Spencer house. She was half surprised the place looked as good as it did.

The grass was green and nicely cut. Flower beds on both sides of the steps had a colorful array of mums and asters. An American flag waved gently in the breeze from a bracket on the porch column. When she stepped on the porch, she noticed three rocking chairs. It made her wonder if only two got much use anymore.

Lily raised her hand to knock but the door swung open.

"Hi, Miss O'Leary," Kayla said, waving her inside. "Thank you for coming."

Lily stepped inside and was immediately greeted by Kayla and the tail-wagging Mr. Butterlickens. Lily reached down and gave Butter a couple pats on the head, much to his delight.

"He likes you."

When she looked up, she almost gasped. Luke was walking down the hall toward her.

Lily hurried to return her gaze to Kayla. "What?" she asked, not sure if she heard correctly.

"Butter likes you."

Lily blushed that they were thinking about two different things. She smiled as Luke approached. He had changed out of his police uniform and replaced it with a pair of blue jeans and a blue Huron Cove Police Department T-shirt. Given his broad chest, she wondered if he was still wearing his bulletproof vest. The strong arms of a man who liked to work out were bronzed from days of running and yard work. She tried not to fan her blushing cheeks.

Luke was drying his hands on a dish towel. "Hi, Lily, come on in. Welcome."

"Thank you." She looked around. She was surprised how clean and tidy the house was. Dark hardwood abounded throughout the front entryway and living area. The wall leading upstairs contained framed pictures of Kayla throughout her life, many of them with an arm wrapped around Butter. "You have a very nice house."

"Thanks. I thought you two could use the dining room. Plenty of table space and good lighting."

"That's sound fine."

Kayla grabbed Lily's hand, and Mr. Butterlickens followed closely behind as they made their way down the hall. Lily was impressed with the dining room and the tasteful chandelier over the table.

"You can sit here, Miss O'Leary."

"Thank you, Kayla," she said, putting her bag on the table. She felt a tender hand at her back.

"Can I get you anything?" Luke asked. "Something to drink?"

Lily smiled. "A glass of ice water would be nice."

"Coming right up."

She watched as he walked into the kitchen as Kayla began unpacking her pencils and paper. *Was this what being a family would be like?* Her thoughts were interrupted when Luke walked in carrying two glasses of ice water and set one in front of her and the other in front of Kayla.

"I'll be in the kitchen so let me know if you need anything else," Luke said. "I'll leave you two to work."

"Thank you, Luke," Lily said.

When she turned her head, she found Kayla sitting up straight, her folded hands resting on the table. She looked like a mini-angel, and the soft smile made Lily think the girl was truly thankful she was there. "Okay, I guess we should get started." She scooted her chair closer to Kayla. "Why don't you open your book to page thirty and we'll go over a few things."

Lily and Kayla worked well with each other. Lily would give her student a handful of problems, and Kayla would do her best to answer them. When she needed help, Lily would provide direction, just enough to get Kayla to the next step. Kayla felt free to ask questions and smiled when she received praise from Lily.

Nearing the end of the session, Lily could smell the beginnings of dinner being prepared in the kitchen. She caught glimpses of Luke walking back and forth, a pot in one hand and a spatula or spoon in the other.

When Kayla showed Lily the last problem, Lily looked it over and smiled. "You got it. See, I knew you would get the hang of it." She patted her on the shoulder. "Just take your time as you work through the problems. And then check your work when you're done."

"Thanks, Miss O'Leary."

Lily winked at her. "I'll give you another set of problems that you can do tomorrow. That way it will teach your mind to remember what you learned the day before." She stood to gather her materials and start putting them in her bag. Once she had everything, she walked toward the kitchen to tell Luke the first tutoring session had been a success.

"How's it going?"

Lily smiled at seeing Luke at the stove, a dish towel thrown over his shoulder. "Kayla's getting the hang of it. I think all we needed to do was take it one step at a time." She patted her student on the shoulder again when she stood next to her. "Before you know it, she'll be a regular math wiz." She looped her bag over her shoulder and prepared to leave, but she caught the blue eyes of Luke staring at her.

Kayla broke the silence. "Would you like to stay for dinner, Miss O'Leary? We have plenty."

Lily blushed and raised a hand. "No, that's okay. I wouldn't want to impose. Thank you, though."

"Oh, please, Miss O'Leary. Stay and eat with us." She turned to her dad. "Please, Dad. Can't she stay?"

Luke stirred a pot of boiling water. He cracked a smile at Lily. "You're welcome to stay if you'd like. We'd love to have you."

Kayla latched onto her arm. "Oh, please, Miss O'Leary. It would be so nice to have you stay and eat with us." Her eyes said it all. "Please."

Lily wrapped an arm around her pupil's shoulder. There was no way in the world she could turn Kayla down. She was too sweet, and her dad wasn't half bad either. "Thank you. I would love to have dinner."

"Yay!" Kayla yelled. Butter even barked at hearing the good news.

After putting her bag on the chair in the corner, Lily walked into the kitchen and stood next to Luke. She looked at the pot on the stove and the tray of frozen fish sticks and tater tots. Her eyebrows rose when she looked at Luke. "Really? This is what you're fixing?"

Luke took a step back. "What?"

"Fish sticks, tater tots, and macaroni and cheese?"

"Yeah, we like it."

Over near Luke's side, Lily caught Kayla's eyes widening with a look as if she worried her teacher was going to bolt for the door, never to return. "We have cereal if you'd like. We even have Frosted Flakes."

Lily smiled and then looked at Luke. "You have enough carbs here to feed a football team. Would it hurt to throw in a vegetable?"

Luke rolled his eyes at the suggestion, but he relented to appease his guest. "Fine, I'll open a can of carrots." He glanced down at the boiling water filled with macaroni.

"Here," Lily said, reaching out her hand. "Give me the spoon. I'll stir, and you get the carrots."

Once the food was prepared, the guest of honor sat at the head of the table with Luke on one side of her and Kayla on the other. After finishing his dinner in the kitchen, Mr. Butterlickens curled up in between Kayla and Lily. The three talked and laughed as they ate, and all of them thought this was what being a family would be like.

* * *

While Kayla was clearing the dishes from the table, Lily looked at her watch. "I hate to eat and run, but I should get going. I have some papers to grade tonight."

"No problem." Luke scooted back his chair and stood. "Would you mind if I walk you home? I have a few things to run by you."

"Not at all."

Lily accepted a hug from Kayla and grabbed her bag. Once out the door, Lily joined Luke on the porch, and they started down the steps. Although she only lived two houses away, Luke wasn't in any hurry to leave her company. And given that Lily was matching his easy pace, he didn't think she was itching to get home either.

"I wanted to thank you again for taking the time to help Kayla. I can't express enough how grateful I am."

"It's my pleasure. Kayla is a wonderful young girl. She'll get the hang of this math and I know she's going to come out of it with flying colors." She reached out and touched his arm. "And thanks for dinner. It's been awhile since I've had fish sticks, tater tots, and mac and cheese in the same sitting."

Luke laughed. "Honest, we don't have that every night, but I'll work on the menu. More fruits and vegetables will do us some good."

He walked her up to the porch of her house. She unlocked the door but didn't open it. They then stood looking at each other in the cool Michigan evening. Although Luke had told himself he was moving on from any thoughts involving Lily O'Leary, that was all out the window now. An evening with her after seeing what she had done with Kayla made him want to ask her out even more. He stuffed his hands in the pockets of his jeans, wondering why the simple act of asking her out was so difficult. Would she say yes? Would she want to think about it some more? Or would she finally tell him she wasn't interested? He had to know the answer. He caught a glimpse of her brown eyes staring at him and he couldn't keep the desire bottled up any longer.

"Have you given any more thought to dinner? Maybe a movie?"

She blushed and smiled. "I have thought about it, and I'd like that."

And with that, his question had been answered.

Although they didn't set a firm time, Lily suggested Luke send her an email or text. Luke agreed, finding it hard to believe he was back in the dating game. Once she went inside, he didn't attempt to hide the smile on his face. He had felt something this evening. Something he hadn't felt in a long time. For the first time in five years, it felt like there was a real family in his household, like the missing piece had been found and inserted into the puzzle.

He knew he wasn't the only one smiling. And by the curtain in Kayla's bedroom quickly being yanked shut, he knew she had been watching. And he had a feeling she was smiling, too.

CHAPTER 20

How about dinner and a movie on Saturday night?

That was all the text from Luke said. Simple and straightforward. Lily received it while reading a book early Thursday evening. She hadn't seen Luke since Tuesday night when he walked her home, but only because their paths hadn't crossed. She looked out her bedroom window and saw Luke's police SUV sitting in the driveway. She got out of bed and started pacing the room, her sock-covered feet leaving trails in the carpet. The man who just asked her out was two doors down. She wondered what he was doing. Was he reading like she was? Maybe watching a game on TV? Or was he pacing back and forth wondering what she was going to say?

Lily stopped pacing and looked at her phone again. *How about dinner and a movie on Saturday night?* With being busy teaching the last couple years and then the move to Huron Cove, it had been awhile since someone asked her out to dinner and a movie.

The pacing started again—around the bed and back to the door. She debated how to respond. The right response was crucial and every word had to have its worth. She rattled a few off the top of her head.

"I would be honored to be your date at the establishment of your choosing." *Goodness, I'm not responding to a request to go to the prom.*

She wondered if she should go with "I'd love to"? But would using the word "love" be too much too soon? Perhaps simply "I'd like that." Or should she be nonchalant and say "Sure" or "Okay"? *Why is this so difficult?*

She thought about calling Rose, but she knew that would

probably entail another lecture and her sister would undoubtedly try to talk her out of going anywhere with Luke. She sat down at the foot of the bed and looked at the text again. It was just dinner and a movie. He hadn't asked her to marry him. *Be honest and up front with him. We're just friends.* She folded her hands, closed her eyes, and prayed. Once her prayers were said, she opened her eyes, and tried not to think more about it as her thumbs typed out a response.

Hi Luke!
Dinner and a movie sound great! Just let me know the time.
LO'L

She was about a second away from hitting the send button when she decided to read her response again. Along with the whimsical play on her initials, it was a typical response—the normal way she would answer an email from any of her friends. But the exclamation points caught her attention. She thought she sounded too excited so she made a few changes.

Hi Luke,
Dinner and a movie on Saturday would be fine. Just let me know when you would like to get together.
Lily

That was better. It was a more businesslike response. She thought Rose would approve of the "get together" language. Plus, it wasn't too gushy and didn't portray herself as being elated beyond belief. She started pacing again, her steps faster this time. Her heart pounded hard against her chest. *Is this what you want?* She thought she couldn't say no or ask for more time to think about it. She had already told him she was agreeable to going out with him. *Why am I so scared? It's only dinner and movie.*

But was there more? Did it have more to do than just dinner and a movie? Was it the handsome gentleman she had met, his wonderful daughter, their rambunctious but lovable dog, and this adorable little town on the shores of Lake Huron? The thought of her time in Huron Cove being temporary failed to register in her mind. She didn't think about the future. All she could think about was today. She took a deep breath and made her decision. She clicked send and watched the response bubble indicate it was probably popping up on a phone two doors down.

Now she just hoped her hands would stop shaking.

* * *

Luke felt his phone buzz in his back pocket at the same time he was pulling the laundry out of the dryer. He didn't reach for his phone right away. He had only sent the text ten minutes before, and he hadn't been able to stop thinking about it since. It was another attempt at dating, and his first via text. And now he really wanted to take the time to once again feel the sensation of asking a woman out on a date—the anticipation, the wonder, the excitement. He had a pretty good idea of what her answer would be, although a part of him thought Lily could surprise him with another request to think about it. Or maybe she would be busy on Saturday night. Or maybe her sister would be coming to town again. Or maybe she had to grade papers or wash her hair. Or maybe . . .

Luke grunted and yanked the phone out of his back pocket. *Only one way to find out.* He clicked on the screen and saw the bubble from Lily. A smile flashed across his face. He was going on a date. *So this is how it feels. Been a long time.* Thoughts started racing through his head. Where would they eat? What movie would they see? None of that really mattered. As long as Lily O'Leary was the one sitting next to him at the theater or across from him at a restaurant, he'd be happy.

Hearing Kayla coming down the basement stairs, Luke hurriedly put the phone in his pocket and turned away.

"Laundry done?" Kayla said as she took the last step.

He fiddled with the knob on the dryer as he tried to suppress his smile. Sharing the news might keep her up all night. He had never been in this position before with Kayla.

"What?" He could feel his cheeks turning red. *Goodness, am I in high school again?*

Kayla looked at the two laundry baskets—one for her and one for him. "The laundry. Is it done?"

"Oh . . . the laundry. . . Yes, yes, it's done." He pointed to the pink basket and then hurried to turn his back, again playing with the knobs and then yanking out the lint screen. There was a silence, and for a moment, he thought he might be in the clear.

"Are you okay, Dad? You seem kind of jumpy."

Busted. He began to feel like one of the myriad criminals he had picked up over the years. Ninety percent of them had guilt written all over their faces. They would inevitably try to weasel their way out of what they had done, but that only made it worse. He reminded himself that he always told Kayla to be honest, and he decided he might as well practice what he preached and come clean. He would have to tell her sometime anyway. Might as well be now.

After cleaning the screen and inserting it back into place, he took a deep breath and turned around. She was still standing there, a quizzical look etched across her beautiful face. *Be sure to tamp down any expectations.*

"Sorry, sweetie. I spaced out for a minute there." Another breath. He realized he was about to say something he had never said to Kayla before. "I . . . uh . . . wanted to let you know that I am going to go to dinner and a movie on Saturday night with Miss O'Leary."

His daughter's widening eyes and the yelp of delight made him realize tamping expectations wasn't going to be easy. She leapt into his arms.

"Oh, Dad, I'm so happy. Miss O'Leary is so wonderful. Thank you."

She was squeezing him so tight he couldn't move. *I guess I should be glad she was happy with his decision.* "It's just dinner and a movie, Kayla. Let's not make too much of it."

It was no use. The hug grew tighter until she suddenly realized she had places to be. "I have to go call Emma!" Before he could respond, she grabbed her laundry basket and was up the stairs in three bounds.

Luke stood in the basement, the whirlwind that was Kayla Spencer vanishing in an instant. If he was lucky, word wouldn't make its way around town until at least the morning. He chuckled to himself. He was going on a date. Although he had his concerns about the final outcome, he couldn't blame Kayla for her excitement.

He was excited, too.

CHAPTER 21

"Well, how do I look?"

With Kayla and Emma sitting on the couch in the living room, Luke spread out his arms and looked himself over.

Kayla was the first to react. She jumped off the couch and clasped her hands in front of her. "Oh, Dad, you look great."

Emma offered her two-cents' worth as well. "You look very handsome, Mr. Luke."

Mr. Butterlickens was wagging his tail at a good clip, so Luke figured that was a good sign too.

The girls had been waiting with great anticipation at the arrival of Luke's "big date" with Lily. Although he thought they were disappointed it didn't take him the grand part of the late afternoon and early evening to get ready, that didn't prevent them from offering their sartorial suggestions and dating advice.

For starters, they demanded he wear his blue button-down shirt, saying it would set off his blue eyes.

"Miss O'Leary will definitely notice," Emma pronounced with great conviction.

Luke decided they were probably right. They also concurred in his decision to go with black slacks and dark dress shoes, although he would have needed to go shopping if they wanted anything else. While they practically begged him to buy Lily a dozen red roses and a box of fine chocolates, he kindly demurred and said that, while flowers and chocolates might be appropriate for Valentine's Day, they might be a bit much for a first date. The two girls did, however, approve of the plan that Luke and Lily enjoy a meal at the pizzeria and they suggested Luke allow Lily to choose the movie—saying it would be "the gentlemanly thing to do."

"Okay, got it," Luke said again and again.

The fashion show and advice session were interrupted by the ringing doorbell. Ethan had arrived to take the girls to the Stone residence for the evening.

"Looks like your ride is here, ladies," Luke said, opening the door for Ethan.

"Oh, Dad, can't we stay and watch you pick up Miss O'Leary? Please, please, please."

Luke shook his head. "No, now you two scoot." He tried to usher them to the door despite further protests. "Try not to think about me and Miss O'Leary." *Fat chance of that.* He looked at Ethan. "Thanks for taking them. What's on the agenda tonight."

"It's movie night with Grandma and Grandpa. I'm sure they'll make some popcorn to go along with it. Hopefully that will keep them occupied."

Luke gave Kayla a hug. "I'll see you tomorrow and I'll tell you all about it. Be good."

"Have fun, Mr. Luke," Emma said.

"Thanks, Emma."

Luke caught a wink from Ethan, who mouthed the words "good luck" and gave him a thumbs-up before marching the two girls to the car. Luke locked the door behind them and, for the first time in a couple hours, he heard nothing but silence. He gave Butter a pat on the head and went back to his bedroom to finish getting ready.

After a final dab of Polo, he looked at his reflection in the mirror. He could hardly believe it. "I'm going on a date," he said to himself.

Feeling lightheaded, he sat down on the bed. *I'm going on a date.* It had been so long he forgot the butterflies that went with it. He focused on the floor, his mind racing through what he and Kayla had gone through since Maria's death. His mind settled on Lily O'Leary—the beautiful, intelligent, athletic Lily. Not to mention feisty and fun. And that smile. Just thinking about her smile made him grin.

Sitting there, he realized he really wanted this to work. He wanted Lily O'Leary in his life. He wanted it for Kayla and he wanted it for himself. He folded his hands, but the words didn't come out. It had been so long since he prayed. He didn't know whether God would even listen to him anymore. But he had nowhere else to turn. He closed his eyes. *Please let this work, Lord.*

A quick glance at his watch made him realize he was about to be late. He grabbed his phone and typed a message to Lily. *I'll stop by if you're ready.*

After hitting send, he smiled as the bubble rose on the screen. It didn't take long for her reply and his smile widened.

I'm ready.

* * *

Two doors down, Lily was standing in front of the mirror on the back of her bedroom door. She decided on her best pair of black jeans and covered her red shirt with her white jacket. Although Rose had told her to wear her pointy red pumps, she decided on her black boots. She made a half turn, gave a look over her shoulder toward the mirror, and pronounced herself ready. Just as she was set to grab her purse, her cell phone buzzed. She glanced at her watch. She wondered if it was Luke with another text to tell her he was on his way. She grabbed the phone, saw the rose petals on the screen, and knew it was her sister with her last-minute warnings.

"Hi."

There was silence followed by a whisper. "Where are you?"

"I'm at the house getting ready for my date with Luke."

"You mean your 'get-together.'" She started to rattle off her list of precautions, but Lily cut her off.

"Sweetie, I have to go. Luke just pulled into the driveway. I'll call you when I get back home."

Before Lily hung up the phone, she heard her worried sister shout, "Be careful!"

Lily shook her head at her sister's concern. It was followed by a slight gasp at hearing the knock at the door. *He's here.* She sucked in a breath and took one last look in the mirror. *It's not a 'date' date. It's two friends enjoying dinner and a movie. That's all.* She yanked two tissues out of the box in hopes of drying her hands before flicking off the light of the bedroom. As she walked to the front door, the butterflies in her stomach felt like they had the wings of a condor. *Two friends enjoying dinner and movie. That's all, right?*

"Hi," she said, opening the door.

"Hi, Lily. You ready?"

Lily nodded and smiled. She hoped her eyes hadn't widened noticeably when she looked him over, but that blue shirt and his blue eyes. *Wow. Such a handsome man.* She quickly looked to the floor so she wouldn't have to start fanning herself. She closed and locked the front door, and they started down the steps.

"I hope you don't mind riding in my work vehicle. The chief likes his officers to drive them around town to give people a sense of security."

"I don't mind at all. It'll be the first time I've ridden in a police vehicle before."

Luke looked at her, an eyebrow arched in wonder. "Really? The first time? With your criminal history?"

"Hah, hah, very funny" she said, playfully slapping him on the arm. "I guess I should be thankful you don't make me ride in the back."

Luke opened the door on the front passenger side and Lily slipped in. They rode in silence until the first stop sign. Luke commented that Lily looked very nice, and Lily responded in kind. With the ice broken, she could feel the tension between them start to subside.

"I hope the pizzeria is okay for dinner."

Lily looked over and smiled. "Absolutely. It's a great place."

Luke found an open parking space on the north side of the

square. They walked south, not in any hurry, talking first about the delightful fall weather. She felt a tingle in her body when his arm brushed up against hers, and the evening was cool enough that Lily wouldn't have minded if Luke looped his arm through hers. She felt comfortable with him, at ease in his presence. Try as she might, she couldn't stop the thought of the two of them as a couple . . . and beyond.

With the restaurant nearly full, Rose seated the two in the corner and handed them menus. Lily decided on the lasagna, and Luke thought it sounded so good he ordered it too. He went with the regular iced tea and Lily ordered the strawberry. While they waited they talked about Kayla. They exchanged smiles and had to lean across the table toward each other when the noise of the restaurant grew louder.

Twenty-five minutes into the date, the phone in Lily's purse started vibrating—buzzing, buzzing, buzzing like an alarm warning of great danger. It caused her to glance at her purse on the chair next to her. Lily knew exactly who it was, and she gritted her teeth. *Rose!* It was her sister's "date safety call." Rose had drilled that practice into Lily's head as soon as she started dating. Depending on how things were going, the recipient could listen with wide eyes as the caller described a fake emergency that required the person to end the horrible date and rush out immediately. Lily couldn't believe her sister, although she really wasn't surprised.

"Do you need to get that?" Luke nodded at her purse that was still buzzing like a hornet's nest.

A half-embarrassed Lily, her cheeks as red as her shirt, decided against it. There was no need to flee the pizzeria in terror, and Luke was definitely not a bad date. She shook her head. "No, it'll go to voice mail."

Two minutes went by before the buzzing started again, and Lily squirmed in her seat. Buzzing, buzzing, buzzing. She was going to give Rose a piece of her mind once the date was over. She tried to ignore it.

Luke drummed his fingers on the table. "Are you sure you don't need to get that? Whoever is on the other end might feel the need to call the police if you don't pick up."

Lily covered her face with her hands, now fully embarrassed. "I'm sorry. I think it's probably my sister."

Luke smiled. "It's okay. Why don't I go ask for a refill on our iced teas. That way you can make sure everything's all right."

Lily nodded, thanked Luke, and then waited for him to get out of earshot. "What?" she snapped in her quietest whisper.

"Are you okay!?" a breathless Rose whispered back. "Say my name if you're being held against your will."

"Stop it!" Lily covered her mouth with her left hand. She couldn't believe her sister sounded so serious.

"Do you need me to call the police?"

"Luke is the police!"

"Do you want me to call the FBI then?"

Lily rolled her eyes, figuring Rose had probably seen that on *Law & Order*. "Will you stop. I'm fine. He's really nice." Seeing Luke on his way back to the table, she ended the call. "I gotta go. I'll call you later."

"Don't kiss him!" was the last thing she heard from Rose.

Luke set Lily's glass in front of her and sat down. "Everything okay?"

"Yes, I'm sorry for the interruption. It was my sister. I just want to let you know that I didn't tell her to call me. Honest."

Luke laughed. "I believe you. So your big sister's worried about you, huh?"

Lily shook her head. "She means well. She's just a little overprotective. She's afraid I'll end up stuffed in a garbage can."

Luke held up his hands. "Well, you can never be too careful in this day and age. Like that woman out in Oregon."

"My sister said the same thing!"

They both shared a laugh over that one.

After a generous helping of lasagna and a basket of warm

bread, Luke and Lily ended the dinner with a final glass of iced tea. Lily hardly took her eyes off him the entire time. He was handsome, rugged, strong. He had a caring heart and a sense of humor. She was beginning to realize he was everything she ever wanted in a man. Her breath caught at the thought. *Is Luke Spencer the one? Is he the one God meant for me?* She flinched when Luke hurriedly glanced at his watch.

"Hey, if we want to see one of the movies that starts at eight, we probably better head over there."

"Sure," Lily said, glad the date was nowhere near over.

Luke paid the bill, and they stepped out into the cool Huron Cove night. Lily zipped up her jacket as they crossed the street.

"I have to admit that Huron Cove has great sleeping weather."

"Yes it does. Just another perk of living on the Sunrise Coast of Michigan."

She thought they were walking closer this time around, their arms brushing against each other. She could almost feel the warmth emanating from Luke's body and her shaking hands were desperate to interlock her fingers with his. If all they did for the rest of the night was walk around the square holding hands, Lily would be content. She had never felt so safe and secure with a man. She wanted him to wrap her in his arms and hold her close.

She gasped when he stopped abruptly at the corner and fronted her. Her eyes focused on his, wondering what he was doing. What was he thinking? *Is he going to kiss me?* She was ready. Despite her sister's warnings, Lily wanted to kiss Luke. She wanted Luke to kiss her.

Her heart skipped a beat when he looked down at her and grinned. He stepped closer. *What is he going to say? Is he going to ask permission to kiss me because, if so, the answer is yes, yes, yes.*

She was a second away from rising on her toes to reach his lips with hers. She couldn't hold the anticipation in any longer. Why was he smiling? She had to know what he was thinking.

"What?"

Luke leaned ever so slightly to his left. "Take a quick glance past my right arm into the ice cream shop across the street."

Without giving it away, Lily's eyes made their way to the front of Lighthouse Creamery. There in the window she saw the faces of her two favorite students. Neither Emma nor Kayla looked interested in eating their ice cream—content to spend their evening spying on Luke and Lily as they walked down the sidewalk.

Lily started giggling and then Luke laughed.

"Those two," he said, shaking his head. "Such troublemakers."

She returned her eyes to his. "It's adorable. I wonder how long they've been waiting."

"I bet they were begging Emma's grandparents to take them for ice cream as soon as they walked in the front door. I'm surprised they didn't bring binoculars with them." Luke chuckled again. "Although I think we could probably have some fun at their expense, maybe we ought to get to that movie."

Lily winked and smiled. "Good idea."

Without acknowledging the girls' spying operation had been discovered, Luke and Lily walked toward the movie theater, laughing all the way.

CHAPTER 22

The next morning, the barrage of questions from Kayla and Emma began as soon as they raced through the front door of the Spencer house and into the kitchen.

"How did your date go, Dad?"

Luke had just finished emptying the dishwasher. He looked at them, appearing surprised by the commotion and the question. "Date? What date?"

"With Miss O'Leary."

He wiped his hands on a towel and looked at both of them begging for information. "Who?"

"Dad!"

"Mr. Luke!"

Luke laughed. He had replayed every second with Lily ever since he last saw her. From the time he picked her up until he dropped her back at her house, he had a wonderful evening. The best time he had in years. But that didn't mean he couldn't have a little fun with the girls. Once he composed himself, he gave them the shortest summation he could think of regarding last night's happenings. "We had a nice time."

Somehow the chatterbox known as Emma Lynn Grayson Stone struggled to find the words before she blurted out, "And!?"

"And what?"

"Dad, you have to tell us more!"

Luke acted surprised. "Really? You need more details. I thought you two would have already known what went on last night." He reached out to grab Kayla and tickle her. "Given the fact you two were spying on us last night at the ice cream shop."

Kayla squirmed and laughed, buckling under the pressure. "We weren't spying, Dad. We were just having some ice cream."

"Yeah, right."

Emma smiled and shrugged, having no qualms with being found out. "It looked like you and Miss O'Leary were having a good time."

Having milked all the fun he could get out of the girls, at least for now, Luke said, "We had a good time."

He then proceeded to give them a few highlights of last night's events. That Lily likes lasagna and strawberry iced tea. He let her choose the movie, just as the girls suggested, and they enjoyed an action flick with a kick-butt heroine. After the movie, they had brownies and hot chocolate at CupKate's Confectionery before he drove her home. Following the five minutes of talking to the captivated audience, he thought he told them almost everything they needed to know.

Except for the fact that he hadn't been able to stop thinking about her ever since. And now he wanted to ask her out again and again and again. He turned his back and opened the fridge hoping the girls wouldn't see the smile that said it all.

Behind him, Emma covered her mouth with her hand and whispered in Kayla's ear.

Kayla's eyes widened before she calmly said, "Dad, we're going to take Butter for a walk."

"Okay. I'll have lunch ready in an hour if you're hungry."

* * *

Lily was sitting on her front porch, the rocking chair that came with the rental becoming one of her favorite spots to spend an early morning or evening. She loved to read, had since she was a little girl, and she made sure to bring a box of books from home to keep her occupied during her time in Huron Cove. Her current read, a Christian romance novel, sat closed on the table beside her. She had tried to crack it open, but it was no use. There wasn't going to be much reading done today. Her mind couldn't concentrate. No wait, it could concentrate. But only on one thing—her date last evening with Luke Spencer.

Once Luke dropped her off and walked her to the front door, sleep had come surprisingly easy after she climbed into bed, although perhaps it was because she was so looking forward to dreaming about her time with Luke. She hadn't been on a date in a while, and this one didn't disappoint. They talked and laughed and enjoyed each other's company. He was sweet, caring, and decent—everything she wanted in a man. She couldn't remember the last time she had this tingling feeling that warmed her heart.

And now she realized she wanted to experience that feeling again. She looked east through the trees, the autumn leaves beginning to rain down from their branches. A smile grew on her face, and as long as she thought about Luke, she knew that smile would remain.

Her thoughts were broken by the phone buzzing on the table. Seeing the rose petals on the screen, she tapped the button.

"Hi, Rose."

"What's wrong? You didn't call me last night. Are you crying?"

Lily rolled her eyes. "No, I'm not crying."

"Did he break your heart? I told you not to let him break your heart, Lil."

A long sigh preceded Lily's response. "No, he didn't break my heart. It was just dinner, a movie, and a brownie after that. We had a good time."

"Did he try anything on you? Did you have to kick him in the crotch?"

Lily offered a silent giggle. She then whispered, "No, Rosebud, I didn't have to kick him in the crotch. He was a perfect gentleman."

After a short silence, Rose added, "Why are you whispering? Is he there? He's not at your house, is he? It's like ten o'clock in the morning. Oh, Lilybean, what have you done?"

"No, he's not here, Rose. I'm whispering because I'm sitting on my front porch and I don't want to broadcast my dating life to all the neighbors."

"Dating life! I—"

Rose was interrupted by a beep from Lily's phone. Lily took the phone away from her ear and looked at the screen. Luke was sending her a text message and, right now in her life, that took priority. "I gotta go, Rose. I'll call you later."

She hung up without saying goodbye, her heart rate picking up the pace. She had wondered when he would contact her again. Would it be today? Would he ask her out again? Was he texting her to tell her he had a great time last night?

Only one way to find out. She tapped her phone and Luke's bubble appeared on the screen.

Be on the lookout. The two spymasters are out walking the dog.

Lily laughed and typed out a response. *Thanks for the warning. I'll be on guard.* It was only a second after she sent the message that Kayla and Emma walked into view with Mr. Butterlickens leading the way. She smiled again. There had been a lot of smiles in the last couple days.

Lily waved from her rocker. "Morning, girls."

"Oh, hi, Miss O'Leary," Kayla said from the sidewalk, sounding as if she was surprised they would run into their teacher on a Saturday morning. The girls and Butter walked up the stairs and joined her on the porch.

The girls stood there looking at her and for once in their lives both were unable to find the right words. Both were smiling, almost giddy Lily thought. The only one willing to move was Butter, and he looked overjoyed when Lily reached out with both hands and gave him a good rubbing.

"Such a good boy." Once she was finished, she looked at her pupils. "And how are you girls today?"

Kayla and Emma looked at each, both of them looking like they were about to burst. Kayla was the first to go. "We're great, Miss O'Leary. Did you have a nice time last night?"

Lily grinned. She was surprised they hadn't yelled the question from the sidewalk when they first saw her. The two girls, and even Mr. Butterlickens, stared at her as they waited breathlessly for her response. "We had a nice time."

"Did you like your lasagna at Rose's?" Emma asked.

"Yes," Lily said, wondering if Luke told them or if they had heard her choice of meals from their spy brethren.

"Did you enjoy the movie?" Kayla asked.

"Yes, we did."

"Did you like your brownie from the bakery?" Emma asked.

"Yes, we liked that, too. Did you two enjoy your ice cream?"

Both girls' eyes widened, like they hadn't realized their teacher had also discovered their little clandestine operation. Their cheeks blushed deeply before they giggled with mischievous delight.

The phone buzzed on the table and the rose petals appeared on the screen. It gave her a way to end the conversation without any more questions—at least until the next time that she saw them. Of course, the girls would probably be on their way to tell the whole town how much she and Luke enjoyed their date. Oh well. "That's my sister, ladies. I probably better take it." She got up from her rocker to answer the call. "I'll see you at church tomorrow."

CHAPTER 23

While Luke and Lily had every desire to go out together again, life got in the way. With several days of heavy rain, one of the county roads was washed away and the sheriff needed some extra manpower to divert traffic around the area and patrol the countryside. So, the Huron Cove Police Department stepped up and helped as much as it could. Luke did his part by working overtime, which meant he didn't get home until late.

Lily had a full schedule as well. Not only did she have to grade papers and organize her lesson plans, she had to help with the upcoming Christmas concert. That meant working with the kids on learning their songs and choreographing their routines. Plus, she spent several days in Detroit attending a teachers' conference and then returned home to Chicago for the long Thanksgiving break.

On the first Sunday in December, Lily sat in her normal spot at church, the third row from the back on the left side of the aisle. She had arrived ten minutes early, and every part of her hoped to see Luke walk into the sanctuary with Kayla. She knew the odds would be long at that happening. She had lost count of the number of times that Kayla came to church without her father. At least Lily could be happy with the fact that Kayla worshipped regularly. It would definitely plant the seeds for continued attendance as she grew older.

But what about her father? Lily looked up high above the altar where the inscription *Lo, I am with you always* was painted in blue. God was always with Luke, even if Luke had trouble sometimes believing it. Maybe he did believe it but needed an extra push to get through the doors. Lily folded her hands and prayed. *Help me help them, Lord.*

Five minutes before the service started, Kayla and Emma walked down the aisle and joined their teacher.

"Hi, ladies."

"Hi, Miss O'Leary," Kayla said. "You look very nice today."

"So do you. I like your jacket." Lily leaned forward. "Hi, Emma."

"Hi, Miss O'Leary."

The service started, and the girls followed along with the songs and the readings. Prior to the sermon, they assembled at the front of the church with their Sunday School compatriots to sing the song they had been practicing. Once the song was over, Emma went to sit with her parents and Kayla returned to Lily's side.

At the conclusion of the service, Pastor Carlton invited the congregation to be seated so he could make a few announcements. The parents of the school children were reminded that practice for the Christmas pageant would continue that week. Lily glanced toward Kayla sitting next to her and noticed the girl was jotting down the time on her service folder. Pastor Carlton also reminded the congregation that family portraits for those that wanted them would be taken next week and noted they would make great Christmas gifts. Kayla didn't write that down. Next up was the family bus trip to the "World's Largest Christmas Store" in Frankenmuth, but Kayla didn't feel the need to write it down either.

Lily looked around the church at the mothers and fathers with their kids. Seeing that and the eleven-year-old girl sitting next to her moved something inside her heart. Kayla Spencer was a smart, sweet, well-mannered young girl. And right now she was all alone. She had no mother, and her dad was working hard at his job to put food on the table and a roof over their head. *But he could be here if he really wanted.*

Lily wasn't sure what moved her to do so, but she reached out and put an arm around Kayla. With wide eyes full of thanks and love, Kayla smiled and leaned her head against her teacher.

Lily clutched her tighter, her heart warming. Once Pastor Carlton had concluded his announcements and the organist finished his postlude, Lily and Kayla sat in the pew while the parishioners gathered their belongings and headed for the exit.

"You doing okay?" Lily asked her student.

Kayla nodded but didn't look at her. Lily squeezed the hug a little harder, thankful God had placed her in that pew at that time. As was often the case being a teacher, there was always a part of her that wanted to do that little extra to help the student turn the corner or see the light. While she couldn't go into the homes of her students to change what was going on inside, she thought this might be the opportunity.

"I forgot to ask your dad about it the last time we talked, but would you like to get together for another math session?"

Kayla looked up to her and smiled. "I'd like that, Miss O'Leary. I think it's been really helpful to do the work with you. I'll ask my dad when I get home."

With the sanctuary clearing out, Lily started to move. "How are you getting home?"

"I'm going with Emma until my dad can pick me up."

As they put on their coats and headed out the back to find the Stone family, Lily asked, "What do you think about coming over to my house on Tuesday night to do our math work?"

"Your house?" Kayla's smile broadened. "That would be great."

"And maybe while we're at it, we could fix dinner for your dad."

"Really?"

Lily nodded. "Sure. We'll fix a salad and maybe some spaghetti and meatballs. Do you think your dad would like that?"

"We love spaghetti and meatballs, but we usually only have it when we go to the pizzeria."

"Great. Ask your dad if it's okay and you can come over a little early. We'll do our math and then we'll get dinner ready and have a nice home-cooked meal."

"Thank you, Miss O'Leary. I can't wait to tell my dad."

Seeing Emma and her parents waiting outside, Kayla gave Lily one last hug. "I'll see you tomorrow."

Lily couldn't hide the smile on her face if she tried. A part of her couldn't believe she suggested fixing dinner for Luke and Kayla, but it seemed appropriate. He was busy, and she could help his daughter with her math and then help them both with dinner. As she walked to her car she wondered if there was more to it than that. She couldn't stop thinking about Luke and the good time she had with him on their date. The thoughts she had of him had not diminished over the last few weeks. Yes, it was only one date, but she felt a connection with Luke that she had never felt before. He was strong, mature, not to mention good looking. And his daughter was an absolute joy.

Her breath caught, and she steadied herself with her right hand against the car. *Is he the one God meant for me?* Then she saw Kayla offering a wave goodbye from the back seat. *Are they the ones God meant for me?* She closed her eyes and wondered what the future would bring.

* * *

"Come on in," Lily said, opening the front door for Luke. She caught the hint of a smile on his face, slightly reddened by the cool December evening. A few flakes of snow dotted the broad shoulders of his coat.

"Wow, it smells good in here," he said, taking off his coat as she closed the door behind him.

"Thanks. Kayla and I have been working hard."

"Everything going okay with the math homework?"

Lily took Luke's coat and hung it on the rack in the corner. She kept her voice down. "It's going great. She's really getting the hang of things. She's learned to take her time figuring out the problem and tackle it step by step. I only have to offer her a few hints here and there anymore."

He mouthed the words "thank you" to her and winked. She smiled.

When they walked into the kitchen together, Lily felt a

tingle in her spine. *Is this what it feels like to be a family? Would this be what it's like if Luke was my husband and Kayla my stepdaughter?* A feeling washed over her. She didn't know where it came from but she felt it deep in her heart. *If this is what it feels like to be a family, I'd be okay with that.*

Kayla was hard at work with a knife and cucumber when she looked up. "Hi, Dad. I'm fixing the salad."

"I can see that. It looks good." He put an arm around her shoulder as she continued cutting. "Miss O'Leary says your math studies are going well. I'm really proud of you."

Kayla smiled and then looked at her teacher. "Miss O'Leary has helped me a lot."

Luke's eyes met Lily's and he gave her another wink. "That's good to hear."

While Kayla finished the salad, Lily drained the spaghetti and then added the sauce and meatballs. Luke asked if he could help, and Lily told him he could get the plates and the silverware. In the close confines, he only bumped into her twice. He apologized both times, and they shared glances and smiles without Kayla noticing. Once everything was ready, Lily sat across from Luke with Kayla at the head of the table. After Kayla said the table prayer, at Lily's suggestion, the three dug in. Luke pronounced the salad "wonderful" and the spaghetti and meatballs "excellent." In between bites, they talked about school, running, and Huron Cove.

Once the table was cleared, the leftovers put away, and the dishes washed, Luke and Kayla thanked Lily for the dinner and headed for the front door.

While Luke was putting on his coat, he said, "Butter's probably wondering where his dinner is."

"Next time bring him with you."

Lily caught Luke's eyes focusing on her. *Next time? Did I just say that?* She didn't think Luke looked like he was going to bolt for the door. She wondered if she was committed to going down that road because she could tell by the look in his eyes that he was beginning to wonder the same thing. Lily blushed slightly and then added, "I mean, if you want to."

"We'll be glad to. I'm sure Butter would like it." Luke smiled that handsome smile. "Say, we like to take a walk around the block after dinner. It gives Butter some exercise." He glanced out the window. "And it looks like the sidewalks are clear and there's still a little sunlight left in the day. You're welcome to join us if you're interested."

"I'd like that."

Luke turned to Kayla. "Why don't you go get Butter ready and we'll meet you down there."

Kayla took off like a shot and left Luke and Lily together. It was the first time they were alone together since their date. In the silence of the dining room, they let their eyes do the communicating. Lily broke first and looked away in a blushing smile.

"I had a really nice time tonight," Luke said. "And the other night, too."

Lily grabbed her coat off the chair. "So did I."

Luke zipped his coat and then helped Lily with hers. "May I take you out again? Dinner maybe?"

Lily took a moment to compose her thoughts. She figured now was as good a time as any to find out what was inside him. Better to find out now rather than later. She fronted him and looked at him in the eyes. "Yes, I'd like to go out again, but I have one condition."

A smile appeared on his face. "Name it."

Lily realized what she said next could lead to bigger and better things or, and it was a good possibility, it could open a can of worms that would create a rift between them that could never be fixed. She looked him in his eyes to gauge his response.

"You come to church with Kayla on Sunday."

Luke's face hardened. He broke eye contact with her and looked off into the distance. She could tell the demand hit him flush in his chest. The smile had vanished as soon as Lily mentioned the word church. Lily could feel the temperature rise in the room, and she wondered if she had struck the nerve that would end any hope of a continued relationship between them.

"I have to work," he said.

Lily waved off the excuse. "Get someone to cover for you. Beth said Mike would be glad to do it."

Luke glanced down at his feet.

"It's time, Luke. It's time to come back."

"You don't understand. It's not that simple."

Lily stepped closer and reached out to touch his arm. "I do understand, Luke. I know it must have been hard to lose someone you loved, your wife, the mother of your child. But she was a gift from God. She was a blessing in your life." She pointed through the window at Kayla walking Butter down the sidewalk. "Look what she brought to your life. Your beautiful and wonderful daughter. Be thankful. Give thanks to the Lord for the blessings you've had in the past, the ones you have now, and the ones you will have in the future."

Luke moved his neck from side to side. Lily thought he was going to come up with yet another reason. She left room between her and the door in case he wanted to storm out. Kayla and Butter walked onto the porch and showed themselves in front of the glass door.

Luke turned his head toward his daughter and then to Lily. "Okay, I'll go."

CHAPTER 24

Luke could feel the collar of his dress shirt squeezing tighter as he looped the tie around his neck. Looking at himself in the bathroom mirror, he thought his face was growing redder by the second and, if he didn't stop sweating, he was probably going to have to take another shower. His head was starting to ache, and the muscles in his neck felt like they were twisting themselves into knots.

Luke Spencer was going to church today.

With his tie hanging loosely around his neck, he leaned forward and placed his hands on the bathroom vanity. He hadn't been to church in years and a big part of him wanted to back out of it. Maybe there would be an emergency at the police station that would require all off-duty officers to report in. Maybe he could pretend to come down with an illness. Giving the profuse sweating and clammy hands, he might be able to pull it off.

The flood of emotions began as soon as he awoke that Sunday morning. He remembered the prayers that had been sent heavenward from the pews of St. Peter's when his wife lay dying in the hospital. He didn't want to lose his wife, and he didn't want his daughter to lose her mother. But it happened.

And he never went back.

Kayla knocked on the bathroom door. "Dad, are you ready?" The voice was soft and laden with worry.

He looked at himself in the mirror. Thoughts of his daughter flashed through his mind. His beautiful and wonderful daughter. She had been trying to move on since her mother's death, and he wondered if he had been the one holding her back. Then his mind focused on Lily O'Leary. She had come into their lives at just the right time. She provided the help Kayla needed in school, and she had rekindled the spark in Luke's heart that he hadn't felt in years.

"Dad?"

Luke cleared his throat. "Yeah, I'm almost ready. Just finishing up." He tightened his tie and then opened the door. The smile on his daughter's face brought a smile to his.

"Oh, Dad, you look so nice."

Luke put his arm around his daughter, who was wearing a red dress with a white bow in her hair. "And you look nice, too."

"Are we going to pick up Miss O'Leary on the way?"

"No, she said she'd meet us there."

With Kayla in the front seat of the SUV, Luke drove past Lily's house and saw her car was not in the driveway. She was most likely already at the church. Even though Luke made the drive to St. Peter's nearly every day to pick up or drop off Kayla, the trip felt longer that morning. He noticed his palms were sweating again. He knew Kayla could feel the tension building because she didn't say a word. She just sat in her seat, her hands folded on her lap. He wondered if she was praying for a miracle.

Luke found a spot in the rear of the parking lot and pulled to a stop. Both of them remained still, and Luke looked straight ahead lost in thought. The stillness and silence were broken when Kayla reached over, touched his arm, and whispered, "You can do this, Dad."

Kayla stayed close to Luke as they walked through the parking lot. Luke nodded to an elderly couple, their names escaping him at the moment, as they shuffled toward the door. He then returned a wave from his friends Alex and Julia Armstrong.

"Hey, Luke," Alex said. "Not working today?"

Struggling to get the words out given his dry mouth, Luke said, "Not today." He put his arm around Kayla and said no more.

Walking into the church was like a giant wave washed over him, flooding his senses with the same sights and sounds he had grown accustomed too when he was a regular churchgoer. A low murmur of voices could be heard as those already seated quietly chatted before the start of the service. The place smelled the same, felt the same. He took a bulletin when one was handed to him.

"Morning, Luke," the usher said.

He remembered the guy, but he couldn't place his name. There was too much going on in his mind. "Morning," he said.

Walking into the sanctuary reminded him the last time he walked out. He looked high above the altar at the painting of Jesus and its inscription in blue of *Lo, I am with you always*. He quickly averted his gaze to the red carpet.

"We can sit over here, Dad," Kayla whispered, gently grabbing his arm and leading him to the left side of the church.

Luke followed his daughter around the end and down the side aisle. His eyes focused on a woman seated on the end, a ray of sunshine filtering through the stained-glass window and giving her an angelic glow. The hair looked familiar. Kayla stopped at the woman's row.

"Hi, Miss O'Leary."

Lily's face broke into a wide smile. "Hey, Kayla. Nice to see you." When she saw Luke, she quickly rose and moved over two spots.

"Hi, Luke," she said, the smile still present. "Nice to see you. I'm glad you could make it."

He returned the smile and then sat down on the end with Kayla seated next to him.

Lily leaned forward. "You look very nice in your tie." The grin was more mischievous this time.

Luke squirmed in his seat as his finger shot up to his collar and pulled it away as if he was being choked. "Not a big fan of the ties."

Kayla and Lily chuckled. Kayla then pointed toward the bulletin. "The Sunday School choir is going to sing right before and after the sermon."

Luke nodded. "Okay." Any further talk was muted by the organist's prelude.

As the service progressed, Luke felt more comfortable. He didn't sense anyone staring at him, and the familiarity with the service made it seem like he never left. When Kayla went down to sing, his heart warmed at seeing her smile—she, Emma, and the rest of the kids looking like they enjoyed being a part of the service as they sung *I am Jesus' Little Lamb*. Lily gave him a smile when they finished.

Pastor Carlton entered the pulpit and started by thanking the Sunday School children for their performance. "The sermon today is based on our Gospel reading from Luke, chapter fifteen, the familiar story of Jesus' parable of the Lost Sheep."

Luke looked over at Lily, and he could tell she noticed his raised eyebrows.

Really? This is the sermon Pastor Carlton decides to preach about on my first Sunday back in church in five years? Really?

Lily suppressed a smile and shrugged. She mouthed, "Just listen."

"I'm sure all of you are familiar with the parable. Jesus asks the Pharisees and those gathered around him what they would do if they lost one of their hundred sheep. The shepherd goes looking for his lost sheep, carries it back home, and rejoices in celebration at finding the wayward animal. Now let's change the players a little bit in the parable. Let's say instead of a shepherd we have a mother or father and the sheep is one of their children. How many mothers and fathers out there would search far and wide to find their lost child? I imagine every one of you would travel to the ends of the earth to find them. So too our Lord Jesus. He's searching for you, no matter how far you've strayed or how long you've been away. We can't save ourselves. But the Good Shepherd is searching for you because He wants you as part of his flock. As Christmas approaches and we await the celebration of our Savior's birth, let us be thankful

He came to search for us, to save us from our sins, and someday, to carry us to our eternal home, where there will be much rejoicing in celebration that you are a chosen child of God."

At the end of the sermon, the children gathered in front to sing their song. When they finished, Lily reached over and gave Luke a quick pat on the arm.

"I'm glad you came, Luke," Lily said as they exited the church. "I know Kayla was happy for you to hear her sing."

Luke smiled. The tie around his neck didn't feel like it was strangling him any longer. "I appreciate the invite. I have to admit I was worried about coming back, but I didn't feel like people were staring at me or pointing fingers."

"You do realize that place is packed full of sinners, don't you?" Lily smiled.

Luke laughed. "I guess so. Maybe that's why I felt so welcome."

They stood outside waiting for Kayla to join them. In the cool Sunday air, Luke noticed Lily's cheeks growing redder. He couldn't remember when he saw someone so beautiful. How glad he was to have her in his life.

"I wanted to thank you for everything you've done for me and Kayla. It hasn't been easy for the two of us, and then you came along. I'm thankful you're here in Huron Cove." He raised his hands to the outside of the building. "I don't know if I'd be standing here right now if it weren't for you."

Lily stepped closer, the tip of her nose now as red as her cheeks. "Maybe God wanted both of us to be standing here right now." She reached out and touched his arm. "And I'm glad I could be a part of your and Kayla's lives."

He wrapped his arms around her. When he felt her arms wrap around his back, he hugged her tighter. He hadn't had these feelings in a long, long time, but it felt right. And he didn't want it to ever end.

CHAPTER 25

Late January

The winter storm that started on Wednesday night and continued through Thursday morning brought six inches of snow to Huron Cove, closing most roads and all schools. The kids didn't seem to mind, most of them out at first light to decorate the streetscapes with a whole host of snowmen and snow forts. The snow angels and snowball fights soon followed.

Lily didn't mind either. She loved snow days, as it gave her the chance to curl up under a blanket and read a good book. But reading only came in spurts because she couldn't stop thinking about Luke. Once the Christmas break ended and she returned to Huron Cove for the spring semester, they had started a regular routine. Dinner at Lily's on Mondays and then at Luke's on Wednesdays. Date night on Fridays usually consisted of dinner at Rose's and a movie. Sundays included breakfast at The Coffee Cove and then church. They made plans to run together as soon as the weather warmed up enough to get outside.

By mid-afternoon, the sun came out and the roads had been cleared. School would be back on tomorrow. Having finally given up on her book, Lily wondered what Luke was doing. Maybe he was called into work. She didn't have to wait long to find out. Everything changed when she heard her phone buzzing on the coffee table. She leaned over, reached an arm out from underneath the blanket, and read the text message.

I have to go pick up Kayla at Emma's house. Care to join me for a drive around snowy Huron Cove?

Her legs shot out from underneath the blanket as she sat up on the couch. Her afternoon just got a lot more interesting.

Gone were the days of hesitation or worries what Rose would say about hanging out with Luke. She enjoyed his company, and what better way to spend the day than checking out the town with a great guy.

She typed out a response. *I'd love to. LO'L*

Once she received Luke's reply that he would be over in twenty minutes, she hurried to her bedroom to find something to wear. She threw open her closet doors and rummaged through the hangers. She settled on a hooded sweatshirt and a pair of jeans. She added her brown boots and a stocking cap. After a check of her watch, she headed for the bathroom for a little makeup and spritz of perfume.

When she came out to find her winter coat, she heard scraping coming from the driveway. She pulled back the curtain and smiled. Luke was making quick work of the six inches of snow in her driveway. She zipped up her coat and locked the front door.

"Thank you," she said, watching her steps off the porch. "You didn't have to do that. I would have gotten to it eventually."

Luke put a hand atop the shovel. "Not a problem. I didn't want you to miss out on school tomorrow."

Once finished, Luke put the shovel in the back of the vehicle. The SUV was toasty warm when she buckled herself in the front seat.

"All ready to go?"

Lily smiled. "Yeah. It's nice to get out of the house. I enjoy a long day of reading but I needed some fresh air."

"Same here," he said, putting the vehicle into gear.

They drove through the mostly empty streets of Huron Cove. The plows had done a good job and a few cars could be seen taking it slow as they traversed the streets. A handful of regulars had braved the elements for some coffee at The Coffee Cove. A few families apparently needed to get out of the house as well because they were buying tickets at the movie theater.

"That was quite a storm last night."

"Yes, it was," Lily said, looking at the white blanket of snow decorating the courthouse lawn. "It was pretty though. And it's pretty now with the sun making it sparkle."

Luke turned left at the northeast corner of the square and headed north. "Once Kayla heard last night that school was going to be cancelled today, she wanted me to take her to Emma's so they could have a weeknight slumber party."

"Sounds like fun."

As they made their way toward the Stone residence, they noticed the evergreen trees heavy with snow weighing down their branches. With the cleared roads and undisturbed snow covering the grass, it created an idyllic scene worthy of a postcard.

Once through the trees, the vast expanse of Lake Huron came into view. The Stone residence sat on the right, and the house and B&B run by Olivia and her family sat on the left. The red-and-white striped lighthouse stood sentry farther to the east.

"It sure is pretty out here," Lily said, her eyes trying to take in the beauty.

Luke turned the SUV to the left and headed north. "I thought you might like to take in the view from the lighthouse."

Lily's head snapped toward Luke. "We can do that?"

"Sure. Olivia's parents act as the caretakers most days and people can go up. The tourists like it. But there won't be anyone out here today most likely."

Luke pulled to a stop. The small parking lot had been cleared, which Luke said was a good sign that the door to the lighthouse would be unlocked. They exited, the cool air quickly turning their cheeks red. They stopped to look at the lake, a gray expanse that looked to go on forever. Luke held the door and Lily walked in and looked up.

"It's a long way up."

Luke smiled. "Seventy-two steps. It's how a lot of the local kids learned how to count."

Lily started up the spiral staircase, holding onto the steel railings with her gloved hands. Luke followed closely behind her until they made the landing outside the lantern room door. Luke gave the steel door a good yank and let Lily go first.

"Wow, it's beautiful," Lily gushed once they reached the windows in the lantern room.

Luke stood behind her, one arm on her shoulder, and the other pointing around her. "You can see the top of the courthouse over the trees there."

"Yep, I see it." She thought of her short time living in Huron Cove. The small-town atmosphere had grown on her, and the people who had welcomed her made it even better. And the one and only person on her mind right now was standing right behind her.

"That's the barn the B and B uses for wedding receptions."

Lily thought the barn looked like a mountain chalet on the shores of Lake Huron. She could imagine her wedding reception down there, the pictures at the lighthouse and on the beach. She closed her eyes to wonder.

She wondered if Luke could read her mind because he let her daydream as she looked around. The lighthouse didn't offer much heat, only a barrier from the cold wind outside, but Lily could feel the warmth from Luke's body. She wanted to melt into his arms.

"That's Emma's house down there," he said pointing. "Kayla and Butter like to come over and play on the beach."

Lily smiled, the thought of Butter running and barking up and down the beach warming her heart. She tried to take it all in. Like the angels had sprinkled the ground with glitter, the blanket of snow sparkled in the late afternoon sunlight. "It really is beautiful."

Luke slowly turned Lily around to face him. She looked up at him, his blue eyes staring back at her. "You're the beautiful one, Lily." He wrapped his arms around her, and she could tell that words straight from his heart were about to be spoken. "I'm falling for you, Lily O'Leary. You've changed my life ever since you showed up in Huron Cove. You've changed Kayla's life. There's more joy in our lives. God is in our lives. That's all because of you."

She could feel the tears pooling in her eyes. Her trembling subsided but only because Luke pulled her closer. Despite all the warnings her sister had given her and all the promises she made that she wasn't looking to find a man, Luke Spencer had touched her heart and she didn't want to be anywhere else but in his arms.

Almost breathless, she was able to say, "You are an amazing man, Luke. And you have an amazing daughter and the world's greatest dog." She chuckled at the thought of the lovable Butter.

Luke smiled, too. He lowered his head. "I'm falling in love with you, Lily."

Her heart fluttered as she tried to catch her breath. "I think I'm falling in love with you, too."

The kiss was everything she thought it would be—soft, gentle, and full of love. She didn't want it to end.

* * *

The next day brought a return to school and a resumption of the workweek. Although with it being Friday, most students and workers were already looking forward to the weekend so they could enjoy the winter wonderland on the shores of Lake Huron.

As Luke stirred the pot of boiling water on the stove, he couldn't stop smiling. The transformation in his life was so profound he could, at times, barely believe it. He hadn't felt such a feeling of happiness since the early days of his marriage to Maria and at the birth of Kayla. Once Maria died, the black cloud seemed to hover over him, preventing him from ever finding joy in his life.

But then Lily O'Leary arrived in Huron Cove.

He had sensed something from the first day he met her, and even though their initial meeting was not under the best of circumstances, he knew there was something special about Lily O'Leary. And it just kept getting better and better. The first date turned into three and then four. There were dinners and movies and cold winter walks. Sure, he wasn't able to enjoy the Christmas holiday with her since she had gone home to Chicago, but there was hope for the future. Combine that with his return to church and worshipping with Lily and Kayla, Luke had been thanking the Lord for blessing him more than he ever deserved. Then there was the kiss in the lighthouse. It stirred something inside him he hadn't felt in years.

Luke was about to dump the box of macaroni into the pot when he heard a rustling of feet in the kitchen.

"Are you going to get Miss O'Leary a birthday present?" Kayla asked, nearly out of breath with Emma right behind her and Butter pulling up the rear.

Luke barely had time to turn his head away from the stove before Emma had her question.

"And a Valentine's Day present? They're on the same day."

Luke went back to checking the timer on the stove·and before pouring the contents of the box into the pot. "They are?"

"Yes," Kayla said, her eyes wide with anticipation. "The same day."

Emma couldn't wait for a response. "Oh, Mr. Luke, you have to get her a birthday present and a Valentine's Day gift."

"You have to, Dad. You have to."

Luke should have known something was up. There had been a lot of whispers in the backseat of the SUV on the way home and then they had darted off to Kayla's bedroom in a rush. That could only mean a plot was afoot. He had come to enjoy the girls' plots considering he was the beneficiary of the one involving a certain sixth-grade teacher. He looked down at them. "I have to, huh?"

"Yes," they said in unison.

He stirred the macaroni some more as the steam began to rise. "Why don't you set the table and we'll talk about it over dinner." He glanced over his shoulder. "Emma, I take it you're staying for dinner."

"Oh, yes, I'm not going anywhere."

The girls scrambled to the cupboards and drawers pulling out plates and utensils like they had received orders from a four-star general. Glasses were filled and napkins were placed. Even Butter got a head start on dinner with a full bowl. Once complete, the girls sat at the table, their hands folded like little angels, and waited.

Luke brought over the bowl of steaming macaroni and cheese and then the chicken breasts. He used the spatula to slide a piece of chicken on each plate. Once he sat down and scooted his chair toward the table, he looked at Kayla.

"You have to get—"

Luke held up a finger. "Maybe we should give thanks for our food first."

A red-faced Kayla quickly bowed her head and said grace, and she tried her best not to zip through it. But once it was over, the girls expected Luke to focus his full attention on the matter at hand.

"Okay, so I have to buy Miss O'Leary a birthday present."

Kayla added, "And a Valentine's Day gift."

"Both?" He looked at Kayla and then Emma. "Can't I just get her one thing for each?"

The look of horror on the girls' faces was priceless.

"No!" they both yelled.

Luke laughed. "Well, I think I remember you two saying that I should buy her some roses and a box of chocolates."

"In a heart-shaped box, Mr. Luke."

He nodded as if giving it great consideration. "Okay, I'll get her some roses—"

"A dozen of them, Dad."

"A dozen!? Can't I just get her one?"

"No!" rang out so loud that Butter even looked up from his bowl.

"Okay, I'll get her a dozen red roses."

The girls gave him a look that said they were satisfied that he had seen the light and wasn't one of those Neanderthals that thinks anything less than a dozen red roses and a heart-shaped box of chocolates will do for Valentine's Day. He didn't need to be told, but he was kind of curious what the girls had in mind for a birthday gift. It had been on his mind ever since they told him Lily's birthday was coming up. The thoughts of something special had been swirling through his head. He wondered if it was time. Had they been going out long enough? Would that be the day to do it?

He was glad to have the two biggest busybodies in the world on the case so he could take the temperature of what the day might bring.

"So, what should I get her for her birthday?"

Kayla looked at Emma and Emma looked at Kayla. Then Kayla jumped out of her chair and ran out of the kitchen. "I'll be right back!"

Luke looked at Emma, who wore a wide smile. She was practically bubbling with anticipation for Kayla to return. Even Butter sat with an expectant look on his face.

Kayla screeched to a halt next to her dad's chair and held the phone in her hand for him to see the screen.

"You have to get her this."

Luke tamped down the shock he was feeling, although he really shouldn't have been surprised. Kayla and Emma loved having Lily O'Leary in their lives as much as Luke did. He figured they saw it, too. And given that they had the finger on the pulse of their teacher, it was a good bet she'd be thrilled at being on the receiving end.

"Jewelry, huh?"

"Yes," Kayla said.

Luke grabbed the phone and scrolled up and down the picture on the screen. He had to hand it to them, he approved of their selection. "It is pretty." When he got to the bottom, he looked at the girls and winced. "It's kind of expensive, isn't it?"

Emma's cheeks rose. "She's worth it, Mr. Luke."

Kayla reached out and put her hand on his arm. With tears

forming in her eyes, she whispered, “She really is worth it, Dad.”

CHAPTER 26

Valentine's Day, February 14th

Lily didn't remember bringing the red dress with her from Chicago, but somehow it ended up in her closet in Huron Cove. Perhaps she'd been distracted, or maybe she had been overly optimistic that there would be an opportunity to wear it. She made a half turn and looked at herself in the mirror on the back of her bedroom door. She raised her foot behind her. All that running had done her calves some good. She gave another half spin to get a look from the other side. It had been a long time since she had gotten all dressed up for a night on the town. And a night out to celebrate Valentine's Day had been so long ago she couldn't even remember where she had gone to dinner.

But tonight was the night.

For the last three months, nearly every spare thought centered on Luke Spencer. They had fun together, and she enjoyed his company, not to mention that of his daughter and their dog. He was everything she wanted in a man—strong, smart, funny, and a gentleman. She flinched at the thought and looked at her reflection in the mirror.

Is Luke the man meant for me?

The time she had spent with him was great, filled with laughs and stories about their lives. But was it time to start making stories of their lives together as a couple? Would tonight be the night to take it the next level? The kiss at the lighthouse told her there was something special going on between them. She thought they were growing closer, and she could tell Luke had feelings for her. But was it long-term? Did he want to get married? Was he going to propose tonight?

She walked over and swiped a couple tissues out of the box on her nightstand. She sat down on the bed and held the tissues tight, hoping they would mop up the moisture of doubt pooling in her hands. With her mind racing through a thousand thoughts per minute, she did the only thing she thought could help clear through the clutter. She folded her hands in prayer. She asked God to give her clarity of mind to help her understand if this was meant to be. Her thoughts were interrupted by the buzzing of her phone.

Are you ready?

Lily smiled. It was Luke. She didn't know whether she was ready for what the future might hold, but she felt God's presence with her. She typed out a response. *I'm ready.*

Luke sent another text saying he'd be over in ten minutes.

Lily put on her red heels and gave herself another look in the mirror. She liked what she saw. She thought Luke would, too. She remembered to grab her purse and her gift for Luke. She looked at the wrapped box and hoped he'd like it.

After one last look in the mirror, she took a deep breath and let it out. *Tonight could change my life forever.*

She walked toward the living room and peeked out the front window. Luke hadn't arrived yet. Thinking Luke would come inside, she waited to put on her coat.

Her phone rang in her purse. She hurried to grab it and saw the rose petals on the screen. A grimace flashed across her face. "Oh, Rose, not now." She tapped the screen and put the phone to her ear. "Rose, I can't talk long. Luke's—"

"Dad's been in an accident."

The words hit Lily so hard she gasped. She felt the blow to her chest hit so hard she thought her legs were going to buckle. Her purse fell to the floor. She had expected a lecture from Rose, but her sister's words sent her mind into a whirring tailspin. *Dad's been in an accident.* She could barely get the words out of her mouth. "What?"

Rose spoke clearly and directly. "Lily, Dad's been in a car accident. He's at the hospital right now. I've talked to him. He's in the emergency room, but I think you should come home."

Lily rubbed her forehead with her hand. A flood of emotion hit her. *Dad's in the hospital, and I'm six hours from home.*

The doorbell rang, startling her. Her voice shook. "I'll be there as soon as I can."

Lily staggered in her heels as she hurried to the front door. Her hand struggled to grip the handle, and when she finally opened the door, a cold blast of February air hit her.

"Lily, what's wrong?"

The question made her realize Luke was seeing the same thing she was feeling. She probably looked white as a ghost. She felt like the blood had drained from her face, and the cold temperature made her shiver. Luke stepped inside, his hands full of roses, chocolates, and a gift box. None of that mattered now. He set them down on the table and reached out his arms.

"What's wrong?"

"My sister just called." Her lips trembled and she had trouble finding the words. "My . . . my dad's been in a car accident."

Luke wrapped her in his arms. "Oh, Lily. I'm so sorry. Is he okay?"

Her shaking increased despite his embrace. "I don't know. Rose said she has talked to him in the emergency room." She looked up at Luke, the tears pooling in her eyes. "I'm sorry, but I have to cancel our dinner. I have to get home."

"Of course," he said, releasing her slightly but still holding on. "Don't worry about it. I can drive you."

Lily took comfort in his concern, but she couldn't ask that much of him. "No, that's okay. I just need to get going." She started to look around and realized the dress and heels weren't conducive to winter driving. "I need to change." She hurried off to her room and was back in less than three minutes wearing jeans, a hooded sweatshirt, and a pair of boots.

She came back to the living room and saw Luke had her purse and coat ready. There was also a bottle of water for the road. "Got you keys and your wallet?" Luke asked, helping her with her coat.

Lily looked through her purse. “Yes, but I know I’m forgetting something.”

“Got your phone?’

Lily grunted. “Oh, my phone,” she said, before finding it on the table next to Luke’s gift. “I really am sorry, Luke.” She gave him a wrapped box. “I was going to give this to you.” She didn’t look at him when she said it. There were too many other things racing through her mind. She never saw him take it or put the box he brought for her in her purse. She just needed to get going.

“Oh, I’ve got to lock up.”

Luke took Lily by the arm and led her out the door. “Don’t worry about it. I’ll lock up. Be careful on the roads.” Once in the driveway, he opened the car door for her. “Are you sure you don’t want me to drive you?”

She fumbled to put the key in the ignition. “No, but thank you so much, Luke.”

“Kayla and I will say a prayer for you. Call or text when you get a chance.”

“I will.”

Luke shut the door, and Lily backed out of the driveway. She only hoped she could make it home in time.

CHAPTER 26

Given her lead foot and the time zone change, Lily arrived at the hospital a little after 10 p.m. She had spent the entire drive praying for her dad's health. She hated that she lived so far away from her family and couldn't be there for him at a moment's notice.

Rose met her at the hospital entrance and told her their dad had broken his leg after a car sideswiped him on an icy road. The surgeon said the operation went well, although a second surgery would be necessary and it would be several months before Mr. O'Leary would be back to normal. Lily, exhausted and drained, let her sister hold her as she reported the promising news.

"Thank the Lord," she whispered.

They walked together to their dad's room where he was recovering. Lily hugged her mom and they gathered around the bed. No one said anything, thankful and content to let Mr. O'Leary rest for the night.

After an hour of whispered prayers, Rose and Lily persuaded their mother to go home for the evening to get some rest. Lily drove her home and Rose stopped by her condo to pick up a few things before joining them at the house. In the darkness of her old bedroom, Lily relaxed for the first time in hours. She had driven for six hours straight, thinking only of her dad and her family. Then there was the reunion with her sister and mother. The emotional ups and downs of the day left her exhausted. She was thankful to be home. She grabbed her phone to put it on the nightstand.

When she turned it on, she flinched at the date. February 15th. It wasn't Valentine's Day any longer. Her scheduled date with Luke seemed like a long-forgotten memory. It felt like a year had passed in the less than ten hours since she had seen Luke. She winced. *Luke.* He had asked her to text or call but she had completely forgotten. It was 1 a.m. in Chicago, which meant it was 2 a.m. in Huron Cove. She debated whether she should send a text or not, but quickly decided it was the right thing to do.

I'm sorry it's so late, but I just got back to my parents' house. My dad is going to be okay. Broken leg. The doctor expects a full recovery.

She didn't expect a response until morning, but the reply came back within a minute.

So good to hear. I'm glad your dad is doing well, and I'm glad you're safe at home with family.

Luke's message warmed her heart. Such a kindhearted man. And she did feel safe at home with her family. Her thumbs typed out another text. *Sorry again for cancelling our Valentine's Day dinner. Hope we can go another time.*

Luke responded. *Anytime.*

She could tell he was typing another message so she waited.

You looked wonderful by the way.

Lily giggled and responded. *Did you mean my red dress or my jeans and hooded sweatshirt?*

Both actually. You look beautiful in everything.

Lily sucked in a breath. Then she chuckled out loud. She couldn't believe she had gone from worrying about her dad all night long to smiling at Luke's text. *Thank you. You were looking pretty handsome yourself.*

She had to wait for any indication whether Luke was typing a response. *Thanks. I should let you get some rest. Let me know how things are going tomorrow.*

I will.

Lily turned off the phone and held it against her chest. What a man. What a day. She didn't even have time to put the phone on the nightstand before her eyes closed and she fell asleep.

* * *

Along with their mother, Lily and Rose were up early, hoping to get to the hospital as soon as possible. When they arrived at the nurses' station, the attending physician was there to greet them. He had checked on Mr. O'Leary and said he was resting comfortably, although he did complain about the fact that he couldn't have bacon and eggs for breakfast. The three women laughed, knowing that the accident hadn't damaged their husband and father's sense of humor.

They all walked into Mr. O'Leary's room and found him propped up in bed with a remote control in his hand and a frown on his face. Obviously, the TV was not putting him in a good mood. His favorite women in the entire world, however, did brighten his day.

After his wife and Rose gave him hugs, he saw his younger daughter behind them. "Lilybean, you didn't have to come all the way down here for me."

She walked to the side of the bed and patted him on the arm. "It wasn't any trouble, Dad. I'm glad you're okay."

"That must have been a long day for you."

Lily managed a tired smile. "It was, but I'm glad I'm home."

Rose sidled up next to her and wrapped an arm around Lily's shoulder. "And we're glad you're home, too. Right where you belong."

Lily couldn't help but think about the fact that her entire family was right here in that Chicago hospital room. This was the city she had grown up in, and she never really thought she'd live too far away from the Windy City. Her plans had changed, but she was beginning to remind herself that plans could be changed again if the opportunity presented itself.

When one of the orderlies entered the room and said it was time for Mr. O'Leary to get an X-ray, Mrs. O'Leary suggested she and the girls go down to the cafeteria for some coffee. As Rose and Lily left the room, their father's request for some bacon and eggs brought smiles to their faces.

In the cafeteria, Rose and Lily sat at a table with their mother, large cups of coffee in front of each of them. Looking around the room, they saw the faces of concerned family members, wondering what the day would bring with their loved ones. The rest of those at the tables were employees—nurses and doctors seeking some caffeine to make it through their shifts.

When two doctors walked in the door and stood in line for coffee, Rose nudged her sister. "There's Nick," she said, pointing across the way. "That guy he's with. His name's Toby. Orthopedics." She raised her eyebrows. "And you know what that means." She rubbed her thumb and fingers together. "Money. Big money."

It didn't take but a second for Lily to see that Dr. Toby had a lot going for him. She could have discovered that by the number of female heads turning to catch a glimpse of the hot young doc in green scrubs walking tall toward their table. *Wow.*

Rose leaned closer. "Wow, indeed."

Lily blushed. Had she said that out loud? She probably wasn't the only one.

Rose stood to embrace her beau. "Nick, you remember my sister."

Lily pushed back her chair, stood, and offered a light hug.

"Of course. Lily, it's good to see you. I'm sure your dad was happy to see you, too. I'm glad he's doing well."

Dr. Toby put a hand to his mouth and loudly cleared his throat.

Dr. Nick caught the not-so-subtle hint. "Oh, where are my manners? Lily, this is Dr. Toby Rayhall. He's the hospital's newest orthopedic surgeon."

Dr. Toby took a step closer. He grasped Lily's hand, brought it to his lips, and kissed it. "It's a pleasure to meet you, Lily. A beautiful name for a beautiful woman."

Lily had to restrain herself from fanning her cheeks, which were now aflame. The man had a chin that looked like it had been carved out of granite. His dark eyes brought her in, and she didn't dare take her hand away.

"I haven't seen you around the hospital before."

Rose leaned in. "Lily's actually going to be moving back to Chicago in May. In case you're interested."

Without having taken his eyes off Lily, he nodded and winked. "I'm very interested." He kissed her hand again.

"Alright, Romeo," Nick said, tapping his buddy on the elbow. "Give it a rest." He looked at Lily. "Toby's actually going to be one of the surgeons operating on your dad."

Given the hunk of a man in front of her, Lily had almost forgotten about her dad's surgery.

"Maybe I could get your number, and I'll let you know how everything goes."

Rose turned around and grabbed a napkin off the table. She took a pen from her purse and then scribbled Lily's number on it before handing it to Toby. "Here's her number. Call her anytime."

With her eyes wide wondering what was happening, Lily saw her sister mouth the words *You'll thank me later* before watching Toby put the napkin in his pocket.

"I will do that," Toby said. "It was nice meeting you, Lily. I should probably get to work."

Rose and Lily watched as Nick and Toby made their way out of the cafeteria. Every other female watched them leave, too. Still trying to figure out what just happened, Lily didn't hear her sister asking a question. Realizing Rose was speaking, she finally shook herself out of the Toby trance.

"What?"

"I said whattya think?"

"What do I think about what?"

Rose's eyes widened. "About what? Toby! He's only the most eligible bachelor in the hospital. Every available woman is maneuvering to try to get his attention. But he comes over and kisses your hand." She fanned herself. "You are so lucky. You two are going to make such a great couple."

Lily would be lying if she said she wasn't intrigued by the

idea. A hot young doc with a successful and lucrative career ahead of him in her hometown of Chicago.

Chicago. Just thinking the word made her wonder about Huron Cove and everything that the quaint little town had to offer. Luke . . . Kayla . . . Butter.

Lily said nothing, which caused her sister to front her. "What is wrong with you?"

"What?"

"My goodness, Toby was practically throwing himself at you and you acted like he wasn't even there."

"No, I didn't. I was just surprised. I've had a lot on my mind the last twenty-four hours and wasn't expecting to be introduced to a guy."

Rose sighed and shook her head. "You're not thinking about that old man, are you?"

When Lily didn't respond, Rose held out her hands, palms up, and weighed the options. "Let's see, you've got an old man with a kid and he's a cop up there in Mayberry." Her left hand went down and the right went up. "On this hand, you've got Toby. Hot, your age, and a surgeon in Chicago." Her right hand kept getting higher. "Did I mention hot?"

Lily looked away and said softly, "Yes, you mentioned it."

Lily said no more, only to ask her mother if she wanted any more coffee. Taking the cups up to the counter for a refill gave her time to think. *What do I want? Is it Luke, Kayla, and Butter in Huron Cove? Or do I really want to be near family and friends with the chance at starting a relationship with the handsome doctor?* It wasn't hard for Lily to think the latter choice might be the best option. She was six hours away from Huron Cove and her sister and parents were right there in Chicago. And Dr. Toby was a definite catch to say the least.

But what about Luke? Kind, considerate Luke. And he was no slouch in the looks department either. But is he who I want? Is he the one I always dreamed of marrying and starting a family with? And was Huron Cove the place that I would call home?

Lily sighed and reached out for the cups full of coffee. Her brain felt like it had reached max capacity in the last two days and she couldn't make sense of much of anything. She didn't know where to turn other than to walk back and set the cup of coffee in front of her mother.

The three then went back to the room to check on Mr. O'Leary. They spent most of the day in the room listening to him replay the accident and its aftermath. He complained some more about the food and the fact that there was nothing to watch on TV. He was quickly going stir crazy at being cooped up in the room.

In the afternoon, the doctors and nurses came in to check on his leg, gave him his medication, and told him to rest. The medication made him drowsy and before anyone knew it, he was out like a light. Rose left to get some sleep, saying she had to work the late shift and she could check on Mr. O'Leary during the overnight hours. Lily and her mother stayed for most of the day, watching nothing of substance on TV and making trips to the cafeteria for coffee. Finally, at seven, they wished their sleeping husband and father goodbye and went home for the evening.

In her bedroom after another exhausting day, Lily replayed her meeting with Dr. Toby that morning. There was no doubting the man was hot. He could probably be a male model. And he did have a bright future ahead of him. She let herself think of being a doctor's wife. Money. A big house. But would he be a good and faithful husband? Would he be a good father? Did he even want kids?

She shook the thoughts from her head and sat on the bed. She opened her purse and fumbled around to find her phone. She found it and then something in the corner caught her eye. She didn't know what it was and knew she hadn't put it in there. She pulled it out and realized it was a small wrapped gift with her name on it. She put her purse next to her and stared at the gift. *Who is this from? How did it get in my purse? Maybe Rose put it in there.* Only one way to find out.

She carefully unwrapped the box and set the paper aside. With her left hand, she opened the lid and then gasped. She couldn't believe it. She let the light shine on it to admire the treasure. She pulled out the necklace and held it in her hand. The jewel, green and blue and looking like a turtle shell, was one of the most beautiful things she had ever seen. She smiled and then laughed at herself when she realized what it was and, more importantly, who it was from.

It was an Isle Royale Greenstone. And it just happened to be the state gem of Michigan. Her students would have known that fact based on their Michigan history lesson. And it would be a certain special father who would have taken the hint from his daughter and her friend to buy it for her for Valentine's Day. Lily got up and put it around her neck. Admiring it in the mirror brought another smile to her face.

She shook when her phone buzzed. She really wanted to text or call Luke to tell him she just found his gift and she loved it. She hurried back to her bed and grabbed the phone. She sucked in a breath when she saw the text.

Hey, Lily. It's Toby. Give me a call.

CHAPTER 27

Luke let Kayla walk into church first. The glaring stares from other parishioners had subsided, replaced by outstretched hands and welcoming smiles. Luke was beginning to feel comfortable in church again. And he had Kayla and Lily to thank for it. But Lily wasn't at the service today. She hadn't been for the last three weeks. Ever since her dad was in his accident, she had made the long trek home every weekend to check on him and help her mother around the house. Now the school was on its spring break and Lily had gone home to spend the week in Chicago with family. So, all told, it would be over a month since Luke and Kayla were able to sit with Lily in church.

And the work week didn't allow for much interaction. At least Kayla was able to see her teacher during the day. But Luke was relegated to a quick dinner with Lily every now and then since she was so busy trying to catch up with her lesson plans and grade her papers. She was less talkative than usual, too, but Luke chalked it up to being concerned over her dad and the demands on her time. But there hadn't been anything like the moment they shared in the lighthouse.

Luke did bring over a pizza early on after Lily returned from Chicago, and she thanked him for the Isle Royale Greenstone necklace. Kayla was particularly pleased that Lily wore it every day. But the interactions with Luke and Lily were slowly getting fewer and farther between, and Luke had the uneasy feeling that Lily's hand was slipping from his grasp.

He worried about Kayla, too. She was doing well in math, but she didn't get to see much of Lily outside the classroom either. He didn't have any answers on how to bring Lily back into their lives on a more consistent basis. As they waited for the service to begin, the only thing he could think of was to fold his hands and pray.

After he opened his eyes, he felt his daughter lean her head against his arm.

"I wish Miss O'Leary was here with us, Dad," she said softly.

Luke's chest fell and his shoulders slumped. Lily was weighing on more than just his mind. He lowered his head and said, "I wish she was here with us too, kiddo."

Following the sermon, Pastor Carlton offered the prayer of the church, wishing certain members of the congregation a happy birthday and offering congratulations to Mr. and Mrs. Gustafson on their wedding anniversary.

"We also pray for Mr. Frank O'Leary, the father of our Lily O'Leary, who continues to recover from his injuries sustained in a car accident. We ask for Miss O'Leary's safe return, as well as for the return of all our school staff and students, following spring break."

With his eyes closed and his heart open, Luke prayed for Lily. He prayed for himself and for Kayla, too. He wanted to be a family again—a family with him and Lily and Kayla and maybe some more. A family that laughed and played and cried and prayed and loved.

"Amen."

And it all depended on whether he could convince Lily that the family he wanted would never be complete without her.

* * *

The warm March sun had started to turn the grass green, and the birds were beginning to fill the air with their melodies. The buds on the trees might be a little behind, but springtime was definitely fast approaching and the people of Huron Cove were glad of it. The running shoes were pulled out of the closet, and the bikes were yanked out of the garage after a long winter's hibernation.

Luke sat on the front porch in his rocking chair and enjoyed the fresh spring air. He had the day off and it gave him time to think. And lately most of his thoughts centered around Lily O'Leary and what was happening between them. He had kept praying, but the closeness between them had yet to return. He wondered if it was gone for good. Lily had said she wasn't sure whether she would go home for the weekend, so that offered a glimmer of hope that they could spend some time together.

He wondered what she was doing at that moment. School had been let out early for a teachers' conference that Friday afternoon so she was probably busy with school matters. The kids, however, wasted no time in getting outside. Kayla and Emma had plans to ride their bikes into town and then the forest preserve. He heard the bell on Emma's bike from a block away. She pulled to a stop in the driveway and hopped off the bike.

"Hi, Mr. Luke."

"Hi, Emma. It's a nice spring day, isn't it?"

"Oh, yes. I'm so glad we got out early from school today. I'd hate to miss a chance to get the bikes out and enjoy the fresh air. It feels so good to get outside again."

Emma leaned her bike against the stair railing and walked up to the porch. She took a seat in the rocker next to Luke.

"Pretty soon, it'll be summer and you two can ride all day long." He looked beyond the yard to the trees across the street. "Kayla was going to change into some shorts. She said she'll be right down."

Emma rocked back and forth, acting like she was in no hurry to leave. "There goes a blue jay," she said, her finger pointing out the bird's flight path. "I saw some cardinals on the way over. I think they have to be the prettiest birds in the world with their red feathers. A bald eagle is nice, of course. But it's not so much pretty as it is majestic. I think scarlet macaws with their red and yellow and blue feathers are pretty, too. It's too bad we don't have macaws in Michigan. I'd like to have a parrot. I'd teach it to say hello, hello, hello whenever someone walked in the room. It'd be fun to have a conversation with a witty parrot, don't you think, Mr. Luke?"

Luke smiled and shook his head. Emma Lynn was certainly someone special—a gift from God, that's for sure. "Yeah, that would be pretty cool, Emma."

The two were content to watch in silence for the next bird to make its way through the Michigan air. But silence was never one of Emma's strong suits, and it certainly was not one of her endearing qualities. Luke could almost sense she was itching to say something, her chair rocking faster and her right leg bouncing up and down. It didn't take but a minute for her to give in to her urge to speak.

She turned her head toward him. "Mr. Luke, may I ask you a question?"

Luke glanced over to her. Emma always asked a lot of questions about policework, and he was happy to impart his knowledge. Of course, he never knew where her vibrant and active mind would take the conversation. "Sure, Emma, you can ask me anything." He then went back to watching for birds.

"What are you waiting for?"

He wondered if he heard correctly. He looked at her again. "Waiting for? I'm just sitting here enjoying the breeze."

"Maybe I should have asked why are you waiting?"

"Waiting for what, Emma?"

"Why haven't you asked Miss O'Leary to marry you?"

Luke's rocking stopped. Emma's rocking stopped, too. The question sucked the breath out of him like no question Emma had ever asked. There was no more thought about spring days or beautiful birds. He was glad Kayla wasn't out there to hear what Emma asked. He looked to the east, out across the yard and into the forest of trees fronting Lake Huron.

Luke had asked himself that very same question what seemed like a hundred times now. *Why haven't I asked her?* With everything that had gone on in the last month, he wondered if it was because he wasn't sure she'd say yes. How would Kayla react if her teacher told her father she didn't want to marry him? He knew how he would react. He'd be devastated, and he didn't know whether he wanted to take the risk. Maybe it wasn't meant to be.

He leaned forward in the rocker and folded his hands. "We haven't been able to spend much time together. She's been going home to Chicago most weekends to be with her father, and we don't have much time during the week to hang out. And to tell you the truth, Emma, I'm not sure what Lily is feeling." He shook his head. "I don't know what to do."

"Do you love her?"

He sat back in his chair and looked at Emma. He didn't need to think about his response. "Yes, I love Lily. I love her with all my heart. But I . . . "

Luke didn't finish his sentence as they both heard Kayla bounding down the stairs inside the house.

Before her friend came outside, Emma pushed herself out of the rocker, turned, and looked Luke in the eyes. "Don't let her get away, Mr. Luke. Once she's gone, she'll never come back. She'll fade away like a distant memory. And you'll have to live with the regret of not asking her for the rest of your life."

Luke sat there looking at Emma, wondering if she was going to say more.

Before he could manage to come up with a response, Kayla and Butter walked out the front door. Then Emma and Kayla were off to ride their bikes. As the girls left his view, Luke sat forward and folded his hands again, his head lowered and his eyes looking at the porch. He sighed, wondering what he should do. Butter walked over and tried to nuzzle his nose in between Luke's hands. Luke rubbed the dog's fur as his mind swirled with thoughts of Lily O'Leary.

Once she's gone, she'll never come back.

The words echoed around his brain. He had thought he had time to make it work, but Emma made him realize that the school year would be over before he knew it. Would she come back next August? What if she didn't? The thought of never seeing Lily O'Leary again tore a hole through his heart. He couldn't let her go. She was too amazing a woman to let leave and never see again. She meant everything to him. She meant the world to Kayla. Luke took a deep breath.

She was the one. Lily O'Leary was the one meant for him. He knew it.

And he knew he had to do something about it.

He stood up from his chair. "Come on, Butter."

They hurried inside, and Luke made a beeline to his bedroom. He opened the top drawer of his dresser and pulled out the box. He flipped open the lid, and the three-stone diamond ring sparkled in the sunlight filtering through the window.

He looked down at the dog, who appeared ready to do whatever necessary to make his master happy. "How about a ride down to the school, bud?"

Butter barked his answer, and Luke smiled. He threw on a new shirt and then checked his watch. Lily would be getting out of her conference any minute now. There was no time to waste. He found Butter by the door, almost willing him to hurry before it was too late. Luke smiled, his heart pounding with anticipation. He couldn't believe what he was doing. He had a proposal to make.

Once she's gone, she'll never come back.

"Not if I can help it," Luke said to himself as he headed out the door.

CHAPTER 28

"I'm getting married! I'm getting married!

The euphoria radiated through the phone. The excited breathless joy of a young woman newly engaged was rarely matched in life. Friends and family had to be called. The big news had to be shouted from the rooftops so that others could feel the excitement and share in the happiness.

Lily had a pretty good idea the question was going to be popped, but she just didn't know when. Although she thought it might happen at Christmas, it was just a matter of time before the engagement ring made an appearance. Valentine's Day was the next logical choice, but then her dad had been injured in the car accident. It was bound to happen, though. Everyone knew it.

"He just proposed! And I said yes!"

The phone call was made a little after three-thirty that Friday afternoon, just as Lily made it to her car after the teachers' conference had ended.

"Just now?"

"Yes, just now."

Once everyone was able to catch their breath, Lily gushed, "I'm so happy for you, Rose. And for Nick. Have you told Mom and Dad?"

"No, you were the first person I called."

"He proposed on a Friday afternoon?"

"Yes, we were finally off work at the same time and we decided to take a walk down by the lake. It was so romantic with the boats and everything. When I said yes, he twirled me around and people were taking pictures. It was amazing." Rose stopped long enough to catch her breath. "You have to come home."

Lily cleared her throat. "What? Come home? I was going to stay here this weekend."

"No! You have to come home! Nick and I are having a party tomorrow night at the hospital. That way all our friends and co-workers can stop by and celebrate. Dad's already getting around in his wheelchair, so he'll be there and you have to be here, too. And there's so much to do. I'm going to have to start looking for a wedding dress. And then Nick and I are going to have to find a place to get married and where to have the reception." Another break to grab a breath. "You have to come home. We'll get started tomorrow and then we'll go to the party tomorrow night. Start thinking about venues on your drive here. And the wedding photos, too. We'll have to have pictures taken at Navy Pier and Millennium Park and the Planetarium and Buckingham Fountain." Not hearing a response, she asked, "Are you writing this all down!? You're going to be the maid of honor!"

Lily laughed at her sister's exuberance. Her eyes were drawn to Luke and Butter walking toward her and she gave them a happy wave. She pointed to her phone and smiled from ear to ear.

"Please, Lilybean, my engagement party is only going to happen once in my life and it wouldn't be the same without you. You have to be there to enjoy it. It'll be so much fun."

Lily looked at Luke and shook her head like she couldn't believe her sister's euphoria knew no bounds.

"Okay, okay. I'll come home tonight. I just have to go home to pack a bag."

She saw Luke look away, like he felt bad for intruding on her conversation or something. She noticed the smile had vanished. She tried to put him at ease by putting her hand over the phone and whispering, "My sister just got engaged. She's ecstatic. Looks like another road trip to Chicago."

Luke nodded and then bent down to pet Butter.

"Okay, okay. I'll leave as soon as I can. It'll probably be

about nine before I get home."

Lily laughed aloud at her sister's parting words shouted into the phone. "I'm getting married! I'm getting married!"

Luke stood up, and Lily was shaking her head. "As you could probably hear, she's pretty excited."

"Sounds like it."

Lily reached down and gave Butter a few pats on the head. "I know we were supposed to do something tonight, but obviously there's been a change of plans."

Luke gave a weak smile and nodded. "So I hear."

Lily could sense a change in mood from Luke, like he didn't find what he was looking for. "Is everything all right?"

"Yeah, it's good. Butter and I were just out for a drive and then a walk. Kayla and Emma were riding their bikes out to the forest preserve."

Lily thought she saw something in Luke's eyes, like he wanted to tell her something but changed his mind at the last second. But her sister's big news quickly changed her focus. "I'm sorry about tonight, but I need to get going. Maybe we can do something next week."

"Sure, sounds good."

Lily gave him a quick hug and a peck on the cheek.

"Please offer my congratulations to your sister."

"I will." Lily reached for her keys and unlocked the door. "I'll see you later. Bye Butter."

* * *

Chicago

The engagement party was scheduled to run from four to eight to give the nurses and doctors on duty a chance to pop in sometime during their shifts. The conference room on the second floor had been commandeered and quickly festooned with balloons and streamers for the happy couple. The punch bowl was full and trays loaded with finger food were laid out.

With her mom by her side, Lily pushed her dad's wheelchair out of the elevator. She had spent most of the morning with Rose discussing the wedding. Magazine photos were clipped, websites were bookmarked, and a list as long as Lily's arm was drawn up for the "wedding of the century," as Rose called it. After a quick nap, she drove her parents to the hospital where they were to meet Rose and Nick.

Dr. Nick was the first person to greet the bride-to-be's father. "How's the leg, Mr. O'Leary?"

"Getting better every day, and as long as you two don't get married in the next week or two, I should be able to walk Rosebud down the aisle without any problem."

Rose gave her dad a pat on the shoulder. "I'm sure you'll be all healed by then."

Lily maneuvered her dad off to the side so he could have room to greet people. They stood and watched Rose and Nick accepting hugs and handshakes. Smiles abounded, and love was definitely in the air.

Mr. O'Leary turned his head to speak to his younger daughter. "Someday it'll be your turn, Lilybean."

Lily said nothing, content to hide behind her dad's wheelchair as the well-wishers streamed into the room. *Someday it'll be your turn.* With all the smiles in the room, it was hard not to think about what it would be like to be the one getting married, to have found the person who makes you happy, the one you want to spend the rest of your life with.

Her thoughts returned to Luke. She chuckled to herself about the first time they met—on the side of the road after he caught her speeding. But he had treated her with respect from day one. And ever since then, they had grown closer. The running, the dinners, the movies. Kayla and Butter. And then there was the kiss in the lighthouse. She closed her eyes remembering his warm embrace. He was such a gentleman. Handsome. Considerate. A good father.

He'd make a good husband.

She felt her hands shaking, and her mouth had gone dry. Her knees felt a little wobbly.

Is Luke the one?

Why couldn't she figure out the answer? She wished she could receive a sign to tell her which direction to take in life.

Just then, Rose burst over, breaking Lily's train of thought, and grabbed her by the hand. "Come here. Toby's here, and I want you to say hello."

Lily felt herself being dragged out from behind her dad's wheelchair. They crossed the room and Lily noticed the hunk of a man in the doctor's scrubs that she had met the day after her dad's accident. By the looks on the faces of the rest of the women in the room, they noticed him, too.

"Toby, you remember my sister Lily."

"Of course," he said, winking. "Nice to see you again."

Lily nodded. Even with the scrubs, she could imagine the ripped chest, the six-pack abs, and the toned biceps. The man was indeed well put together. "Nice to see you, too."

"Quite the shindig your sister has put on," he said, looking around the room.

Lily smiled. "Yeah, and I imagine it'll only get bigger from now until the wedding."

Rose smiled like it was true. She gave a little bump to Lily to get her closer to Toby.

Toby didn't back away. "I just finished my shift. How about we get together for a drink later on?"

A twinge crossed Lily's face. Maybe it was a wince, but it showed she hadn't expected to be asked out. She didn't know how to answer. The guy was a hunk for sure. And he was a doctor. Her heart beat faster at the uncertainty of it all. Finally, she looked around the room and saw her mom and dad. She gave a shake of her head and pointed. "I'm sorry, I have to take my parents home. I'm their ride."

Rose waved it off. "I'll take them home. You two go have a good time."

"Yeah, I know a little place that has great jazz music. We could have a few drinks, maybe do a little dancing."

Lily felt like the room was closing in on her. A flash of heat hit her face and her hands started shaking. She didn't know what to do. She shook her head and said, "I'm seeing someone."

Rose leaned in. "Not for much longer, though."

Lily gasped and slapped her sister on the arm with the back of her hand. "Rose."

Rose held up her index finger and looked at Toby. "Excuse us for a second, Toby. I have to talk some sense into my sister."

Rose hustled her sister into the corner of the room for a bit of privacy. Through her gritted teeth, she said, "What is wrong with you?"

"What are you talking about?"

Rose gestured with her thumb over her shoulder toward Toby. "The guy is an Adonis," she said softly enough that only Lily could hear. "He is practically falling all over himself trying to ask you out and you blow him off."

"What about Luke?"

Rose grunted and rolled her eyes. "You cannot be serious. He's too old for you, Lily. I don't know how many times I have to say it. Forget about him and his kid. You're going to move back to Chicago anyway."

"How do you know that? I haven't even heard back from any schools yet."

"There are million teaching jobs in Chicago, Lily. One is bound to open up any day now. So, stop thinking about the old man and start thinking about Doctor Hottie."

Lily broke eye contact and looked at the floor, her fingers fiddling with her necklace. *What if I can get a new job in Chicago? It would be closer to home and family. No more six-hour drives to get home. And what about Toby?*

Her head was beginning to ache from the overload of the past several months—her dad's accident, the trips to the hospital, her sister getting engaged. She didn't want to think about all this now.

I don't know what to do.

CHAPTER 29

Huron Cove

Luke spent most of Saturday pacing the house, his mind deep in thought. He was glad Kayla was at Emma's because she would have wondered what was wrong with him. He didn't have anyone to talk to and he wasn't sure what to do.

His first attempt at proposing to Lily had been cut off by her sister's phone call on Friday afternoon. The fact that she had to return to Chicago to be near family was not lost on him. Would her family be the reason she left Huron Cove for good? Or did her heart belong in Michigan with Luke Spencer? If he asked, would she say yes? What if she said no? Hadn't he been through this before?

Once she's gone, she'll never come back.

Emma's warning had echoed through his brain the entire weekend. The pacing didn't help much. He wished he could know what Lily was truly feeling in her heart. All he knew was he couldn't imagine the emptiness in his life if Lily were no longer a part of it. But what if she left? Luke realized he'd have to start over in hopes of finding someone to share his life with. But he didn't want to start over. He found the one he wanted to spend the rest of his life with. And he realized he had to figure out a way to convey to her that they were meant to be together.

Once she's gone, she'll never come back.

Kayla returned on Saturday evening, and they were both up early for church. Given the warm morning, Luke parked his SUV across the street from the police station so they could walk the two blocks to St. Peter's. With the sun up over Lake Huron and the temperatures on the rise, storms were forecast for later in the day.

"You can really feel that humidity today," he said to Kayla as they passed Rose's Pizzeria. "It's about time for spring to roar in like a lion."

Kayla, however, had her mind focused on more than the weather. "I wish Miss O'Leary didn't have to go to Chicago this weekend."

Luke put his arm around his daughter. "Me, too. Maybe she'll be here next weekend."

But what if she isn't? And how will Kayla react if Lily decides to move back home at the end of the school year?

After they found their spot in church, Luke stood when Emma arrived, and he let her down the pew to sit next to Kayla. While they chatted quietly, Luke folded his hands. *Please God, help me figure out what to do. Help me understand what Lily is feeling.*

During the prayer of the church, Pastor Carlton asked the congregation to pray for police officers, firefighters, and those serving in the military.

"We give thanks for Carl and Barb Stanton on their fortieth wedding anniversary."

Try as he might, Luke's mind began to wander at the Pastor's words. He wondered if he would ever have an anniversary to celebrate. He could still have a fiftieth anniversary, but he realized he had better get started soon. Lily flashed through his mind.

"We also pray for Dale Bowen at the death of his wife, Janet. Give Dale and his family comfort as they mourn Janet's loss and help them to remember Janet's faith in Christ and her eternal rest in her Savior's arms."

Luke felt Dale's pain. He had been through losing a wife. But as much as the pain of losing someone happened to be, sharing a life together was worth it in the end. Luke wanted that feeling again. He didn't want to wait any longer. He didn't want to lose Lily.

Once she's gone, she'll never come back.

Before the prayer ended, Luke had made his decision. He would ask her to marry him as soon as she made it back to Huron Cove. He couldn't wait any longer. Proposing on her front porch may not be the most romantic spot in the world, but he loved Lily and he wanted her to be his wife.

After the service ended, Luke and Kayla said their goodbyes to their friends and headed down the sidewalk to Luke's vehicle. His phone buzzed in his pocket. He gasped, but not enough to catch Kayla's attention. That it was Lily brought a smile to his face.

> *Luke, would you use the hidden key and go to my house and shut my bedroom window? I think I left it open when I left in such a rush and I saw they're forecasting storms today for Huron Cove. I'm heading to church. See you soon. LO'L*

Luke typed out a quick reply.

> *Sure, no problem. It does look like storms are on the way. I hope we can talk when you get back. I need to ask you something. Safe travels. Luke*

There. He told her. He was going to ask her that night. He looked at his watch. She usually left around two in the afternoon. That meant she'd be back in Huron Cove between seven and eight. Luke sucked in a deep breath. Tonight was the night.

* * *

Chicago

Strong thunderstorms in central Iowa up through Minnesota had Lily wondering whether she should get an earlier start on her return trip to Huron Cove. She didn't like driving in storms, and white-knuckling it for six hours to the eastern side of Michigan was something she hoped to avoid.

But before she could think about getting on the road, she had to go to church.

With her dad in the front passenger seat and her mother in the back, Lily drove them to their home congregation of St. Paul's. It made her feel good that she could help her parents, and she knew they appreciated her help when Rose was at work or out of town.

She typed the message to Luke after they arrived in the parking lot. As she pushed her dad's wheelchair toward the door, she wondered if Luke and Kayla were on their way home from Sunday service at St. Peter's.

She winced at the thought. She forgot Kayla and the rest of the kids were supposed to sing in church that morning. She hated to miss it. They had been practicing during school all week.

She hated missing out on sitting by Luke, too.

They sat in the back so Mr. O'Leary could have some space with his wheelchair. His wife sat next to him and Lily next to her. During the prelude, Rose and Nick arrived and sat next to Lily. The whole family was there, safe and secure once more in the house of the Lord.

Following the service, Pastor Morton greeted the parishioners at the front door to the church. Frank O'Leary received the well-wishes from his friends who were glad to see him. Lily smiled and thanked all of those who said they were glad to see her, too. They let the others exit first so they didn't hold up the line.

"Lily, why don't I take over pushing your dad," Dr. Nick said, offering to take over wheelchair duties.

Lily thanked him and joined the line with Rose by her side.

Once Nick had pushed Mr. O'Leary's wheelchair through the front door, Lily extended a hand to Pastor Morton.

"So good to see you again, Lily," he said. "Heading back this afternoon?"

"Yes," Lily said before peeking her head out the door and looking up to the sky. "Hopefully, I'll beat the storms."

"Well, I pray you have a safe trip." Pastor Morton looked behind her and, seeing Rose was the last in line, he spoke loud enough so that only both could hear. "I didn't mention this in the announcements because it hasn't been officially announced, but Mrs. Janokowski told me yesterday that she's going to retire at the end of the school year."

Lily's eyes widened.

Rose gasped, knowing the significance of the announcement. "So that means there's going to be a job opening!"

"Sure looks like it. I wanted to let you know right away in case you're interested."

"Of course she's interested, Pastor." She grabbed Lily by the arm. "Can you believe this? It's perfect. Now you can come back home!"

Lily felt a whirring rush in her ears, her mind trying to figure out whether she was really dreaming what Pastor Morton had just said. Her sister's excitement made her think she too should be excited. But was she? Is this what she wanted? It was a great opportunity, but was it the path God wanted her to take? The decision was going to have to be made, and sooner rather than later.

She managed to thank Pastor Morton for the information, and while she and Rose walked down the sidewalk to the parking lot, her sister rattled off all the great things that would happen once Lily moved back home in a month.

"We'll be able to do all the wedding planning as soon as you get back! And then someday you'll be able to babysit your nieces and nephews!" Rose gasped and grabbed Lily by the arm, stopping them both in midstride. "And you can go out with Toby! And then we can plan your wedding and our kids can have playdates!"

Lily looked at her with wide eyes, her mathematical mind trying to calculate all the information overloading her brain. *Is this what I'm going to be doing? Has the decision already been made and I don't even know it?*

Her sister hugged her, giddy at the good news. Lily felt it but didn't offer much of a hug in return.

"Call me on the road if you can," Rose said. "We'll do some more planning. I gotta get to work. Love ya, sis."

Lily was left alone. She managed to mumble, "Love you, too," but there wasn't much feeling behind it. She looked at the church she'd just left. Would this be her home again? She closed her eyes and prayed. *Please, lead me down the right path, God.*

She hit the interstate at one in the afternoon. She'd be back in Huron Cove by seven as long as the weather cooperated. The skies were growing more ominous, and she wondered if the dark clouds would follow her all the way back.

Two hours from Huron Cove, Rose finally called. Lily punched in the button on her dash. "Hey, Rose."

"I'm on my break. Are you excited? Have you called Principal Macaron yet?"

Lily squeezed the wheel tighter, the rain picking up. "No, Rose, I haven't." She could feel water pooling in her eyes. *What do I want to do?*

"Well, hurry up. You want to be the first in line when the announcement's made." Lily heard voices in the background. "I gotta go, Lily. I'll call you back when I get the good news."

Good news? Lily didn't have time to ask what Rose meant because her sister hung up. Lily turned off the radio, hoping the silence would help her sort out everything that was bombarding her mind. The green grounds of Michigan in spring passed by as she drove closer to Huron Cove. She smiled at the thought of that quaint little town, so welcoming to her and inviting to all. It was such a peaceful place.

And then there was Luke. Handsome and wonderful Luke with his super sweet daughter and their lovable dog. She chuckled at the thought of Mr. Butterlickens. Her finger went toward her neck and rubbed the Isle Royale Greenstone necklace Luke had given her.

The water cascading down her windshield was no match for the tears running down her cheeks. What would she say to them if she decided to leave? When the crying became too much, she pulled off into a rest area and sobbed.

Am I ready to give up my life with Luke in Huron Cove? Please God help me make the right decision.

CHAPTER 30

Luke busied himself in the basement doing the laundry for the better part of Sunday afternoon. He was going to ask a woman to marry him tonight, and that would make any sane man a nervous wreck. The pacing started again. He walked back and forth, hoping Kayla and Emma didn't come downstairs and start asking questions. They were in Kayla's bedroom doing some homework and, at least outwardly, they hadn't suspected anything amiss.

He looked at his watch for what seemed like the thousandth time. It could be less than two hours until Lily arrived back home in Huron Cove. He wished he could take her someplace romantic. Maybe by the lake or a fancy restaurant or up in the lighthouse. But he couldn't stand waiting any longer. He couldn't risk something coming between them. He had to ask her.

Today.

When he wasn't looking at his watch, he stopped pacing long enough to look out the basement window toward the south. If she parked outside, he would be able to see her car in the driveway. It was empty at that moment.

Just walk over there and tell her you have something important to ask her.

He prayed again. He lost track of the number of prayers he had made in the last couple of days. All of them centered around Lily O'Leary. The woman who could be his fiancée by the end of the night. The first rumble of thunder made him look out the window again and up toward the darkening sky. He grunted at the thought that popped in his head. He hurried up the stairs and stopped in the doorway to Kayla's bedroom.

"Kayla, I forgot to close Miss O'Leary's window, I'll be right back."

Luke walked down the front steps and took a look at the ominous clouds overhead. The weather radio had been sending out alerts for the better part of an hour advising residents that storms were in the forecast and they should make plans.

Stepping up on Lily's porch, he looked around to make sure no one was looking. He unscrewed the top of the porch light and reached in for the emergency key. After unlocking the door, he went inside and started in the living room, checking all the windows to make sure they were locked tight. The window over the kitchen sink was shut, too. He tried the faucet and it still worked like a charm.

In the silent house, he walked toward Lily's bedroom. He had never been back here, and he smiled at the pictures of her and her sister on the hall walls. He flicked on the light to her bedroom. The bed was made, and a stack of books sat ready on her nightstand.

There were more pictures on her dresser, but he shook at the sound of the phone ringing in the kitchen. He had forgotten Mrs. Fossan still had a landline. He was about to head to the window when he heard a male voice coming through the answering machine. Luke stepped back into the hall to listen.

"This is John Macaron at St. Paul's. I hope this is your number. Your sister gave me a couple so I thought I would call them both. I just got off the phone with Rose and she said you'd accept if we offered you the job once Mrs. Janokowski leaves. I can't tell you how happy it is to hear that. It's always great when one of our former students comes back to teach the next generation of students. I know you'll be a wonderful addition to the school."

Luke staggered before reaching out to steady himself against the wall. *She's leaving? The woman I was only hours away from proposing to is leaving? Without even telling us?*

Once she's gone, she's never coming back.

And it appeared the decision had already been made. Before Principal Macaron ended the call, he welcomed Lily to the faculty and said he'd be in touch with the necessary paperwork. The machine clicked off, and the house fell silent again.

All the prayers. Think of all the times I prayed to have Lily in my life.

An angry rumble of thunder rattled the windows.

Stunned, Luke walked toward Lily's bedroom, his right hand on the wall trying to brace himself from the shock of the news overwhelming him. He looked toward the open window, the curtains swaying in the growing breeze. As he stepped by the dresser, his eyes caught sight of the calendar on top, the red Xs filling the boxes. His shaking hand reached out for it. He flipped over a page for the previous month, all of the boxes full of red. He continued backwards until the previous August.

His jaw clenched, his teeth grinding together. *Days until I'm out of here.*

"She had no intention of staying," he whispered to himself. She had played him and his daughter. She had given them false hope, led them to believe she wanted a relationship with them. He tossed the calendar back on the dresser in disgust.

The phone buzzed in his pocket. The last thing he wanted to do now was talk to Lily O'Leary. Maybe he'd never speak to her again. He pulled the phone out of his pocket. It was his boss.

"Yeah, Chief."

"Luke, with all the rain we've had in the last few days we're worried about the road over Huron Creek. There are big storms rolling in, and I need you out there to divert traffic until the street department can get some barricades out there. It's all hands on deck. Keep your eye on the skies, too, just in case you have to report a tornado."

Luke was almost relieved at the job calling him to duty on his off day. Anything to keep his mind off Lily. "I'll be out there as soon as I can, Chief."

“Thanks, Luke. Be careful.”

Luke clicked off the phone. His head wiped a river of sweat off his forehead, his mind quickly returning to Lily and her lies. *How could she do this to us?* He turned around, slammed the window shut, and stormed out. After locking the front door and replacing the key, he hustled back to his house. His face felt like it was on fire, but there was no time to gather his thoughts in hopes of calming down. He found the girls in Kayla’s bedroom.

“Girls, I just got called in to work. They’re worried about the bridge over the creek, and they want me to divert traffic. You stay here. If it gets windy, get to the basement. Emma, I’ll call your parents and let them know where you are. If they want to come pick you and Kayla up, that’s fine. Just take Butter with you.”

The girls stood from the bed. “Okay, Mr. Luke, stay safe.”

“Dad, is everything all right?”

He wiped more sweat off his forehead with the back of his hand. *No, everything was not all right. But he didn’t have time to talk about Miss O’Leary now. It would have to wait until later.* “Everything’s fine, baby doll. I’m just in a hurry to get out there. Keep an eye on the weather radar on TV and listen to the radio. I’ll have my phone with me.”

Kayla hurried over and gave her dad a hug. “Be careful, Dad.”

Luke gave her a good squeeze and then rushed into his bedroom to change into his uniform shirt. On his way to the Huron Creek bridge, he slammed the steering wheel with his fist. *How could I be so stupid? What is this going to do to Kayla when she finds out?*

Luke pulled to a stop and blocked the intersection to divert traffic. He radioed the station that he was in position. He stepped out of his vehicle and looked to the sky. The rain had stopped for the time being, but the clouds to the west were getting blacker by the minute. There was nothing for him to do now but wait.

He pulled out his phone and typed out a message to Lily.

I shut your window. Your new principal called and left a message about your new job while I was there. You're leaving? Thanks for telling us. I would have thought we meant more to you than that. Guess I was wrong.

He didn't think twice about whether he wanted Lily to read it. He stabbed the phone with his finger and sent the message to wherever Lily was. He shoved the phone back in his pocket, the low growl of thunder turning his eyes back to the skies.

* * *

Lily was only ten minutes outside Huron Cove when she heard the ding of a message on her phone. She had been exceeding the speed limit for the last fifty miles, hoping to make it back to her house before the storm rolled through. The headlights of the cars heading in the opposite direction were on, and the lightning flashes brightened the horizon. Thankfully there weren't many cars going toward Huron Cove so she had the road to herself. But there was a good reason for that. On the radio, she heard the mechanical voice from the weather service warn of large hail, damaging winds, and a possible tornado heading for Huron Cove. Residents were told to seek shelter. She pressed the gas pedal harder, picked up her phone, and looked at the message.

It was from Luke. Trying to keep her eyes on the road, she had to read it twice. She gasped once she finally understood. *But how can that be? I haven't accepted anything.* The thunder shook the ground, and she refocused her eyes on the road. She hit the speed dial for Luke, but it went to voice mail. She put the phone down so she could hold the wheel and turn up the windshield wipers.

When her phone rang, she picked up.

"Are you home yet, Lilybean?"

"Rose, what have you done?" Her voice was frantic, shaking.

"Lily, are you okay? What's wrong?"

Lily sniffled back her sobs. "I just received a text from Luke. He said he heard a message from Principal Macaron and said I accepted the job at St. Paul's."

The silence made Lily wonder if the call had dropped. "Rose?"

Rose sighed through the phone.

"Rose, what did you do?"

"I called Principal Macaron and told him you'd accept if he offered the job."

"Rose! How could you do that!?"

Rose started crying when she heard Lily crying. "I'm sorry, Lilybean. I just want what's best for you. You need to come home so you can be near family."

Lily's hand started shaking so badly she could barely hold the phone. She tried to take a deep breath but only choked on her sobs. Her eyes filled with tears. *Is this the end? Has the decision been made?* Her intention from the first day she arrived in Huron Cove was to leave as soon as possible and move back home. But that was before Luke Spencer came into her life and swept her off her feet.

The hole forming in her heart made her realize she didn't want to leave Luke. He was the one she wanted, and she had a feeling she was what he wanted, too. Her plans had changed.

But could she convince him that she wanted to be with him forever in Huron Cove?

"I gotta go, Rose. The weather's getting bad."

She tossed the phone into the passenger seat and hit the accelerator.

CHAPTER 31

Luke felt his phone vibrating in his pocket not too long after he sent the text to Lily. The only reason he looked at the screen to confirm his suspicions was because of the emergency situation. But once he saw Lily's name on the screen, he put the phone back in his pocket. He didn't want to deal with her now. Maybe ever. He thought it might be best if she just left town without saying goodbye because, by the looks of things, she never wanted anything to do with the place anyway. Or with him.

How could I be so stupid?

He didn't let himself answer the question because he knew the reason. He had fallen in love with her. She was everything he ever wanted—perfect for him and his daughter. He had opened the door to his heart, and she had slammed it shut. With the water running off his raincoat, he pounded his fist against the side of the vehicle.

After the street department arrived with the barricades, he hurried back into town, the rain picking up and the wind swirling the leaves on the trees. The storm was close, and the town was going to get hit hard any minute now. The streets were empty, the residents taking heed of the warnings. Bolts of hot, white lightning zapped the ground, followed quickly by thunder shaking the entire area. It was followed by more lightning. The storm had to be on top of them, but who knows how long it would last. He drove past the police station, water filling the gutters, and then north of the town square.

Three blocks from home, the windshield wipers struggled to keep up with the rain and hail started pelting the SUV. *God, please help us weather this storm.* Leaves and branches blew across the road, and the wind rocked the vehicle. He kept an eye out for falling trees or downed power lines. He peered out the driver's side window and then his stomach sank at what he saw. He slammed on the brakes. Off to the side of the road, he saw a young girl struggling to keep upright in the wind as the rain pelted her face. He gasped and hit the gas to get closer. He lowered the window and yelled into the howling wind.

"Emma Lynn Grayson Stone! What on earth are doing out in this weather!?"

Emma, her eyes wide, rushed through ankle-deep water to the SUV. "Oh, Mr. Luke! It's Butter! We let him out to go to the bathroom before the storm, but the thunder scared him and he ran away. We can't find him!"

Luke felt like a sledgehammer hit him in the gut. *Kayla and Butter are out in this?* "Get in!"

A drenched Emma hurried around to the passenger seat and jumped in. She struggled to close the door in the gusts.

"Where's Kayla?"

"She went north," she said, pointing out the window. "We called for him, Mr. Luke, but he was gone so fast. There's no sign of him!"

Luke could only think of his daughter—out in the pouring rain with a severe thunderstorm barreling down on Huron Cove. He did the first thing that came to his mind. He prayed. *Please God be with her and help us find Butter.*

"It's going to be okay, Emma. We'll find them. Did you try Marvin's house? He likes to go there."

"I called Miss Julia, but she said she hadn't seen him."

Luke edged the SUV slowly up the street, both he and Emma searching in the darkness for Kayla or for Butter. Luke flicked on the spotlight and maneuvered it against the trees swaying in the gusty wind. Nothing.

"Emma, I want you to use the loudspeaker and call for them."

They drove by Lily's house and continued up the street. The darkened interiors of all the houses told Luke that the power was out. Lightning flashes lit up the area offering them a chance to see, but the rain kept them from seeing far. In between thunderclaps, Emma called for Kayla and for Butter.

But there was no movement. No signs of Butter or Kayla.

Please God, help us find them.

* * *

Lily could barely see through the tears in her eyes, and the rain didn't help any. She was so close. She just wanted to get home to Huron Cove.

Home?

She couldn't stop the feeling that safety and security were only two miles away. If she could just make it back to her house, she thought she'd be okay. She quickly changed her mind. If she could just make it two doors to the north of her house, then everything would be all right. She could find Luke and tell him how she really felt. She knew he would protect her. She knew he would love her. She wanted him to take her in his arms and never let go.

Please God, help me get there.

The water on the road was rising at an alarming rate. She pressed the gas some more, hoping to, at least, make it into town. The lightning flashes showed the trees bending almost to their breaking points. The wailing tornado siren filled her ears, her heart pounding with fear. She gripped the steering wheel tighter. She couldn't stop. It wasn't safe to be in her car. She had to keep going.

She took a short cut, bypassed downtown, and was north of the square when she slowed for a stop sign. There were no other cars on the road. She hurried on, her car plowing through the standing water. She leaned closer toward the steering wheel, trying to stay on the road.

Only three more blocks.

She flinched when she caught a glimpse of pink out of the corner of her eye. One swipe of the windshield wipers and a flash of lightning revealed the face of a young girl looking directly at her. She knew that face.

"Oh my goodness."

Lily pulled the car over to the curb, jammed the shifter into *Park*, and threw open the door. With a wall of rain drenching her in an instant, she ran over to the girl crying on the side of the road. "Kayla, what are you doing out in the storm!?"

Scared, alone, and unable to find her lost dog, Kayla sobbed, "I can't find Butter!"

"What? What happened?"

"He . . . He . . . He got out . . . And he ran away!"

Lily grabbed Kayla, who was shivering in the cold rain. "It's going to be okay, Kayla. We'll find him."

Kayla latched on with all her strength. "Please don't leave me, Miss O'Leary. I'm scared."

Lily held her tighter, the closeness warming them both. "I'm not going anywhere, Kayla." She gently kissed her on the top of her head. "Now, let's go find Butter."

* * *

Luke turned down another street. His head looking left and right in quick fashion made him realize he was getting nervous, scared even. Butter got out a lot, but they always found him. He had friends and neighbors around town who would give him shelter. But he expected to find Kayla. She wouldn't have ventured too far off the sidewalk unless Butter was in trouble. Or maybe she stepped in a swollen creek or a drainage ditch. He couldn't live without his daughter.

"Please God," he whispered.

He didn't know what else to do except plead for God's help in finding Kayla. As he let out a pent-up breath, a calmness washed over the car—the only sounds being the steady rain and the thumping of the wipers whooshing back and forth. In the near silence, he felt a hand reach over and touch his arm. He looked over and saw the sweet eyes of Emma looking at him.

"It's going to be okay, Mr. Luke. We'll find them."

He nodded and looked out the window. *Focus. Use your training.* "Does Kayla have her phone with her?"

"I don't think so."

Luke was about to push the speed dial for his daughter's phone when headlights caught his attention up ahead. The car had pulled off to the side of the road. He worried there had been an accident. As the SUV grew closer, he felt a jolt in his heart. *That's Lily's car.* His hopes of finding Lily and Kayla quickly vanished when he realized the car was empty with the lights still on and the engine running.

"We might be getting close, Emma." They looked in every direction. He drove to the end of the block and turned east, hoping to find them heading toward home. Near a grove of trees, he stopped the vehicle, and they both got out. Before shutting his door, he pulled out a second flashlight and handed it to her. "Stay close to me."

The roaring wind lessened, giving them a chance to focus on the search instead of watching for falling trees. They wiped the rain out of their eyes as they sloshed through the water. Luke and Emma took turns yelling out names.

"Kayla!"

"Butter!"

"Lily!"

The storm was beginning to pass, and the sky to the east lit up with lightning that illuminated the trees. Luke's heart leapt at the flash of pink off in the distance.

"Kayla!" he yelled. At the sight of his daughter, he broke into a run through the soggy grass that slowed his progress with every step. But there was no stopping him. Not even quicksand would keep him from Kayla.

From the darkness in the dense trees, Lily and Kayla, along with a wet and muddy golden retriever, emerged into the beam of Luke's flashlight. Luke ran to his daughter and threw his arms around her. The hug she gave him never felt so good. He didn't feel the need to lecture her or scold her. He was just thankful to have her in his arms again. *Thank you, God.*

"Are you okay?"

A shivering Kayla managed a smile and a nod. "I'm okay." She looked to her left. "Miss O'Leary helped me find Butter, Dad."

Luke released his embrace of Kayla and looked at Lily. She was drenched from head to toe, her designer boots covered in mud. The streetlights kicked back on, giving the surroundings a soft glow. Luke and Lily looked at each other, both of them debating what to say first and who should say it.

Luke took the lead and cleared his throat. "Are you okay?"

Lily looked down at her mess of clothes before smiling. "I'm fine. I just happened to be driving by when I saw Kayla." She gave the leash she was holding a little tug. "We found this guy hunkered down under that old dead tree over there. I think he was waiting out the storm."

Luke didn't respond. He was too busy taking in the beauty of Lily O'Leary. Even soaked to the bone, she was gorgeous. He wished he could walk over, wrap his arms around her, and hold her forever. And kiss her like there was no tomorrow, too.

But he couldn't because she was leaving, skipping out of town as soon as the school year ended.

"You didn't answer my call," Lily said.

Luke narrowed his eyes and tried to choose his words carefully. "I didn't need an explanation. Your new principal spelled it out pretty clear over the phone. You got a new job, and we're the last to know."

Kayla looked up at her teacher. "You're leaving, Miss O'Leary?"

Lily handed the leash to Kayla. Then she took a step closer to Luke. "I'm not leaving, Luke. My sister told the principal I accepted the job, but I turned it down when he finally got hold of me on my cell phone. I'm not going anywhere, Luke. Huron Cove is where I want to be."

Luke struggled to understand what he was hearing. He didn't believe her, figuring she was just saying it to save face in front of the girls. "What about the calendar on your dresser? It said days until you're out of here."

Lily grimaced and shook her head. "It's something I started when I first arrived in Huron Cove. I thought my job at the school would be for a year and then that would be it. I don't know why I kept marking off the days. Maybe because my sister kept asking me how many days were left in the school year. Or maybe it was because I didn't know what I wanted in life." She reached out and touched his arm. "But I know what I want, Luke. I want to be a part of your life and Kayla's life." Her smile widened. "And Butter's life, too."

Butter barked at hearing his name.

"My family's in Chicago, and that's where I thought I would return. But that was before I fell in love with this wonderful little town. And that was before I met the most decent and caring man in the world. I found my heart in Huron Cove, Luke, and I want to stay here with you. And I want to be around these great girls." She looked deep into his eyes. "I love you, Luke."

Luke's eyes left Lily's when he saw movement behind her that caught his attention. It was Emma. She was holding the flashlight up to her face. She nodded and gestured with her head toward Lily. Luke's eyebrows scrunched together, wondering what she was trying to tell him. She did it again, the nod and the head movement toward Lily a little more pronounced this time. Her eyes might have widened a little more too, like she was telling him to get on with it.

Luke sucked in a breath. He read the message perfectly this time. He couldn't believe it. *How did she know?* Luke suddenly remembered he had planned on asking Lily to marry him that very night, and he still had the ring in his pocket. He reached and pulled out the box. There, in the wet grass and mud of Huron Cove, Luke knelt in front of her and looked up at Lily. "Lily, you've meant the world to me, and I don't think I can live without you. I need you in my life. Would you be Kayla's mother and my wife?"

Lily brought her hands together. "Yes, I will."

Hearing the good news, Kayla and Emma rushed over to hug their teacher and Luke. The embrace warmed them all. They walked back to the safety of Luke's SUV and Lily took the front passenger seat with the girls and Butter in the back.

Once everyone was inside, Luke reached over and grabbed Lily's hand, never wanting to let go.

Just then, Butter shook the rain off his wet fur throwing water everywhere.

"Butter!"

CHAPTER 32

During June of the following year, Luke and Lily had their wedding at St. Peter's. It felt like the right place to become man and wife. The reception was held at the Huron Cove B&B's barn, and Emma and Kayla made sure to supervise the decorating to get everything "just right." It was, and those in attendance marveled at the beauty of the surroundings as well as the look of love in the bride and groom's eyes.

After the wedding, Lily moved two doors up the street, and they started a home. They took frequent trips to Chicago to visit Lily's family and even enjoyed an interleague matchup at Wrigley between the Cubs and Tigers. The Cubs lost, and Luke and Kayla made sure to rub it in as much as possible.

Although Lily didn't have Kayla and Emma in class any longer, they were never shy of showing up in her classroom to help in any way they could. She didn't want it any other way. Luke and Lily ran a lot and road bikes out to the lake. Their favorite routine was taking a walk into town to enjoy the summer breeze and have some ice cream at Lighthouse Creamery.

"I'll never get over the beauty of this place," Lily said, as they walked toward town with Emma, Kayla, and Butter leading the way a half block ahead.

Luke squeezed his wife's hand tighter. "And I'll never get over how such a beauty like you decided to be my wife."

Lily rose on her tiptoes and gave him a peck on the cheek. They thanked God every day for every minute they had together.

A potato chip truck rumbled toward them.

Emma was the first to see who was driving and pointed at the truck. “Hey, look! It’s Bubba Nuts!”

They all stopped and waved as the truck drove by, the big meaty arm of its driver waving out the window. “Hey, girls!” He yanked on the cord a couple times, and the truck’s horn blared much to the girls’ delight. Then he was off to his next delivery.

They kept walking—smiles on their faces. Luke looked at Lily and shook his head, his sly grin widening. “He could have been yours, you know.” He gestured to the truck behind them. “Funniest guy you’ll ever meet. Just think you could have been Mrs. Bubba Nuts.”

Lily smiled. She looped her arm around the crook of Luke’s elbow. She leaned in close and looked at Luke. The man for her. “I think I made the right choice.”

THE END

Rob Shumaker is an attorney living in Danville, Illinois. *Learning to Love Again* is his fourth Christian romance novel. He is also the author of *The Angel Between Them*, *Turning the Page*, and *Christmas in Huron Cove*, the first three books in the Huron Cove series.

Did you enjoy *Learning to Love Again*? Readers like you can make a big difference. Reviews are powerful tools to attract more readers so I can continue to write engaging stories that people enjoy.

If you enjoyed the book, I would be grateful if you could write an honest review (as short or as long as you like) on your favorite book retailer.

Thank you and happy reading.

Rob Shumaker

To read more about the Huron Cove series,
go to
www.RobShumakerBooks.com

Made in the USA
Monee, IL
23 December 2020

51459454R10152